th
hair
ed
, was
apsed amongst
the wreckage of
waterdry trees...

Jenny
"So this is a potion..."
Sara
"Say, Ann. Do you want to stay together with him forever?"
Deneb
"Ish sho good!"
"Whoa, it's positively delicious~"
Ann

"It looks like you've been assigned to Labyrinth #228, Kousaka-san."
Misato Karumi
Aoi Kousaka
LABYRIN
"Ah, so it is an eShop catalog..."

My face feels hot, and there's a tingling feeling inside my chest. I wonder why...
The faint and mysterious light of the glowing moss shined into the room from the window...

AUTHORED BY:
Shinobu Yuki

ILLUSTRATED BY:
Itsuwa Katou

PUBLISHED BY:

STRONGEST GAMER: LET'S PLAY IN ANOTHER WORLD VOL. 1
SHINOBU YUKI

Translated by J. "Bango" Colmenares

Sol Press, LLC.
P.O. Box 6593
Fullerton CA, 92834
www.solpress.co

Quantity sales. Special discounts are available on quantity purchases by corporations, associations, and others. For details, contact the publisher at the address above.

Sol Press, LLC. is not responsible for websites not owned by Sol Press, LLC.

First Printing, May 2018

ISBNs: 978-1-948838-02-3 (paperback)
978-1-948838-00-9 (ebook)

10 9 8 7 6 5 4 3 2 1

Table of Contents

Illustrator: Itsuwa Katou

Prologue

You must have heard the phrase "Life's just a bad game" before, right? I'm sure you have. Does "You can't hit the reset button on life" ring any bells? How about "Life's just shovelware"?

It all sounds so depressing, doesn't it? Just hearing those words would drag down any semblance of good vibes, so let's think about it for a moment. If you compared real life to the countless amount of 'good games' in the world, you'd probably be hard-pressed not to discount it as just another 'bad game.' Ah, but there's more to it than just that.

See, life may be a 'bad game'—I don't disagree with you—but it all comes down to perspective, don't you think? You're only going to find one of those so-called 'good games' by going through life itself, after all.

So what if you can't hit the reset button on life? There are a myriad of games without them. It's a little old-fashioned, don't you think? What I'm trying to say is... If you're a gamer who thinks life's just a 'bad game,' then maybe you just need to level up a little, and find some new ways to enjoy it. I may be coming off as high and mighty, and maybe a tad bit overbearing; but if you got thrown all the way down to the bottom of a ravine, that was so deep it looked like a natural wonder without any trace of civilization—all while wearing a business suit—anyone would want to escape from reality. It kinda feels like: "Damn, this game's hard mode is tougher than I thought."

◇

Anyway, let's slow down and take a look around. The guys that panic always die first in movies, novels... and FPS games. Being in a bit of a hurry would be the natural reaction if you fell down a ravine after a car accident or something, but I couldn't help but remain calm given these circumstances. After all, I was a gamer that had spent his whole life playing games, and I intend to keep it that way.

There was one thing that caught my eye while I surveyed the bottom of the valley. A translucent character board, similar to those UI (User Interface) windows you see so often in games, was floating out near my right hand. Even with so much reality right in front of me, the game-like window near my right hand gave me a curious sense of security.

—Well, at least I wasn't thrown down to the center of the earth.

I got a better picture of the situation as I observed the surrounding area. I was at the bottom of an extremely deep ravine that was being bathed in sunlight. Up past the horizon line was a cliff face that went as far as the eye can see. And from what I could tell, the bottom of the ravine ran down about 30 to 40 meters. The walls all around me were also nearly completely vertical. Climbing something that steep was out of the question. It looked to be about 50 meters to the top of the cliff, and I was a good 100 meters down into the valley itself.

The ravine looked almost as if someone stabbed the earth with a giant knife. From where I was standing it seemed to be about 100 meters out to the farthest point off in the distance, and probably went even further. You'd think it'd be difficult for sunlight to reach the bottom of a ravine this deep unless it was right above it, but the smooth polished surface of the ravine's walls acted like giant natural softboxes, and diluted the sunlight through the forest's trees.

The walls themselves were made of hard rock, but the ground was just soft black soil. You could even see a few weeds and a bit of moss here and there. Overall there didn't seem to be that much water, but a small amount oozed out of the walls in scattered places, and created tiny waterfalls and small pods in the soil. The confluence of the tiny water streams created small rivers and ponds that led down into the ravine's floor.

The water looked crystalline and safe to drink, so I wouldn't have to worry about thirst, at least. Curiously, there were a few tiny trees sprinkled about with twisted trunks, and beautifully bright soft leaves spread out over the valley, too. But there didn't seem to be any animals around.

It was like the whole place one big walled off garden.

—If this place was naturally occurring, it'd definitely apply for world wonder status. Heck, if it was made by people, it'd be an effort worthy of a god.

If it wasn't for the handmade cabin standing behind me, which disrupted the tranquility of this otherwise beautiful microcosm of nature, I would have believed it if you told me this place was called Paradise or Eden. Between the seemingly randomly generated topography, climate, and vegetation, this idyllic mountain forest almost looked like something straight out of "Forest Simulator 2012 ~Botany Glory~". The sheer magnitude of the overflowing green miracle around me was nothing short of staggering. All in all, I didn't think it would even be possible to replicate this wonder of nature in a game and do it justice.

I turned my attention to the strange translucent UI window next to my right hand. When I touched it, the window started displaying alphanumeric characters based in English.

—Huh? This window states I'm inside a game... But everything around me looks way too real. It also shows my real name as my display name. I'm not one of those that people who puts their real names in games. This can't be right... Can it?

Pretty polished UI for a game, but it wasn't quite all there still—not newbie friendly at all. It would be so much nicer to look at if it was just a little bit more graphical. It was going to bug me every time I looked at it, surely.

I may have been thrown into a really strange situation, but having fun wherever you find game-like elements was what I would call a gamer's duty. I tried operating the translucent window filled with characters, and pushed my fingertip against a spot that said 'Status.' A window popped up to display:

Aoi Kousaka <Apprentice Labyrinth Manager> **Vitality**: 21/21 **Stamina**: 56/58 **Willpower**: 13/14 **Skill(s)**: <Dungeon Management Tool> <Appraisal>

Pretty standard looking character screen. So standard that it seemed like something designed for an MMORPG (Massively Multiplayer Online Role-Playing Game). No, it was more like one of those tabletop role-playing games (RPG). You know, the ones where you wrote things down on paper and roll a die.

Let me be honest with you, I couldn't care less about the situation I was in right now. Going nuts over a potentially fun element was what being a gamer was all about. If this UI floating above my hand was set to be a menu, then I was used to it already. You could even say it was simple compared to recent games, nowadays.

I opened the configure settings in the UI window.

I sort of relied on my intuition to navigate through all the options, and customized the interface. I managed to come up with something rather similar to an internet browser interface that I was used to, called "WaterRacoon". The UI window didn't have much of a force feedback response when I touched it. It seemed more like a typical smartphone touch screen.

I fixed the status screen in place and brought up a new tab, scrolled through the menu's summary, and clicked on the 'Skill List' option. My heart felt as if it was going to beat its way out of my chest as my fingertip touched the <Dungeon Management Tool> skill.

I'd played countless dungeon, farm, and city management games by now. The goals and objectives may change depending on the game, but the basics were always the same: Raise monsters as guardians of the dungeon to go against the pathetic intruders that dare set foot into it, expand the dungeon with the power of magic to confuse trespassers, install vicious and beautiful traps causing mental fatigue of the intruders from the surface, et cetera. Administering an evil dungeon was a genre that really kicked off in recent years.

When I pressed the <Dungeon Management Tool> a separate window popped up. The new window had various new settings, such as <Terrain Improvement Tool> and <Structure Creation - Outer Wall> next to it.

—Heheh, so the <Dungeon Management Tool> has all these bundled into one skill, huh? Pretty cool.

I selected the <Terrain Improvement Tool> among all the options and tapped the 'Execute' button. All of a sudden my body felt heavier, and at the same time something fell in front of me with a metallic clunk on the floor.

—Is that an iron pickaxe? And a shovel?

The two items that fell right in front me were a metal pickaxe, and a shovel that looked big enough to wield with two hands. When I took a look at the status screen, I noticed my 'Willpower' had decreased from 13/14 to 3/14. It seemed the magical Willpower thing acted as some Magic Points (MP) of sorts, and was depleted to activate the skill.

—Yep, these definitely are terrain improvement tools, alright. You can change how the world looks with the pickaxe if you keep at it long enough.

More specifically: Digging into the ground, breaking stones, and shoveling dirt.

"I-Isn't this a little *too* hardcore!?"

My yell echoed out across the sunlight-bathed ravine.

Aoi Kousaka
<Apprentice Labyrinth Manager>
Vitality: 21/21
Stamina: 56/58
Willpower: 3/14
☆ Skill(s)
- Dungeon Management Tool
- Appraisal

Chapter 1

When you boiled down my profile, it was comprised of about one or two lines: Aoi Kousaka, Age 22; fresh out of some minor science university, and hardcore gamer.

Pretty straightforward, don't you think? So straightforward it hurts, though. It wouldn't be an exaggeration to say I had spent more than half my life so far playing games. Ever since I touched my first game at the age of three, I'd become completely obsessed, and dedicated my life to playing them. Although games were my lifeblood, I still worked hard to maximize the amount of time I had to play.

When I was a kid, I would set a time limit for playing games on the television because it wasn't good for eye development. Instead, I would either play card or board games. Both my parents liked games and were very understanding, but I knew they wouldn't be so understanding if my test scores dropped as a result. And so I did my best to keep all my grades above average in every subject.

When I got to middle school, there weren't too many jobs available to someone my age, but I managed to find part-time work as a newspaper delivery boy, and saved money to buy the computer I'd so badly wanted—and games too, of course. When I finally bought the computer, I discovered that foreign PC games were cheap, so then I put all my efforts into learning English. In about a year's time, I was able to understand all the English games I wasn't able to get in Japanese. I had seriously lived to game my whole life thus far, but I came face-to-face with the harsh realities of life not too long ago.

Job hunting had started pretty early in the summer for third years at my university. There weren't that many jobs that would let me secure not only a decent salary, but also enough time to still dedicate to playing games. The whole 'large companies and corporations were life-sucking leeches' wasn't a joke. What good was earning loads of money if I couldn't play games? Nevertheless, I managed to get a job offer from a nearby facility as Location Management and Security. The pay wasn't great, but at least I had a lot of free time for my hobbies. I lamented not being able to play a certain MMORPG that came out around the time due to taking certain qualification courses that would benefit said job, too.

Unfortunately, at the end of March, I received news that there was an accidental fire that had occurred at one of the facilities managed by the head company I was working for. As a result, the management staff was held liable, and subsequently downscaled. I was told that after my training period was up I was going to be let go as well since I was just a temporary contractor.

And so, I kept job hunting from the end of March, all the way until our graduation ceremony. Unable to find anything that met my criteria, I became a jobless university graduate.

Life's 'hardcore mode' was so hard that I couldn't even muster a laugh.

I resumed job hunting the next spring, but still struggled with a lack of offers for two whole months post graduation. By then, the rainy season had begun.

One day I came across a random leaflet that had gotten caught in one of the newspapers I usually got at home. It was really small—smaller than the normal advertisements for the supermarket itself, but there looked to be a job offer on that leaflet that said...

Work Details:
- Facility Management position
- Salary: Starting from ¥140,000/mo
- Prior experience not required
- Traveling expenses covered
- Note: People with high stamina and proficient with games will have priority.

The details checked all the boxes I was looking for. The salary was a bit low compared to ones typically offered to graduate students, but it was definitely not low enough that I couldn't live off it. I understood why they would want to hire healthy people, but people with an affinity for games? What did that have to do with managing facilities? Either way, I couldn't have hoped for a better job than one

I could use my love of games for, so I immediately got in touch and agreed to have an interview.

“I trust you’re familiar with our institution?”

The briefing and interview took place in an office building across the street from the train station closest to my house. I wondered if the person interviewing me had foreign parents. She had seemingly beautiful blonde hair that didn’t look to be bleached or colored at all, but also black-colored eyes. Her facial features seemed more like those of a Japanese beauty than not.

“Yeah, it’s an institution that’s aimed at building public projects,” I replied.

I was wearing my business suit that I had grown so used to wearing. The institution in question built community buildings, libraries, and even auditoriums for events. They used tax money to do so though, and it resulted in fighting over who was going to pay for maintenance costs.

“Yes, that’s right. We are generally in charge of the management and property maintenance in regards to the community projects our company develops.”

—I see. They would even manage a community building despite problems related to its use and maintenance costs. Interesting.

“So I was wondering… What does this have to do with preferring people with stamina, or those good at games?” I asked.

“Well, since there are a good amount of properties in remote places, having good stamina is beneficial in being able to reach their locations. Now, in relation to games, our company doesn’t just go out to perform general maintenance; we carry out managerial duties as well. We’re well aware that hiring management experts for our projects won’t improve some aspects of our business, though. That’s where the proficiency with games comes in. Wouldn’t a person who is good at games be more adept at improving our management? That’s the idea the company’s President came up with, at least.”

—Remote places? I guess it was dumb of me to assume it would be something more local just because it was in the advertisement stuck in the middle of the newspaper. Nonetheless, if there’s internet and

home delivery you can still play all the same.

"I don't have really anything to lose by giving management a try, but would I be able to move beyond that if things went well?"

"Yes. At the end of the day, the job you'll be performing is maintenance and management of the location you're assigned to. If you think maintaining the status quo management-wise is too difficult, then you can change things around as you see fit. And if the situation of the operation improves, you can expect it to be reflected in your salary."

It wasn't a bad offer. The fact that I'd be in charge of administration duties on top of the management was surprising, but I wouldn't mind a salary raise if it went well. Although... it may be a bit presumptuous of me to expect much since they weren't hiring a professional.

"The trial period before official employment is three months. Salary will be paid out as per the exhibited conditions, but please think of this as your trial period."

The employment conditions weren't bad, and it seemed like the interview was a success after some easy questions, so I decided to sign the contract on the spot. As far as formal employment went, this seemed a bit easy to get in, but since they had this trial period thing to test people, I guess that's how they truly verified applicants.

"There, my signature... and my stamp. Is this the last document?"

"Yes, that's fine. We'll be colleagues from here on out. Let me introduce myself, I'm Karumi. We'll be counting on you, Kousaka-san."

—Ah, getting hired means we're colleagues now. That makes sense.

My first condition with people was that they were gamers as well, so I never had this kind of opportunity before. But it wouldn't be so bad to share a workplace with a beauty like her, even if it meant I needed to cut out any untoward feelings. Her last name was the same as the company name. Maybe it was a family-run management business. That was rather common among smaller companies.

"Thank you very much. Let's get along together."

I shook her hand and returned her smile.

Gamers generally had a bad image as far as personal relations went, and to be honest, I was like that too a long time ago. But there was a vast amount of multiplayer games with player-to-player interaction nowadays; not to mention all the clan or guild events that happened inside them, so I did my best to improve my communication skills.

I hadn't really read any of those how-to books or anything about it. I just had a lifetime of experience meeting and talking to a lot of people. It really came in handy for job hunting and everyday life, so I figured it was a nice skill worth having, even if you didn't like it. But, well, it still didn't help much to overcome the hurdle of dealing with a pretty lady as a healthy young man.

"Well, then. Let's introduce you to your workplace at once."

Karumi-san led the way and we walked to the door opposite the room we were just now.

—Was that the entrance on the other side? Maybe it leads to the parking lot, the stairs, or even to an elevator.

The door squeaked as she opened it, and in came an unusual wind from the other side. It smelled of overflowing vegetation that reminded me of a time I had traveled to the mountains. A second ago I had been walking over hard ceramic tiles, but all of a sudden it felt like I was stepping on soft soil.

—Huh...?

Before I had even noticed, I was met with an awe-inspiring view from the bottom of the ravine.

"It looks like you've been assigned to Labyrinth #228, Kousaka-san. The conditions may prove to be somewhat harsh, but please do your best. Well then, we'll meet again when your training period is over."

"Eh? Labyrinth? Excuse me, can you repeat that?"

When I turned around, the only thing I managed to catch was the door getting slammed shut behind me. Upon closer inspection, all that was left in its place was a rugged wall of solid gray rock. There weren't any traces of the door or the office I had come from mere seconds ago.

—And that's how it went.

"Hard mode, huh..." I sighed.

I recalled everything that had happened so far while I checked the pickaxe and the shovel that fell on the floor. You could say I was trying to escape reality as well.

"Wait. A community building labyrinth? Could this be a..."

I walked into the log cabin-style house nearby me. The metal hinges on the door were difficult to budge, probably because it hadn't seen much use. The interior seemed to be about 20 square meters wide. There was a simple bed, a cabinet, and a round wooden table which stood in the middle of the room. The interior somehow managed to look even cheaper than the cheapest hotel, in the cheapest city, in the cheapest country.

I noticed a brown A4-sized envelope on top of the wooden table.

"Ah, right. They're a management company, so there should be things to manage."

If Karumi-san's words were to be believed, then my training period would last three months. She said we would meet again after the training is over, so the pickup should be in three months at best. I didn't really have any guarantee that she was gonna keep her word, but I guess thinking positively would make it a little more bearable.

From the look of things, it didn't seem like I was going to be able to just waltz back home, so I guess I should be grateful my merciful employers had the decency to provide me a room to stay in. There was nothing man-made around here aside from the cabin. But if this place was a labyrinth, it wouldn't surprise me to find a huge structure sprawling out underground.

I opened the envelope and took out the contents; I found a stiff and seemingly old starchy paper with official looking information handwritten with a fountain pen. It read:

<Labyrinth #228>
Purpose: Foster an environment to ensure inter-clan engagement, collection of military goods, and deposit base. This structure is also designated as the neighbor residents' evacuation point.
Scheduled Completion: Mid-scale Labyrinth — Class 3.

I supposed this wasn't that much different from a building. Rather, a labyrinth being classified as a 'community building' wasn't too unrealistic a proposition.

Total Construction Status: 2% — Construction of cabin for worker completed.
Current Construction Progress: 100% completed.
Interior Design Progress: 100% completed.
Facility Equipment Installation Progress: 100% completed.
Deployment of Golems for Facility Protection: Completed.
Awaiting for manager to take up their post...

—Hmm? There's two progress sheets here, but their contents are completely reversed.

Additional Notes: Person in charge of the labyrinth's construction, Barald Gain (49), has been arrested under suspicion of corporate embezzlement.

"Hahaha... This sure happens a lot with public projects, huh?"

So he hadn't even started working, and pocketed all the money intended for the construction. If I'm unlucky, he might have even stolen the money for management and maintenance costs; which meant the company thought they needed a management administrator because it was completed on paper, but in reality it was actually incomplete—I had nothing to manage.

I was at a loss for words. Managing a facility like this seemed more and more like a punishment game. I wanted to break down and cry, but attempting to escape my reality wouldn't get me anywhere, as unfortunate as it was.

"Did we need the embezzlement feature!?"

My scream echoed out into the ravine.

Screaming helped me calm down a little bit. This was unbecoming of someone as tempered a gamer as I, who had experienced countless RPG challenge runs. You know, challenges like 40-hour time limits, or game overs meant you had to start over with no resets or data backup. They were masochistic challenges that pushed even the most ruthless of frame-timed, auto-save limited experts to their limits.

I felt pleasure every time I got wiped out towards the end. The only truly masochistic thing were the challenges themselves. The games were innocent and magnificent pieces of work on their own... I wasn't playing because I'm a masochist or anything, if that's what you were thinking. All that aside, I wasn't particularly pessimistic despite the actual lack of a building to manage, or the obvious corruption.

Couldn't I make my own labyrinth if there wasn't one to begin with? They said they would raise my salary depending on how well I improved the place, so I figured it was pretty safe to say whatever I did would be an improvement over this shabby cabin. Besides, the idea of making my own labyrinth seemed like fun. Fortunately for me, the house was already kinda furnished... But I think I would have to give up on the dream of living in a comfy room with water service, gas, or heaters of any kind.

"So what am I supposed to do about food...?"

First of all, that translucent window that floated over my hand made me doubt whether or not this world was the same as the one I came from.

—There may be squirrels, mice, or even birds for all I know around here. It may not be much but it can make for a decent meal.

I looked in and around the cabin for about half an hour, but didn't manage to find even a trace of any of those.

—This is quite a problem, there's no fruits or anything either... I guess it's time to eat grass and leaves.

I did find some butterflies with glassy-looking wings, and I may be able to find some worms if I turned over some rocks or dug a little, but I'd rather not have to resort to doing so if I could help it. There was also the concern of hygiene as well, but there were a lot of ponds and little rivers nearby, so getting water wouldn't be that hard.

There were no fish shadows in any of the ponds or streams, though. The ponds themselves were several meters deep, and so transparent you could see all the way to the bottom with no problem. Maybe the water was too clean for fish to live. It didn't look like it could be dangerous to drink. With an environment with so many bodies of water, but no fish in sight, it was gonna be hard to get anything in the way of food.

I may have to give up on the hope of surviving by normal means. This seemed like one of those survival games where civilization collapsed and aimed way too hard for realism—they were so overused a setting that no one really liked them anymore.

“Throw away your dignity as a person in order to survive...”

Or so it went with those sorts of games. The only thing I learned about them was that you could postpone the time to starving if you focused on just surviving, but you’d lose something important as a human being.

To be specific, I was talking about a technique which involved cutting out the waste of nutrients by recycling and ingesting your own... Yeah. Let’s be clear here though, that was truly the last of last resorts. That feature was in a game developed with the help of professionals with real-life survival skills they had hired for reference, but I think that was the very same reason the genre didn’t really kick off to begin with.

I looked around inside the cabin in hopes of finding some kind of stash of any kind, when I found something unusual hidden in a corner.

There was a complex pattern drawn on the surface of the floor—I wondered if they were letters or something. I also found some kind of box that looked big enough to fit two people inside. And there was what seemed to be a porcelain piggy bank standing on top of it, as if it was enshrined there on purpose.

When I tried touching it, a translucent window popped up. It displayed ‘Delivery and Payment Box’ on it. The separate window that appeared looked like something out of an online catalog. The title of it said “Regional World Catalog: Tundra”. I wondered if the person who made this thought the end users would be able to read English right away.

The catalog itself was written in English and had illustrations all over. When I operated it a little bit, the display changed to ‘Foods > Seasonings > Salt... 1 kg Salt == 120 DL’.

—Ah, so it is an eShop catalog. This DL thing seems to be a form of currency, but I’ve never heard of it before.

But I couldn’t be called a gamer if I let something like that confuse me. The fact this catalog popped up as soon as I touched the delivery box probably meant that if I put something of value inside the box... I might be able to get some currency. And if I put in currency, I could get goods... It was a pretty typical system in games.

As typical as it may be, with the <Dungeon Management Tool> thing I had, it was kind of hard to really piece it all together properly. Plus, there was this vague 'Willpower' stat thing that got consumed to make the shovel and pickaxe appear earlier. It was amazing and whatnot, but... how did all this stuff tie together?

—I really want to try it out, but what should I put inside?

The rocks and fallen leaves scattered about around here didn't look like they held much value to them. I tried to fish something out of my suit pockets, and found a piece of mint bubble gum I normally used to keep myself awake. Now that I thought about it, it was still unopened. I put the bubble gum inside the delivery box, and a metallic sound resounded from within it, almost like the sound of coins dropping.

When I opened the box again there was no bubble gum to be seen; in its place were two metallic looking yellow-minted coins. They appeared to be worth 100 DL and 5 DL respectively. They weren't quite gold; they seemed to be made of some kind of yellow-metallic material, maybe some kind of brass? On the other side of the coins was a demon-like face motif carved out into it. Under that it read "100 DarkLord Coin".

DarkLord... As in a big bad demon? Did this mean it was the currency of the demon lord? I didn't really know how they appraised the value of the gum, but it was good news regardless. Now I could use the delivery box thing to get money. If only the <Dungeon Management Tool> itself was even as remotely decipherable as the delivery box was.

I opened the translucent window again and chose the 'Natural Salt' that was listed with a price of 50 grams for 55 DL. When I had confirmed the order in the eShop, a popup which said "Please Insert Fee" appeared, so I put the two coins I had inside the piggy bank. Right as I did, a 50 DL coin dropped from below the piggy bank, and at the same time a slot suddenly appeared in what was a seemingly empty gap, and burst open. An unusually heavy looking A4-sized paper envelope fell to the ground with a sonorous plop.

"Thank you for your purchase!"

A strangely high-pitched voice came out from the box, followed by another bursting sound, to which the opened slot unceremoniously closed back up. The word "Tundra" was printed on the envelope, and under it was decorated with what I assumed was their logo.

—Tundra? As in the biome?

There was also a note, which seemed to have been written with magic pen that stated the "Administrator of Labyrinth #228" as the recipient's name.

—How can this thing be so convenient, yet the <Dungeon Management Tool> wants me to do literal manual labor!?

I needed to report this. There came a time in a man's life where he must report broken features.

—I need to calm down, come on. Look at the bright side...

I managed to regain my composure in less than a minute. There was this one time I had stayed with some university friends, and we marathoned a bunch of games that were listed on a site called "The Worst of the Worst", which aggregated all of the worst games in the history of humanity. We played them one after another for God knows how long, so I should be able to cope in these kinds of situations.

Freezing after every battle in an RPG... Freezing while saving... Saved games disappearing just because... Final bosses that didn't spawn in the last area because of bugged scripts... Compared to that hell, this was still pretty tame. I had been living my life for games this whole time, and it had been of real use ever since I came to this place, at least.

After opening the A4 envelope, I found about 50 grams worth of salt inside a plastic bag, which was cushioned by a material similar to cardboard.

—So I can order food from this Tundra thing, huh? So the objective is use this box to get DL coins, and use those get food to subsist...

Nevertheless, there weren't many things around here that looked like they'd be worth much. My pickup was approximately three months out. Even if I'd sold everything I had on me, namely my suit, wallet, and shoes, I doubt I'd be able to get by more than one month at best.

"Valuable stuff, eh? Can't I use **that** thing..."

I looked around the room, and my eyes went straight towards pickaxe I'd created a while ago with the <Dungeon Management Tool>.

—Depends on if I can even sell it to begin with...

I tried putting it inside the delivery box, but instead of turning into coins, a message in red letters popped up which said "Cannot Be Exchanged".

—What a shame. It's never that easy, is it?

It consumed a stat called Willpower, but it was also common in games to make it so you were unable to resell equipment you could create as many times as you wanted, or at the very least, make it sellable, but only for incredibly cheap.

"Let's try with a stone next."

I took my suit jacket off and headed out, pickaxe in hand.

You may not know this if you didn't live in Japan, but stone was often used as a building and interior material. The prices went up and down depending on the type and rarity, but they were always quite pricey to buy.

Once, I got addicted to this one game called "Moss Decoration Meister", in which putting moss on stones was considered a decoration of the highest order. I'd participated in a contest sponsored by the developer and won the silver medal in the 'Free-sized Garden' category. I even wanted to make some moss decorations in real life as well, but the cheapest stone bases would go over four figures a piece. I would be hard-pressed to find a memory more bitter than that one. Even if what I could find around here wasn't some fancy stone used for decorations, I could crush it and turn it into gravel. There was a lot of demand and uses for that as well.

I went to the closest rock to the cabin and held the pickaxe I'd created using the <Dungeon Management Tool> with both hands... and pierced the rock! It made a satisfying sound. In its wake was a clean cross-shaped crack in the stone.

"Ohhh..."

I unintentionally dropped the pickaxe. My hands went numb due to shock. I'd never taken up one of those part-time jobs that had you doing heavy manual labor, like making holes in asphalt, so it was the first time in my life I had used a pickaxe. I figured I had a knack for it, but was kind of hesitant due to the resulting muscle pain. I tried using a bit less strength and struck the rock again... and again... and again. It had slowly become easier on my hands. The cross-shaped crack expanded as I continued to strike the stone. Along with the sound of my strikes came perfectly cut square-shaped pieces of rock.

—Huh? Pickaxes don't normally cut into stuff like that, right? Why are they all so square?

When I pulled apart the perfectly cut pieces, a heavy gray-colored stone cube covered with dark spots fell out. It was exactly 10 cubic centimeters. They would be easy to pile up as building material in this shape, but the fact that they could be cut up with such precise symmetry with just a pickaxe was downright bizarre. Rocks normally were supposed to crumble apart and break down into irregular shapes when struck with a pickaxe.

—The whole ravine is littered with regular rocks. Is this related to the pickaxe I have?

What was with the mysterious pickaxe that ate up my Willpower? I wanted to try the <Appraisal> skill I first saw back on my status screen.

—This UI is really easy to use. I haven't seen this kind of polish before, even in overseas games.

I was impressed by my handiwork as I maneuvered around the translucent window to enter the Skill Menu. I'd customized the UI to be like my favorite all-purpose internet browser for smartphones and touchscreen computers, "WaterRacoon". The only thing that I didn't seem to need to change to be more user-friendly was the simple character information screen from before. The UI screen which displayed a player's various information, and reflected their every action, needed to be perfect. It heavily influenced the amount of enjoyment one would derive while playing.

Usability played a huge part, but I found the most important thing was to make it intuitive enough so that one could understand everything at a glance. Something that made you go "Whoa, this is easy". The translucent UI window was perfect from the get-go. It was easy to use, and I could manage everything without any kind of explanation. Presumably, if you could use it as a computer to send emails and browse the internet, it would be a piece of cake, too.

I registered the <Appraisal> skill to a vocal shortcut, and set the trigger keyword to "Execute Appraisal", while I pointed towards a target with my finger. In an actual game, it would be pretty difficult to setup, but in such a fine-tuned place like this, it was child's play.

I turned my right finger towards the pickaxe and said "Execute Appraisal". The sound of an electronic buzzer went off in my head, and a translucent window popped up near my index finger.

Name: Novice Iron Cube Pickaxe
Creator: Aoi Kousaka
Durability: 498/500
Special Effect: Effective against inorganic matter. Turns target into cubes.

Oh, it sure looked like a real appraisal. It consumed some Willpower because it was a skill, but I would say one point was pretty reasonable, all things considered.

—I see, so the pickaxe effect is what's cutting down the rocks into cubes. They seem like they'll fetch a higher price like that, instead of just crushing them, so that's a plus.

I kept digging afterwards and managed to gather up 20 stone pieces with the pickaxe. The fatigue of manual work was not something I was used to. After a while, my hands started to ache from the constant shock of digging into the rocks with the pickaxe. Seeing the 20 pieces of rock made me feel a sense of accomplishment, though. But there remained another problem.

—The cabin is 20 meters away or so. It's not that far away... But carrying 20 of these is gonna be a little...

Don't underestimate these mere 20 meters. To carry so many pieces of stone without a wheelbarrow or a backpack of some kind was going to be painful. True to that thought, I was out of breath and sweating bullets by the time I was done carrying them. I had left the suit jacket back in the cabin, but I still felt manual labor was twice as tiring wearing formal clothes like I was.

—Alright then, I hope these things actually fetch some sort of price.

Even if they didn't fetch a good price, I could make a furnace or a workbench with them. There were a bunch of ways to use them, so there wasn't really any loss.

I placed one of the stones inside the delivery box and closed the lid. The metallic sound didn't take long to follow. There were several coins inside. The total amount summed up to 802 DL. That was quite the price compared to normal stuff like gravel and rocks. It seemed like being turned into cubes was beneficial after all.

I sold the other 19 rocks.

The price didn't change even if I sold two or three at the same time. The estimated value for each was always 802 DL. The total amount for the 20 of them was 16040 DL. I would have gotten the same amount selling 150 pieces of bubblegum. The thought of that made me happy, for some reason. I couldn't help but be concerned as I saw the mountain of coins piling up. There didn't seem to be any sort of paper currency here.

"First, food. Then, some light. And finally, some blankets. I'll be happy as long as I have those."

Fortunately, it seemed like summer was right around the corner here. Despite there being a bunch of water nearby, I didn't feel all that cold right now. It would get cold from here all the way into tomorrow morning though, so it would be nice to have at least one blanket. I also figured it'd be safe to expect that one could see the moon and stars in a nature-filled place like this, so it wouldn't hurt to have a lantern and some candles.

I operated the translucent window and opened the catalog.

There was nothing in the eShop like magazines, games, or anything that reminded me of the civilization I came from—but it was full of fantasy-like stuff. There were cast iron swords starting from 30000 DL. There was also a seemingly old introductory book to summoning evil spirits for 280000 DL. I also found an 'Automated Defense (Golem)' that looked like a plain piece of armor, for the special bargain price of 300000 DL...

"Y-Yeah... There's a lot of fantasy items, alright."

Although, I was awfully curious about whether the book for summoning evil spirits was the real deal or not. My motivation to get it slowly dissipated when I thought about how many stone pieces I had to carry here to get the money.

—Let's see, food... A set of 'Hard-baked Barley Bread and Beef Jerky (Adult Male, Std. 5 Meal Set)' is 3000 DL. That seems pretty reasonable, all things considered.

Preserved meals like this usually didn't need to be cooked and could last for a long while, but 600 DL per serving was kinda high. Even if it was the cost of just one piece of stone, I needed a lot of stuff besides food, so I'd like to reduce expenses as much as possible.

"Hmm... Are there buyer reviews? It would be nice if they had impressions of the taste."

The display switched immediately as I touched the 'Review' button.

Rating: ★★★★☆
Reviewer: Manager, Labyrinth #112
- Water is a must, but the taste isn't bad. The hard barley bread is pretty hard, but does last for a long while. That, coupled with the salty pork taste of the jerky, will really make you want some water to go with it. You can eat it as is, but it's kind of difficult. You can get some vegetables and make a stew to make it really delicious.

Rating: ★★★★★
Reviewer: Manager's Family, Labyrinth #48
- The meat is yummy~ The meat was delicious~! ♥
I definitely would eat it again~

Rating: ★★☆☆☆
Reviewer: Manager, Labyrinth #28
- the cold district sux. the climate around here makes the bread so hard i think i could break my teeth if i tried. be careful if ur in a cold place like me. u wont be able to eat it without heating it up 1st.

"They actually have buyer reviews!?"

After having lost my composure for a second, my shoulders dropped with a sigh.

—What's with this halfway point between reality and fantasy... Oh well, it's always convenient to get the impressions from people who have tried it if you haven't.

In the end, I got five meals, a pitcher and cup, and a piece of animal fur, since that was cheaper than the blankets—also a lamp with oil, and about 10 matches to light it up. The total for all that ended up being 15120 DL, which meant I had used up almost all of my budget. The blanket was really pricey. I almost didn't have enough to buy a piece of fur big enough to work as a blanket. When you were in a survival setting like this, the first thing you needed to put on your list was to improve your bedding situation.

I kept putting coin after coin inside the piggy bank, but the large amount of coins made it a slow and tedious process. If you cashed in all the stuff you had at once, you'd get more high-value coins, so

I resolved to try to putting it all together the next time I used the delivery box.

"Thank you for choosing us!"

There went the mysterious home delivery again. Everything I had ordered came in a single cardboard box. I wondered if that was because I ordered it all at once.

—Oh? Couldn't I put together a makeshift blanket of sorts if I took apart this box?

I opened up Tundra again and hurriedly ordered a utility knife, and promptly used it to dismantle the box. The cardboard was a bit stiff, but you could use it as a mattress, as well as a blanket, so it was rather convenient.

—"What a beautiful sunset..." Is what I would say if I could actually see it from here.

After I took apart the cardboard, I placed it on the wooden bed. I chose a nearby pond to use as my water source, and dug a hole near the attached downstream river to set up a simple bathroom. Before I knew it, it was already evening. I managed to secure food, clothing, and a place to stay... But I guess that was kind of the standard procedure for survival games. By all accounts, I had 'made it' for the night.

Typically around nightfall, there would be dangerous spawns like zombies or dinosaurs, but that depended on the level of realism the games aimed for. That said, anything could end up difficult if the development teams put some real thought into it. Nowadays, survival games aimed more towards putting players into scripted events, and not so much into random variety in the way of dangerous creatures roaming around. The environments weren't even harsh snowing mountains or deserts. It was kind of ironic that real life was easier than the games themselves.

As I sat on a rock, I saw the reflection of the sunset hit the ravine's stone walls, which dyed the whole area an orange hue. There might be nocturnal carnivores, so I kept my eyes and ears peeled, but there didn't seem to be even the slightest hint of any animals around, big or small.

"Wow, the reviews weren't joking, eh..."

I tried eating some of the food I'd bought from Tundra. The bread was so hard I could barely make a dent in it with my teeth, and the jerky didn't fare much better either. I could only muster putting a little bit in my mouth to consume slowly. I guess preserved foods really were this salty. I wasn't expecting the damn bread to be salty too, though. They were right when they wrote I would need water for this. It wasn't inedible, but it was trying really hard to be. The unappetizing nature of the food made me crave for fruit or a chocolate bar.

I tried to think about my work while I chewed for dear life. First of all, what was with that door in the office building that brought me all the way here? I couldn't think of a good explanation for it aside from it being some sort of hypnotism trick.

I was sure I'd remember if such a breathtaking ravine like this place was part of a list of natural wonders; but I didn't recall any television shows, documentaries, or videos on the net about it. Between the ravine and the eShop with its delivery box, it didn't seem likely I was in the same world as I came from.

There was also the possibility that I was drugged out of my mind and was actually being tied down in a basement somewhere inside the office, or that this was some sort of fever dream. Somehow, I figured being transported to another world still made the most sense. With that in mind, I needed to figure out why they would bring me here in the first place. If I could sort out some sort of goal, it would be easier to work towards it.

So, let's assume this was all real and was part of the training Karumi-san had mentioned. The training period itself would last approximately three months, and it would be safe to assume that a typical Japanese person, who was well-versed in games, would find it difficult to last long in such a natural setting. There weren't many people who were able to survive in this kind of harsh environment, let alone seek out a job for one. Even if their purpose was to kidnap or kill me, it wasn't like I was rich or had good insurance policies, or anything. There was nothing to gain from doing either to me.

If it was just for the thrill of killing, then I would think there would be more effort put into doing so. If I went by those Tundra reviews, there were at least a hundred people out here who lived normally. Which meant there wasn't any sort of conspiracy behind this, and it was truly just backed by a normal company. Realistically then, I really was just stuck in the middle of an evaluation period to see if I could adapt to the labyrinth manager life or not.

Now, if this training was to see if I was fit to be a labyrinth manager in another world, then the survival setting clashed with that. But if I could unravel the true meaning behind all of this, then the whole situation would fall into place.

Then there was the two documents I found today. One with a truthful report which stated there was nothing but a beat up cabin here, and a false one which listed the labyrinth as completed and fully operational. Was that not what caused this confusion in the first place? Which meant the labyrinth was indeed truly finished, according to the documents Karumi-san and the company had. If I went off that, then putting a newbie like me on a three month trial period, with nothing to go off of but a crappy cabin to live in, didn't seem too strange a proposal—like I was expected to do well enough given the circumstance.

This place being located at the bottom of a ravine was pretty poor as far as transportation was concerned. It was like this labyrinth was made to lure in travelers and surprise them with demons and traps. It was safe to say that the possibility of this place being even remotely convenient to travel to, or even find in the first place, was low. It made no sense. All in all, the possibility that Karumi-san sent me here in the first place, under the impression I wouldn't have any difficulty for three months, seemed high. And so, this wasn't really any sort of trial to see if I could become the master of a labyrinth, or a special event to see if I could actually live in another world—I just got unlucky. It would seem that having to survive was the result of a bunch of misfortunes piled up one on top of another. The end goal of this whole ordeal was to just stick it out until the end of the three months.

—Hah, were you expecting a management sim? Well, too bad, it's actually a survival sim! Talk about switching to hard mode...

And so I continued to grind my teeth away on the bread and jerky.

—My first survival gameplay, eh? If I was recording everything I did, it would be like one of those ultra-realistic let's play runs people do sometimes.

Although I had seen them before, I'd never actually streamed one myself. I couldn't figure out how to have the viewers only listen to my commentary, especially when I played them in a multiplayer setting. And if I stopped talking altogether, then it wouldn't be a game stream, but just a normal gameplay video.

Despite all the gripes and concerns I had, this type of living wasn't so bad. It was more challenging than I could have hoped for, too. If this was my training, then managing the facilities would be rather fun, in the end.

The nighttime darkness had finally started to settle in by the time I was done eating the hard bread and smelly jerky, so I put some oil in the lamp, and took out the matches to have them on standby. The ravine quickly went from orange to red as night crept in slowly, but surely.

"Wow..."

The soft evening glow bathed the bottom of the ravine for about five minutes before night finally took over. The night scenery had a phosphorescent tinge of white and blue. The gentle cobalt blue glow seemed as if it were emitted by some sort of creature, and was spread out across the ravine.

—Are those glowing things some sort of moss... or weed? There so much of it.

When I tried looking for the source of the light, I found it was from moss which stuck to stones, and tiny weeds which sprouted from the soil, that emitted the dim glow. The light wasn't that strong, though. Like you probably couldn't read a book with it, for example. But it was bright enough to walk around, or scoop water out of the pond, or even do some light work.

—I guess I'll just use the lamp indoors. I don't wanna ruin this natural view with it.

After I got my fill of the magical view that was the naturally lit ravine, accompanied by the soothing sound of the flowing river, I headed back inside the cabin and fell asleep on top of the cardboard I had placed previously, and covered myself up with the fur blanket.

—Preparing a good place to sleep was the right choice. It's pretty humid around here, so the mornings are pretty cold.

I awoke as the cool breeze of the early morning entered through the gaps in the cabin and across my skin. When I went outside to gaze upon the sky from the bottom of the ravine, I found the left side to be mad with red, while the right was dyed in blue.

My head was clear now, so I thought about the time. If I assumed this world's day lasted 24 hours, and I was at the same latitude as Japan, then sunset started around 6 to 7PM, and I watched the local scenery for about two hours and went to sleep around 9PM. If this place really was another world, then I wasn't sure how far a normal Earth's calendar would go by comparison, but the hands on my wristwatch told me it was 5AM right now, so I would have slept about eight hours in total.

"Ah, if only I could use some of that excess sleep to play games instead..."

A game I recently downloaded for the PC back at home came to mind. It was set in a post-apocalyptic desert world, and you had to explore the desolate land and scrap for materials to craft your own weapons; all this while looking for the remnants of humanity which were said to be below the ruins of the desert, and held a giant stash of weapons and vehicles. There were Non-Player Characters (NPCs) that were people that had survived the collapse of civilization and cooperated with the player, but could also be hostile depending on various parameters. It was a pretty lonely game if you wanted some sort of online multiplayer interaction.

It was said that the average playtime before actually getting the hang of the game's systems was 80 hours, but I had 'played' here for about 12, and I was already having fun. Despite being in what I presumed to be a fantasy world survival game, you could say I was already set for life at this point, but that was all a matter of perspective.

—If the sun rises in the same way it does on Earth, that means the ravine goes from north to south, and the entrance of the cabin is facing the south.

I vaguely predicted my position while I looked up at the sky.

Then again, if this really was a natural environment, then one might be able to discern the same information at this depth using the way the surrounding vegetation and trees turned towards sunlight. But it was kind of hard to calculate the direct angle of said sunlight since it bounced so many times across the walls of the ravine.

"I want to take a look around the ravine today, better get some weapons first..."

I saw medieval swords, lances, maces, and some metal armor in the Tundra catalog. I didn't really feel the presence of dangerous animals yesterday or anything, but if they sold them in this world, then it was because there was something dangerous you might need protection from.

—Alright, let's use the morning to search the same rock I got the stones from yesterday, then buy up the metal weapons, and go exploring.

After I repeated the task of digging up 20 pieces of stone, I sold them to the delivery box four times, and bought a wooden wheelbarrow, a lance with an iron top, and a cast iron dagger from Tundra. By then, the sun had peaked at one side of the ravine, so it must have been close to noon. I looked over the valley while I gnawed on some of my hard lunch. With my cabin as the center, the ravine extended about 700 to 800 meters, north and south respectively. If my calculations were correct, then that was approximately 1.5 kilometers. The steepness of the cliff didn't diminish at all across the length of the ravine, and there didn't seem to be an easy way to descend down here from the surface.

The width of the precipice looked to be consistently 30 meters across, although it seemed to expand up to at least 50 meters high in the few spots where the cliff went down slightly. It looked like I didn't have to worry about dangerous animals, or a surprise attack from enemies inside the ravine, but escape was also impossible.

Before I went to work in the morning, I used the <Dungeon Management Tool> to get some info on the pickaxe. I found that my Willpower had been restored when I checked the status screen. Somehow it seemed to refill over time. The rate of recovery for Willpower was such that it filled one point per hour if I moved around or worked, two if I was resting. A full recovery was made if I slept for at least seven hours.

Aside from conducting experiments with Willpower's restoration rates, I tried using the <Appraisal> skill on the various plants around the ravine, and found two promising varieties of plant-life.

Name: Waterdry Tree
Description: A tree that grows in lands of plentiful water. A natural bag is said to be used for storing water inside its trunk, and no moisture is found within its branches. Removing the water results in withering of the tree. Useful for processing as firewood. Reaches maturity quickly. If a branch or seed is planted, it can reach a few meters in height within one week.

Was what I got when I appraised one of the shrubs with thin, twisted trunks near the cabin. Apparently it stored water inside, so it was pretty useful for when you needed clean water, and it could be used for firewood as well.

—But the trunk itself is twisted and thin, so wouldn't it be hard to use for construction?

I gathered up about 30 branches and planted them close to the cabin. With this, I should be able to secure firewood, provided things went well.

> **Name**: Bluelight Moss
> **Description**: Moss which grows in lands of abundantly clear water. Capable of growing in some environments without sunlight so long as there is a supply of water. Can emit a pale light. Will not wither in places without water and will continue to emit its characteristic light, but will not propagate.

The other thing I appraised was this moss. It seemed like the magical view of the whole ravine was due to countless amounts of these growing all over the place. If one put a piece inside a glass container, it would become an easy source of light. I wasn't really mining underground, but if I were to make a labyrinth, then I would plant them at set intervals to provide better lighting than any exhaustible torch would.

Even if the light was a bit on the weak side, it was bright enough to illuminate the area in which it grew. That made it a strong contender as a light source compared to the sort of lightmoss one would find on Earth. Since it wasn't uncommon in the valley, the fact that it was easy to obtain was a real godsend. As for the appraisals, I was expecting that it wouldn't be necessary to reappraise the same type of item if it was done before, but it looked like that wasn't the case. You had to use the skill every single time regardless.

I planted some of the waterdry tree branches I'd picked up earlier around the cabin, and dug out more stone with the time I had left. It was already evening by the time I was done selling them to the delivery box. It was a bit hard to move the wheelbarrow around as the wheels were made of wood, but it sure beat carrying stone pieces back and forth by hand. The usefulness of tools could not be underestimated.

I felt as if the days here went by faster than those on Earth. Although, it may have just seemed that way because I moved around constantly, compelled by the sheer enjoyment of the 'gameplay.'

"Hmm... Farm work sure seems tough..."

After dinner, I took a look at Tundra's catalog. While I sat there in front of the cabin, the sun went down and was replaced by the bluish glow of the moss. I still gnawed away at my jerky and bread, but remembered that relying solely on preserved food was not only bad for the economy, but also for overall health. Tundra sold fresh vegetables, but the price made you think twice, and they sold out fast despite that.

As I calmly perused the eShop, I noticed something. While the actual process of collection and delivery of Tundra was still very much a mystery, the quantity of goods sold through the service was basically updated in real-time as people bought from, and sold goods to, Tundra. I could tell because the stone cubes I sold were in the 'Stone' category.

Black Shadow Stone - Building Stone (10x3 m.) == 1300 DL
Seller: Manager, Labyrinth #228

Rating: ★★★☆☆
Reviewer: Manager, Labyrinth #172
- Good quality stone, although the amount for sale is too low. It's a high quality black shadow stone, so it's suitable for building interiors. You can also give it a good luster with a little bit of polishing. I wanted to make a stone wall, but the amount available for purchase was too little so I gave up. I expect an increase in production output in the future. You could also make stone pavings if they were a little smaller.

In Tundra's system you didn't gain additional remuneration even if your item sold after it was placed in the catalog. But seeing someone had bought the stone I sold, and left a review, made me feel kinda happy. Before I noticed, I was grinning like an idiot.

I resolved to keep that comment about increasing production in mind. I checked up on food ingredients next. I could tell vegetables were a popular product from the reviews. It seemed like they constantly sold out right after being put up in the catalog. And so much demand, meant an increase in price.

I searched for seeds and saplings to see if I could raise the crops myself, but from the outset, proper agriculture still seemed difficult in this world. I tried to find more specific examples of fruits and crop seeds in the catalog.

ating: ★★
Reviewer: Manag
- Good quality stone,
It's a high quality black s
building interiors. You can also
little bit of polishing. I wanted to
amount avai le for purchase was t
expect an increa se in production o
could also m pavings if t

Rating: ★
Reviewer
PER

rinth
!! i
ca
whol
ardr

Ice Fruit Seedling == 800 DL
Seller: Manager, Labyrinth #28

Rating: ★★☆☆☆
Reviewer: Manager, Labyrinth #35
- impossible to use in the desert. I thought it would be okay if I planted it underground deep enough since it's cold, but it withered out by the 10th day, it might have something to do with water quality here

Rating: ★★★★★
Reviewer: Manager, Labyrinth #785
Environment: Permafrost
- Sweet, delicious! - After about 40 days from planting it you can get get about 10 fruits so big they won't fit in your hand, per harvest. The skin is kinda hard, but it's sweet and delicious. The fact it doesn't freeze even in my environment is the best!

Dry Land Rice Seedling == 3000 DL
Brand: ~Devilish Glance~
Seller: Manager, Labyrinth #421

Rating: ★★★★★
Reviewer: Manager's Family, Labyrinth #48
Environment: Savanna...ish?
- Everything excellent besides the brand name - It took 80 days to harvest after planting. I'm happy it's resistant to dryness. The harvest amount wasn't bad and neither was the taste. I shared some of it around the nearby village and it became pretty popular, but couldn't answer when they asked me about the brand's name...

Rating: ★★★☆☆
Reviewer: Manager, Labyrinth #601
Environment: Temperate humid climate - plateau
- It's resistant to dryness but weak against cold? - Harvested after 65 days from planting. I raised them in a prototype field. The fact they don't need much time for watering is a plus. The same day winter started was the same day they became out of season, and some of them froze and withered, so I had to wipe my tears as I harvested while most were still not ripe. The taste was nice but my climate might be too harsh for them.

As you could see, it looked like there was nothing fantasy-esque with regards to the growth of crops. There were lots of games aimed at casual players in which crops could be harvested in about one to five days after planting. But here? It took a while for them to grow. It was useful when the reviewers would put the climate and time to harvest in their comments, though. My training period would be over before I had time to harvest some of these crops with long periods of growth. I didn't really have the luxury to grow and harvest them with my current time allotment.

Raw meat and fish were cheap, but sold out. Items of luxury and processed goods remained in stock, though... From what I had gathered, managers with labyrinths located in places like meadows or other calmer climates were the ones participating in agriculture. There didn't seem to be any type of greenhouse cultivation, so the seasonal influence affected everyone. We were in the early part of summer right now, so edible wild plants were rather abundant, but most of them were bitter when compared to normal vegetables. And most of all, it took more time and effort to process said plants to remove the astringent tastes.

"Hm? Maybe this one might be good for me, eh?"

My hand stopped upon one of the seasonal items as I checked the catalog.

Lantern Pumpkin Seed == 150 DL
Left in Stock: 3 remaining

Rating: ★★★★★
Reviewer: Manager's Family, Labyrinth #601
- For seasonal interior use. Careful you don't leave anything raw inside! It sprouts as soon as you plant it and you can pluck off a pumpkin big enough to make a lantern in about a day. Their skin is pretty hard so you'll have to have a tool ready to process these. They're also packed full inside so you'll have to take it all out. I repeat, be careful not to leave anything raw inside the lanterns you make, there'll be bugs and mold if you're not!

Rating: ★★★★☆
Reviewer: Manager's Family, Labyrinth #48
- i had a blast making them with my mom but theyre kinda scary when theyre done!!!

Like the ones found during Halloween, right? Those seemed to be in a lot of online games.

—Yeah, the ones they implemented for seasonal events and didn't bother deleting the data so they can use it next year too, hah.

Surely they must have felt lonely being ditched like that. There sure seemed to be a lot of comments suggesting to throw away the insides of pumpkins used for lanterns. They all said it wasn't tasty. Not like it was poisonous or anything, though. They almost seemed like event items. You could even plant them and have it ready the next day.

I ordered the remaining three in stock, and used the light of the moss to help me put the money into the piggy bank.

“Thank you very much!”

—You know... Hearing that voice every time really ruins my immersion.

“Whoa, these sure are big.”

When I opened the envelope that was delivered, I found seeds as big as an eraser inside. I figured I should try to plant one for now. I thought that actual soil would be better for this, so I used the <Dungeon Management Tool> and selected the ‘Soil Improvement Tool’ from the Terrain Improvement System.

—And that’s it.

If this was a dungeon creation game, I could maybe create designated plots of land and switch up the field’s soil. But instead, what fell in front of me, like that shovel and pickaxe before, was a simple metal-edged hoe. I didn’t mind actually cultivating a big plot of land, but how long would it take to ‘improve soil’ with a single cheap hoe like this?

I chose a patch of ground near the cabin, used the hoe to till a bit of it, and planted the lantern pumpkin seed inside. I grabbed the remaining water I had from dinner earlier and sprinkled it onto the ground.

—I hope it’s actually edible. Not expecting much since it was so cheap, but still, that would be nice.

I patted the soil I planted the seeds in and prayed for a good harvest. With a loud yawn, I headed to bed afterwards. I’d been moving non-stop ever since this morning so I was pretty beat. The next day I woke up to find an enormous pumpkin was born in front of the cabin.

“Nice.”

Boring remark, I know. It looked like it was about 50 centimeters across and 25 centimeters tall. I was surprised it grew this much overnight. It looked more and more like a game's seasonal event item with each passing second.

"I have to see if I can eat it or not... Umm... I don't really have a pot to cook it in. Maybe I can just grill it?"

I selected the <Dungeon Management Tool> and chose the 'Forest Processing Tool' from the Terrain Improvement System. As I expected, a hatchet then fell right in front of me. The waterdry trees that grew around were pretty thin, so the hatchet should be enough to cut some down.

I cut down three tree trunks, snapped off the branches, and stuck them in the soil. Although it was just out of consideration to prevent running out of resources, I still felt a level of reverence for what nature had provided me. Very much a Japanese-type thing to feel.

I easily chopped a bunch of pieces of firewood to about 20 centimeters long, then I took one and chopped it into finer pieces. With the smaller pieces surrounded by the longer ones, I lit them both together using matches I had bought from Tundra.

Waterdry trees really were useful, as they were easy to make into firewood without having to dry them first. Normally a tree wouldn't catch fire so easily, let alone start smoking. I remembered one time I played a game where humanity had collapsed due to a zombie outbreak, and if you tried to set a live tree on fire, you would fail pretty quick. Should you have managed to even light one though, the amount of smoke that billowed out would draw the attention of the zombies, and even other players. So me and my friends would carry a bunch of wood into a big church on the map, dry it out, then wait for another player to come by, and then we'd go...

"Welcome, would you like to worship the wood?"

Ah, the memories brought a tear to my eye. Being the crazy heretics we were, we would beat up anyone who wouldn't submit to the sacred wood.

Cooking the pumpkin proved to be very simple. I tossed the whole thing, skin and all, into the open air fire. With a moderate flame, it should be edible if you peeled off the scorched outside bits... I think. It would save time from having to crack it open since I didn't have a frying pan or wire mesh handy. Anyway, I roasted it directly on the fire for about 30 minutes before I peeled off the skin with the hatchet, red insides to come out.

"Welp... Nothing inedible in here, but..."

There was practically no sweetness to it. Maybe a slight amount, but the overwhelming vegetable smell completely drowned it out. The texture and subsequent feeling of it going down your throat was also anything but pleasant. It felt grainy and rough, almost like a sand pear, and it left an awful aftertaste that was reminiscent of sawdust in my mouth. While it was edible, it was also far from tasty.

—I'm glad it's kind of edible... But I think I'll pass.

While every passing meal of consuming this wretched pumpkin might prevent you from starving, you'd slowly edge more and more towards just wanting to be starved.

—Now that I think about it, characters in survival games don't care about the flavor of anything, do they?

Among all the survival games I'd played so far, it was commonplace to eat stuff like canned sardines or cold amoeba cells for every meal. But when you became the affected party, then of course you'd want a change in meal types even if it wasn't lobster or caviar. All that aside, at least there was still a lot to eat... So I guess I didn't have to worry about running out food...

The days went by as I continued to dig out stones, plant more waterdry trees for firewood, and pondered purchases while browsing Tundra.

When I looked at the various reviews, it dawned on me that many of the labyrinth managers were Japanese or lived in Japan. Among the typical things that were manufactured by them, the ones which stood out more conspicuously were things like modern underwear, cat ear accessories, and soft-looking robes. Of course, the fact that they were hand-made meant there was little stock to go around, and what little there was sold out almost immediately.

Strangely enough though, there was still lots of stock for convenient and reasonably priced items. Presumably all of them were provided up by local denizens of the world, which seemed to imply that their level of civilization wasn't all that modern.

Most clothes seemed to be made out of linen, sometimes cotton. There were simple dyed shirts, and even some with some sort of detailed designs, too. There was a level of regional disparity;

everything looked more like it came out of middle-aged European society, than not. A period of time you'd be all too familiar with if you played a lot of fantasy-themed games before.

Right as I had started to settle into the groove of waking up everyday to gather stones and any other valuable items, and buying food and clothes from Tundra with my profit... an incident occurred. Maybe it was because I had gotten fed up with my newfound lifestyle, but one morning I found myself oversleeping, only to be awoken by the sound of something rolling across the ravine, followed by a big bang.

"Wha... Did some rocks fall, or something?"

I ran out of the cabin while rubbing the drowsiness from my eyes. About three of four meters out were some waterdry trees I had planted. I thought they were about the age to be cut down, but they were now shredded to pieces.

"Well, I guess that saves me the trouble of cutting them down... What the hell happened here?"

I made out what looked to be a person's silhouette among the mess of broken trunks and twigs that were the waterdry trees.

"Is that a person? Don't tell me someone fell all the way down here!"

I looked up, but all I could see was the usual steep cliff and the unreachable sky. I couldn't imagine falling from that high up straight onto the ground would be anything but dangerous to one's life.

—A girl...? Wait a minute. A girl falling from the sky is a game scenario flag for a new character introduction. But what's the point of that if the person died from the fall!?

A young girl with chestnut-colored hair and a dress, covered in dust and soil, was collapsed amongst the wreckage of waterdry trees...

"Ah..."

I was so unexpectedly captivated by the girl that I had forgotten the gravity of the situation for a moment.

She was like a budding rose. Her innocent face was a captivating combination of a young girl's cuteness and a grown woman's beauty. Although her clothes were dirty, she didn't seem like a doll or one of those smutty 3D game models. No amount of dirt and grime could obscure the fact that she was a spunky cute girl full of life. I wouldn't keep my composure even if you had told me this was just a game event, so I rushed to her side.

—I don't care if you're an illusion or if I've finally lost my mind thanks to those pumpkins. I don't care what happens afterwards, just please be alive...!

I reached out to her as gently as I could, and touched her soft-looking cheeks. I felt the warm and soft, yet somewhat rough, sensation of her skin.

"Thank goodness, she's still alive."

The warmth of life in the girl which ran through my fingers relieved me from the bottom of my heart.

—But I still need to treat her. If we were in Japan, I would carry her to a hospital so they could take a good look at her, but...

There were no such things as hospitals in this fantasy ravine that I didn't even know how to get out of. But first aid from a rookie like me was better than no treatment at all.

—Did the fragile waterdry tree branches cushion her fall? Well, it's good that the soil where she fell is also close to the wet, marshy part of the valley.

The waterdry tree trunks were scattered all over the damp ground. They might be useless as firewood now, but it was a cheap price to pay for saving the girl's life. Though... Wouldn't it be rude to say the poor trees were cheap?

"Oh, she's pretty light."

I placed my hands on her back and her legs to hold her up and looked back at the broken waterdry trees.

—Thank you for saving her. I'll be sure to come back and dry all of you off. No one's life will be lost in vain while I'm around.

I thanked the broken waterdry trees before I carried the girl back to the cabin. I had raised the trees to be used as firewood, so it wasn't like they were going to thank me or respond in any way, but I didn't want to seem ungrateful. Maybe I was being a little too Japanese, but I liked being this way.

—Right, I want you to live, and I did say I wouldn't mind whatever came after, but...

My strength was dissipating quickly. I felt my legs were on the verge of collapse and soon I would find myself on the ground, too. Did this world have to throw me a curveball every time?

I placed the girl on top of a table in front of the cabin that I had cobbled together from piled up stone. I had to clean the dirt off her before I did anything else, so I went inside to fetch a towel from the cabin. I dipped it into water and wrung it out. When I returned, the girl I had placed on the table was nowhere to be found. In her place was a tawny, fluffy dog-looking thing!

It wasn't possible that they switched places. The dog-looking thing was wearing the same dress as the girl had. How could this furball of a pet be such a cute-looking girl? I almost wanted to drop to my knees and cry out "Why!?" at the top of my lungs. Maybe I was just so tired that this was a hallucination.

—A... god? No, it's more like a human...

The tawny dress-wearing ball of fur was about 130 centimeters long. The palm of her hand seemed to have a paw pad, but she still had five long fingers. There were also a lot of joints, so I supposed she could use tools like a normal person. Her bone structure from her spine down to her legs looked more like a human's instead of an animal's too, so she must be able to stand on two legs and walk around. Nothing about it really made any sense to me, but there wasn't any time to process what had happened. I had more pressing matters to deal with.

"Maybe I really haven't gotten used to this life after all..."

Why did this doggy look like a cute girl? I couldn't believe it myself.

—Wait... I don't remember ever having a preference for furry things, could it be that I—

From all the games with heroines that I had encountered so far in life... I was confident that human companions always beat out furry ones, according to me that is.

—No! Now's not the time to be thinking about that!

The girl turned dog didn't change the fact that she needed treatment. She just looks a little... No, it would be terrible of me to change my attitude just because her appearance was different. After I slapped some sense into myself I cleaned the parts of her which were dirty, while I checked out the condition of the rest of her body. There were severe cuts and bruises, but there didn't seem to be any fractures or heavy bleeding. I was glad there was nothing that needed to be sewn or operated on.

—She looks okay, at least.

"Execute Appraisal."

Ann Half-Kobold **Vitality**: 4/18 **Strength**: 5/28 **Willpower**: 8/25

Kobolds were a pretty famous monster race in fantasy games, right? It had decreased a lot, but she still had some Vitality left, and it didn't seem like she had any severe injuries as it wasn't decreasing. What a relief. According to my fantasy knowledge, kobolds were monsters, but this girl had such a gentle look to her, and her fangs weren't even sharp. She also seemed to groom her claws as they weren't really long. If anything, she looked more like a gentle herbivore than a carnivorous beast to me.

She was also wearing clothes, so it was safe to assume her species was intelligent enough to talk, at the very least. I felt like this would be one of those game events in which a window popped up and I would need to choose between "End Her Misery" or "Save Her". But the thought of ending the life of a fluffy creature in pain seemed too much for me.

I wasn't sure what kind of higher being this labyrinth had, if any at all, but after seeing her as a normal cute girl, the consequence of choosing "End Her Misery" would be too much for me to bear. She didn't seem that strong status-wise, and I probably could manage even if I got attacked, so let's choose "Save Her".

I took her inside so I could treat her easier. There was something I noticed as I held up her fluffy kobold body. If this was a normal RPG then just placing her on the bed would be more than enough to restore her Vitality, but in this case I would have to take her clothes off in order to wipe down her whole body with the cloth.

—She smells like an unwashed dog...

You may think I was being rather harsh, but I was having second thoughts about putting her on the bed. I took off the dusty dress and wiped her fur down with a cloth until the dirt started to come off. Eventually the cloth would become pitch black with soot, so I rinsed it out and pressed onward. By the end of it, her fur seemed to be more glossy than before. Once she was clean, I carried her to the bed and laid her down, and continued to monitor her situation.

"Execute Appraisal..."

—Her Vitality's still four, huh? The fact that it's been a few hours since I found her, yet she has shown no signs of recovering, is worrying. Even if we are in a fantasy RPG-like world, isn't it bad that she isn't recovering over time?

I had been watching her the whole time since I laid her down on the bed, but her condition remained the same. The only thing I had heard come out of her were strained gasps. If you discounted old game systems, it was very strange she wasn't recovering with rest here. Even if they wanted to take a more realistic approach to recovery time, it just didn't make sense not to regain anything after all these hours.

The only possibility I could think of was... Maybe some of her internal organs were damaged? If so, then the amount of Vitality she regained and lost would be almost the same over time. Should I rely on Tundra again? It didn't seem like something I could solve with just first aid. Next time, I'd like to get a book on herbalism and memorize it. In the end, I opened up the catalog and looked for something that would be useful.

—Hm, I see magic potions, vitality potions, and revive potions in the Medicine category here.

Amazing, they sold potions right next to the usual stuff like compresses and disinfectant, as if it was the most normal thing in the world.

"The simplest Grade 9 Vitality potions costs 20000 DL. It's a pretty hefty price, but I don't think I can do much about it. The cheapest Grade 10 Revive potions go for 45000 DL. Good Dark Lord..."

The price made me spout out something pretty weird just now. It wasn't like I couldn't pay it, but my savings would melt after getting both.

—Dang it. It'll hurt my wallet, but I'd feel bad later if she dies like this.

As I looked at her fluffy fur getting cold… The only thing that went through my mind was how I wanted to avoid having to bury it into the ground if it got any colder. I could save money again, but I couldn't do anything but face regret when it came to an actual living being.

"It's better to regret what you've done, than not doing anything at all, I guess."

If it was all about the money, I could always dig out more stone and sell it again. It was better to try and help now, rather than living on wondering if I could have—should have—done something. Rather than missing out on a limited availability game and regretting it, isn't it better to laugh all the way home after finding out it's shovelware?

I ordered the vitality and revive potions from Tundra. Both of them came inside separate blue and green pots, with a dubious smell. Well, I wasn't expecting less from magical medicine.

From the reviews, it was the sort of medicine you drank that had lasting effects, so it would be pointless to drink it all in one go. It also said you could apply the potion to an affected area, but ingesting it had a stronger effect.

So there was one problem now.

The potion was like a normal medicine, and she wasn't conscious… How can I have her drink it? I could just pour it into her mouth, but if she choked or spit out something this expensive I think I would just cry. The traditional method to get unconscious people to drink medicine was doing it mouth-to-mouth, but she had a dog muzzle… And I had no experience with kissing at all. Do you understand my dilemma, now?

—My first kiss will be with a dog… No, this doesn't count, right? I'm just closing her mouth with mine so she doesn't spit the medicine out!

If you compared mouth-to-mouth between humans and someone with a long and thin dog muzzle like her, I think I would have to give her a very deep kiss to make her drink the medicine.

—This sure is hardcore... No! This is where a gamer has to be brave!

I remembered the words I learned in a certain guild of a war-themed online game I was part of for many years. "When the going gets tough, the tough get going!" So I got a mouthful of both potions. Despite the dubious smell, they tasted like mint. When I placed my lips against her muzzle and poured the liquid right into her throat, she tried to spit it back out. But I still forced it in... Yeah, the hurdle to have had such a passionate kiss was high even for lovers.

—Hehe... I did it, I really did! I got over the difficult challenge!

After I was finished making her drink both potions, the mental fatigue was so great I ended up with my hands on the floor. But I still wanted to praise myself for doing it well. I never thought I would have to overcome giving medicine mouth-to-mouth to a dog-faced girl. Cross-species communication sure sounded like it was gonna be hard... I just prayed this kobold was really a female; I didn't want my first kiss being with a boy.

I didn't know if it was a hallucination or something, but I was sure she seemed like a normal girl at first. I wanted to believe she was a female since she wore a dress at first, but then I realized our cultures might be different. Maybe I got a little careless. If it turned out to be a male... Then I guess I would just seal away the memories of the past hour.

"If she really turned out just to be a cute trap, I don't think I could laugh it off. I really don't!"

I felt as if some sort of flag had gone off as a pretty nasty word had come out of my mouth, unintentionally.

—Oh, right. I need to order some clothes, don't I? I can't really put those dirty clothes back on her without washing them first, can I?

The clothes she was wearing at first were torn off in a corner and were dirty, so I didn't really want to put them on her again. I opened Tundra yet again, and used nearly all of my remaining savings, after the potions, to order a simple children-sized linen dress for her to put on.

—I guess I'll be eating grilled pumpkin for a while longer...

I started to notice the effects of the potion as my mental fatigue wore off.

Two hours later and her Vitality had gone up past 10, and her Strength and Willpower had recovered considerably as well. I sat on a simple wooden chair I had made using the trunk of a waterdry tree and watched over her now restful sleep while I flipped through a book.

I entered the <Dungeon Management Tool>, opened the 'Monster Management' menu, and chose the <Monster Translation Tool> under the 'Japanese to Monster Language' dropdown... And out popped a dictionary and a practice textbook. I wasn't even surprised anymore. I thought it would be really convenient if it translated everything for me with a magic tool or something, but of course it would just be a dictionary.

The monster language seemed easy enough to understand, so at least that was good, I guess. There were some sort of dialects in different places, but it was almost like modern Japanese. They even had the same characters and all that. I can only assume this monster language used Japanese as a base, but who in the heck spread it into this world? Whatever, it was convenient to say the least.

The kobold finally woke up right as sunset began to turn into night.

"Wh-Where... am I?"

Her voice was cute, and you could sense the intelligence behind her words. If we were talking voice only, there wasn't much difference between her and a normal Japanese girl. The kind of cute I like... Now that I thought about it, it was pretty close to one of those cute anime voices.

My chest was filled with relief. If she had that kind of voice then the chance of her being a female was high. My whole rescue act wouldn't become something I'd want to pretend never happened. I was pretty secular myself, being Japanese, but I'd like to offer a prayer of thanks right now.

"Good morning, this is Labyrinth #228. I'm the manager. I think you fell down from above. Would you happen to remember anything about that?"

It was important to be polite in every first meeting; just common sense as a working adult.

“Labyrinth... Fell... down...”

She seemed a little confused. Might be because of the shock of the fall. But the fact she could communicate at all, and wasn’t hostile, made me happy.

“You still look kind of tired. Take it easy and sleep a little more, please.”

I gently patted her head until she finally closed her eyes. She seemed pretty pleased and fell asleep right away. I prepared grilled pumpkin for dinner, if you could call that dinner, but the kobold didn’t wake up again that night.

Since she occupied the only bed, I worried about what to do for a moment, but I figured it would be like sleeping with a dog, so I slipped into the bed as well. Maybe it was because I dedicated my whole life to play, but I had never owned a cat or a dog myself. I’d always wanted to sleep with a pet, though. That night I fell soundly asleep while wrapped in the soft blanket, with the warm and fluffy kobold as a body pillow. Having lived a completely solitary life in the bottom of a ravine for a week, the sensation of having someone close by was really appreciated.

I was awoken by a pleasant shake—I wondered if it was morning outside already. I could feel the gentle sunlight pouring onto me from the gaps of the closed window. The one shaking me awake was yesterday’s kobold. The soft feeling of her paws on my shoulder was pretty comfy.

“Hey, hey! Wake up, Mister. It’s morning already!”

Being woken up by such a sweet voice sure was nice. I wasn’t really interested in the actual goods, but I kind of understood how the guys that bought alarm clocks that woke them up with the voice of game heroines felt like.

“Hgnh...!”

I got up and stretched out. I felt like I slept a thousand times better than every night since I arrived here, thanks to the blanket and furry body pillow.

“Good morning. You’re looking better now.”

I greeted her with a smile on my face. Smiling while greeting was an important part of communication.

"Good morning. Say, where are we? Heaven?" she asked.

Something felt kinda off when such a cute anime girl voice was let out by this furry little thing. There were lots of talking animals in shows aimed at kids, but actually seeing it in real life felt more uncomfortable than exciting.

"This place is called Labyrinth #228. I'm the manager here, my name's Aoi."

It might not be my fault, but I felt kinda embarrassed to call this place, with nothing but this shabby cabin, a labyrinth.

"I think you probably fell down here from above around midday yesterday. Do you remember anything about it?"

I wanted to say "Boss, a girl fell from the sky!", but I doubt a girl from a completely different species, in another world, would catch the reference. Man, I wanted someone around that understood my jokes.

"Fell down... Huh...? So I'm alive even though I fell down from the Great Saredo Rift bridge? And in a labyrinth? Are you one of the Dark Lord's subordinates!?"

Now that was quite the info dump. The only thing I caught of that for now was that this ravine was apparently called Great Saredo Rift.

"Maybe we should slow down a little. Would you tell me your name first?" I asked.

"Huh? Oh, okay... I'm Ann, from the Kobold clan. I forgot to say it, but thank you so much for saving me, Mister!"

"You're such a polite nice girl, aren't you?"

Ann's polite but friendly words made me smile unexpectedly. Ann let out a strange sound, almost like an "Awoo!?" all of a sudden when I did. I wondered if human smiles were creepy for kobolds... Interspecies communication sure was difficult.

"I am the manager of Labyrinth #228, but I started pretty recently, so I don't know much about this world. Do you think you could tell me what you know about this place, Ann?"

“Yes! I can tell you everything I know, leave it to me!”

As a person that couldn’t get enough of fluffy animals, I was unable to resist from patting Ann’s head after she replied with so much energy.

“Let’s see… There’s a lot of clans in this world, like mine, the Kobolds…”

According to what Ann told me, this area was called the “Berkud Border Dominion”. And there apparently was a land route that continued east into the continent, but we also were surrounded by sea in the remaining three directions. I assumed it was something like a peninsula, but Ann told me she didn’t really know its shape since she hadn’t traveled very much. It seemed like this country’s leader was a certain Mister Dark Lord, and they had various races living together in this world, including humans like me and kobolds like Ann.

There were familiar fantasy game races like elves and dwarfs living in harmony with races that would normally get classified as monsters like ogres, cyclops, and even goblins. It was a multi-ethnic land with many races, but since the Dark Lord united them together, all the races and cultures joined under the new demonic banner of the country of Daemon. It seemed that any differences between the clans got resolved in not so amicable terms by the Elingald clan that was composed of cyclops from the north. I guess it was easy to understand why they ended up all together that way.

There were various races living peacefully even in the pioneering village Ann was from. It was kinda surprising to me since the Earth I came from couldn’t seem to get out of conflict because of cultural differences or history. The political system seemed to be a feudal system made up by the Dark Lord as the King, and the nobility. They valued power higher than bloodline around here, so that meant nobles were beings that showed outstanding physical or mental prowess to claim their pedigree, and were considered special from the common citizens.

It seemed the Berkud Border Dominion was governed by a Feudal Lord named Spirit King that ruled the land. That Spirit King was one of the Demon Lord’s vassals, but it seemed that the Demon Lord also took orders from the Great Dark Lord. The power structure went something like this: Great Dark Lord -> Demon Lord -> Nobility -> Town Mayor -> Commoners.

Pretty straightforward, huh? The Great Dark Lord being higher than the Demon Lord wasn't that strange in fantasy settings, but I wondered what that was like in reality. When I asked Ann, the only thing she had to say was that the Great Dark Lord was "The person above the Demon Lords", so I guess I could only imagine. So maybe Demon Lords were like Governors and the Great Dark Lord was more like a Prime Minister. The village where Ann lived was in a remote spot to the west side of this Berkud Border Dominion. Since the area around here was still being pioneered, there were small villages just like hers scattered about.

If you went even further west, you'd find the "Polaris Channel" and the "Polaris Fort" standing in between. And west of that was a nation of humans with a different type of culture than the other races, yet still looked like a region of just human tribes. And then there were the labyrinths, like #228, that I was supposedly running, which were also under the direct control of the Great Dark Lord; making the managers running them also belongings of the Great Dark Lord, and as such they were given special treatment by the people of Daemon.

I kinda overlooked it because a bunch of cool words like Great Dark Lord and Demon Lord came up, but the ideology of using the country's budget to create community buildings and tend to the people by the person in charge was a pretty Japanese thing to do... The tension kinda wore off once you noticed that.

"I see, then by that classification I think it's safe to assume this 'Labyrinth #228' is under the Great Dark Lord's jurisdiction... Ah, you seem more relaxed now."

"Huh? Yeah. I don't think you're a bad guy or anything anymore, so it's okay," Ann replied.

"I was hired not too long ago. You said this is the Great Saredo Rift, right? I'm the apprentice manager of Labyrinth #228, located at the bottom of this ravine."

I wasn't sure they had any concept of company training with their level of civilization, so I thought that apprenticeship was a better term for it.

"Oh, there's a rumor that there was a labyrinth around here, but the manager wasn't anywhere to be found."

"I saw everything I could from down here, but I don't really know anything about what's up there. Do you know anything about that, Ann?"

"Um... A long time ago they were building something at the bottom of the Sareno Rift, like a giant scaffold. But I haven't heard anything about them aside from none of them are around anymore, and that no one returned after they fell apart, so I don't think it's possible for anyone to know..."

"Right, so you need to build a scaffold or a staircase to go up at least, huh? Ann, do you wanna live here until we find a way to go up?"

"Really!? Umm... You don't mind?"

"No need to be stiff. I'm still an apprentice, even if I'm supposed to be a manager. It would be stupid to kick you out of here when there's not even an exit from the ravine, don't you think? It's the first time I've met someone that's not human, so I don't really know much about kobolds, but you're still a girl, I'm sure of that."

And she's pretty soft, too. It would be a shame to lose my body pillow.

"Thank you, Mister!"

I embraced Ann as she jumped into my arms. She's so small it felt like I was hugging the little sister I never had. Although, she looked more like a large dog right now.

"Let's eat first. I take it you're hungry, right?"

I took Ann with me and lit the fire. I started heating up the grilled pumpkin, and threw in some salt and pepper, for breakfast. Even though there was a lot of it, it was still pretty bad. Yet, Ann just happily ate it, and let me know how tasty it was. She was such a cute girl. After seeing her eat it up so happily, I couldn't tell her how tired I was of eating them.

"Well then, I should get to work. What are you gonna do, Ann?"

I asked her while she drank water after finishing her meal. The water quality in this ravine was pretty good so it must have been tasty, huh?

"I'll help too! Um, what are doing?"

"Well, I say work... but it's really just digging out stone. Oh yeah... The village you live in is to the east, right?"

"Yes, Milt Village. It's about an hour from here on foot."

"Then how about I dig up stone in the east wall and make a stairway? We'll need a way to go up first, anyway."

It would be really nice to make something like the stairs of a mansion, but I didn't really have any experience, besides games, in making something like a multi-storied cavern. It seemed like all I had to do was dig up a staircase pattern on the wall, easy enough.

"Are you sure? You helped so much and I haven't even done anything..."

"No need to worry. I can do business if I get to the village as well."

Not a very childish thing to worry about, so I patted her head to reassure her. Now that I thought about it, how old was she anyway? She seemed more like a girl than a woman, so I guess I could treat her like a little sister. Besides, I wasn't lying when I said I want to connect with the village as well. They should have crops and peddlers around there. It was my chance to break away from the pumpkin diet.

"By the way, you're a half-kobold, right, Ann?"

"Y-Yeah... I am."

I wondered why she looked so nervous all of a sudden.

"I don't even know about the Kobold clan to begin with, can you tell me about it?"

"Well... Our clan is said to be filled with dog demons. We don't grow very tall even when we become adults. We're not usually very strong, but there's a lot of us who are very good with our hands, so I guess that's our best trait? We can even see when we're in dark places. I've heard that's really useful when making stuff like basements or other things in the dark."

"I see, are half-kobolds different from normal kobolds?"

"Erm... maybe I'm a little weaker than a normal kobold."

So she's delicate, huh? I guess it depended on which race you were a half of.

"I'm kinda good with my hands too, but nothing compared to a real kobold."

Looks like kobolds specialized in dexterity. Watered down traits was natural for a half breed.

"Ah, but I seem to be smarter than normal kobolds. I can calculate and read and write stuff that's too difficult for the rest of the villagers."

"You can do all that? That's amazing."

Being able to deal with numbers and read and write in a fantasy world that went "Literacy, is that tasty?" was pretty good. Although it won't help much for the problem we have currently.

"How about your stamina?"

"Normal kobolds have more stamina... and I'm kind of a female, so..."

Oh, yeah, I guess it made sense for males to have more stamina.

Well, what should I have Ann help with then? Your first helper having lackluster stats in games was pretty much cliché at this point, but I didn't think it would worry me as much as it did. But I couldn't tell her to not do anything when she looked at me with such eager eyes. They practically screamed "I'll do anything!" at me.

"Let's see, this labyrinth's special product is stone. Maybe I can show you how to deliver it... Come with me."

I took her into the cabin and showed her the delivery box in the back.

"This is the delivery box. The materials you put inside of here will get converted to money."

I put one of the stones I'd left beside the box to show her how the conversion worked.

"You put the materials inside the box like this, close the lid, and there'll be money next time you open it. One piece of stone is worth 802 DL."

"Amazing, I've never seen anything like this before. This is really the Great Dark Lord's labyrinth!"

So this box was rare even by this world's standards, huh?

"I have something I'd like you to do with this. Do you think you could polish the stones that I bring here?"

"Polish?"

"Yeah, it seems like they get a nice luster when you do. I think the selling price will go up a little bit if we polished them properly. Wanna give it a try?"

"Yes, I'll do my best!"

I gave Ann a cheap cloth I bought via Tundra. I had been digging west this whole time, but I went the opposite way this time and started digging a 20x20 meter staircase in the east wall of the ravine. I'd like to leave the stone carrying to Ann, but the whole kobold thing aside, I couldn't really let a girl that was injured recently do physical labor all of a sudden. Assuming this ravine's depth was of about 100 meters, I calculated I'd roughly get at least 200,000 stones from making it to the top.

—Let's take it easy, I'll lose the drive to work if I think too hard about it.

"Mister, look at how pretty it looks after I polish it!"

Ann waved her paws at me while I carried the stones I'd dug out of the wall closer to the delivery box. Yeah, not being alone is really nice, after all.

"Ann, what happened to the stone?"

"Look, it's sparkling so much!"

I looked at Ann's paws while pushing the wheelbarrow closer to where she was.

"So they get that pretty when you polish them... Now that's a surprise."

The stone Ann was holding looked so smooth and brilliant. It was somewhat darkish. Compared to stuff from my world, I'd say it was close to the granite they use for tombstones. It took about two or three hours to dig out the stones and carry them back. I was amazed she got them all polished up in that time. Despite being only half-kobold, I was in awe of the race's skill.

"You're amazing!"

Patting Ann's head to praise her had a really relaxing effect.

"Let's try putting one in the delivery box. I wonder how much your effort adds to the price... Ah, why don't you keep the first one?"

"Umm... Well, I want to put it in the delivery box now. I want to know how hard I worked."

"I see, let's try it out then."

So soft... Yes, the sweet and fluffy creature right in front of me was so nice. When Ann put the stone in the delivery box and closed the lid, the clanky sound of coins was louder than usual. Upon opening the lid, there were obviously more coins than I used to get when selling the stones before.

The numbers added up to 5800 DL, seven times higher than the normal stones.

"This is amazing, this sells for way more than normal stone."

"Eheheh~"

Ann was so happy her smile hooked me right in. Before I noticed, I was smiling as well.

"Oh, right."

I started up the <Dungeon Management Tool> and accessed the 'Tundra Manager > Purchase Authority' options and gave permissions to Ann. I also opened up Tundra's catalog and purchased a leather purse with a cord to strap around your neck, and put all the money from Ann's first sale in it.

"Ann, this is a memento of the first time you came here and worked. So you have something to remember it by. Use it carefully if there's anything you want."

"Eh... Ah... Huh?"

I could see the surprise on her face as her eyes went between the leather purse hung around her neck and my face repeatedly.

"I... Uh... Mister...!"

She suddenly hugged me, crying, while burying the tip of her nose in my clothes.

"Wh-What's wrong, Ann? Did I say something bad?"

"A'm sho japy... Wai ar shu sho goot me...?"

—Erm... "I'm so happy, why are you so good to me?", maybe?

"W-Well... I-I didn't really mean to. I just... Oh yeah! I-I just did what I would if I had a little sister... That's all."

She was like a human, even if she was a little dog-ish. I wasn't really used to girls, and even less so to other species. That was why I couldn't shake away the feeling that she was kind of like a pet. Really, the only reasonable route for me was to treat her as if she were my little sister.

"A-Awooo!"

—Oh man, she is really crying.

She might have had a lot of sad memories in this fantasy world. I enjoyed the fluffy feeling as I stroked her head until she calmed down. That night, I found Ann trying to sleep on a bunch of cardboard pieces which happened to be on the floor as I was about to go to bed.

"Hey, Ann. Isn't that a little hard?"

"Yes..."

"I bet it's cold without a blanket."

"Y-Yes..."

"Well, I know you might feel a bit embarrassed, but it would be bad if you got a cold."

"Huh? Wai— Mister!?"

I held the sulky Ann in my arms and carried her from the cardboard to the bed, and embraced her the same way I did yesterday.

"We're different races, so it shouldn't be that big of a deal, right...? Ah, so soft."

I yawned right after hugging her.

"U-Uuuh...!"

Ann seemed like she was about to complain for a moment, but it took less than 10 minutes for the both of us to depart to the land of dreams. The softness of blankets, and the warmth of another person's skin—or fur in this case—was truly a fiendish thing...

I suddenly woke up in the middle of the night. This soft and warm thing was... Ann? It seemed like she was hugging me back, but she was just sleeping while burying her face into my chest.

"Auntie, it's still sour... Sara... the wind feels so nice today..."

Ann's sleep talk made its way into my ears. I wondered if she was dreaming about when she was still on the surface... Her sleep talking voice had a pretty funny tone. Seemed like she was having a good dream.

—I have to return Ann to her home...

I stroked her fluffy head while she murmured. Although I would be happy if she stayed with me forever, I didn't want to make her feel lonely from losing her family and everyone she's known all of a sudden. Even if she ended up going home... It was way better than carrying the sin of keeping her from everything she loved. I tightly embraced the softness within my arms and thought about working as hard as I could to build that staircase tomorrow.

The next day I started making the staircase with more conviction than ever. First, I used the stone I dug out already to pave the wet ground connecting the entrance of the cabin to the stairway. It was hard to move around when the wheel of the wheelbarrow got stuck in the mud thanks to exposed soil. I couldn't really afford to keep all the stone lying wherever since the valley of the labyrinth wasn't all that big to begin with. And even if I could do that, I needed to turn this stuff in to make money. Ann still took care of polishing the stone. Since her injuries had healed completely, I got her a wheelbarrow from Tundra, and was having her help carry the stone as well.

Anyway, my training would be over in three months. I didn't think I would be able to build these stairs all the way up by myself in that time, and if I waited for Ann to finish polishing each and every one of them, the terrain around the cabin would be completely filled with stones before we could even finish. Ann's strength and stamina might have made the job a tad difficult, but I didn't want to leave Ann alone down here without a way out when they came to pick me up in three months. The deadline might be a bit tight, but I'd like to complete the stairs.

"Munch, munch... This is tasty, delicious!"

Ann's eyes sparkled as she bit into a big sandwich. After three days of starting the stair digging in earnest, our muscle pain was too much to stomach, despite our best efforts to try and keep going. I decided to splurge a bit and bought some white bread and bacon from Tundra. I also managed to nab a lettuce-like vegetable and made something akin to a sandwich.

I used a whole 20 centimeter diameter piece of bread to make the sandwich, and observed as the tiny Ann wolfed it down, with a smile on my face.

Even though they were simple dishes, the ingredients made up for most of the taste. I felt some kind of joy as a chef... No, more like a househusband. Yeah, there was this one game about a housewife taking care of her husband and children. This was like the gender-swapped version of that... Man, my head is really hardwired to games, huh?

"Hmm... Yeah, it's really tasty."

I was hungry after a hard day of work, so I ate a sandwich the same size as Ann's. Albeit, at a much slower pace.

"Oh...?"

As the number of people increased, so did the amount of wood we used. On a certain day, when I was gathering firewood to prepare today's breakfast early in the morning, I found a clear, pale amber stone in the ever-growing plot of land I used to plant waterdry trees I used for wood.

"It's quite pretty, but I wonder what it is... Execute Appraisal."

Name: Waterdry Amber
Description: The solid state of waterdry tree sap. It's rarely produced when raising waterdry trees with abundantly clear water. The higher the water quality is, the higher the transparency of the amber and the rarity of the same will be.

So it was some kind of amber. I was surprised when a jewel fell out of a tree all of a sudden. Ambers on Earth were fossils of tree sap, but the fact it was produced inside the tree made it something more akin to a pearl. Or like kidney stones, if you wanted to think of it that way. They were really pretty, so I added collecting waterdry amber to the daily ritual of gathering firewood.

Since we had been selling tremendous amounts of stone every single day, we were kind of well off money-wise, so I bought a glass container that looked very much like a goldfish tank, and decide to decorate the room with them. Maintaining peace of mind with interior decoration was important, too.

It was nighttime after work was done for the day.

When we had started working on the stairs, both Ann and I would almost pass out in the bed each night, as we had spent all of our stamina during the day. But as we repeated the same routine everyday, my body gradually adapted, and the effort needed became less and less. And with more time to spare, my lifelong craving began to surface.

In other words: I wanted to play games.

There were many games you could make in places where tools and materials are limited, but playing those said games by yourself was kinda restricting. Fortunately, I wasn't alone. I had my trusty Ann with me. At first we played tic-tac-toe using the bluelight moss and branches to draw symbols in the soil.

"Umm... A circle around here... Ah, I lost!"

"It was a good call, but you're rushing to win too much."

I bought a parchment from Tundra and drew a 8x8 grid on it, cut out circles out of a piece of thick leather, and coated half of them black to make a makeshift othello board.

"I got you now, Mister! The four corners are mine. Heheh! Huh? Why are you doing that when you have no place to move? No! Don't!"

"You're smart, Ann, but you're too upfront as well. You have to match your movement to your rival's."

Unsatisfied by only board games, I created my own primitive RPG that only needed paper and pen to play, no need for computers. If I wanted to play with someone, said person would need to be able to read and calculate, but Ann was qualified enough for that.

“I take two steps ahead and attack the thieves. Umm… I attack for eight points. It’s a critical hit!”

Ann absorbed things like a sponge. She familiarized herself with the game I made from scratch, and got hooked right away.

“Man, you’re amazing, Ann. You have the qualities to make a genius gamer. World tournaments aren’t just a dream if you keep up this pace.”

“I don’t really know what a gamer is, but I’m happy when you praise me! Hey, hey, Mister! We still have some time before bed, right? I wanna play that ‘Labyrinths and Dragon’s Feast’ thing again!”

“I see, but it’ll take a while, okay? It’s not good for your eyes at your age to create characters with only the lamp’s light.”

“Yeah, I know. Let’s hurry, then!”

I hadn’t realized it at first, but at the time, the main factor in retaining my sanity in this unfamiliar environment, where I worked myself to the bone everyday, was that I had Ann as my Player 2.

It hadn’t crossed my mind initially, but after overworking my body every single day for one month to build the stairs in this unfamiliar, nature-filled environment, I felt my technique and my strength had improved a lot compared to the first day. It wasn’t like I had huge muscles or a six-pack all of a sudden, but my body felt strangely light. At first, I could only dig out one stone at a time, and had to hit the stone with the pickaxe several times. But now, if I put some strength into it I could dig out eight at a time, and my hands didn’t even get numb from the shock, like the very first time.

Ann’s limit at first was five or six trips back and forth of carrying stone back to the delivery box, but she carried so much stone now that the wheelbarrow was the one screaming for help.

—I’m not imagining this, am I…? Oh, I forgot I have an easy way to check myself.

It had been a long while since I brought up the translucent menu and checked on my status screen.

Aoi Kousaka
<Apprentice Labyrinth Manager>
Vitality: 121/121 **Stamina**: 640/872 **Willpower**: 60/80
Skills: <Dungeon Management Tool> <Appraisal>

The reason I was able to spend my time well and keep my sanity was due to having Ann as my game partner. Yes, our daily efforts were being rewarded. My Stamina increased so much it was almost scary. My stats, which looked like a stamina-specialized tank in an RPG game, was not what came to mind when you considered I was supposed to be a labyrinth manager. I wonder if I'm the only one who thought like this... My mental image of a labyrinth manager was more like an intellectual, or a magic user, or something... I felt like all of that was crumbling inside my head.

"I wonder if Ann's the same. Execute Appraisal."

She was on her sixth wheelbarrow replacement by now. They became broken right away if they got overused since they were made purely out of wood. We didn't have the means to repair them ourselves, so we would just get a new one from Tundra. I got a really sturdy one this most recent time. It even had a load-carrying tray which Ann made good use of to load the stone.

Ann
Half-Kobold
Vitality: 42/42 **Stamina**: 206/226 **Willpower**: 28/28

Ann's gotten pretty strong, huh? Seems like her race's tendency was to lack in the power department, but as far as I could see, she was way stronger than I was just a month ago. I continued to dig up the staircase afterwards as Ann kept carrying the stones back to the new stone storehouse near the delivery box. She cashed out some stone when there was no room in the storehouse, and so our days continued.

It had been about a month and a half since we first started building the stairs, and by the second month since I'd first come to this labyrinth, we had finally reached the surface.

Chapter 2

"So this is the surface... It's lot less green than I thought it would be, almost like a wasteland, really."

"Monsters hate living in places like these, so it's easier to build fields and villages. There's a forest at the other side of the bridge, see?"

I looked to the west and saw there was grassland spreading out on the other side across the bridge, just like Ann said. I could just make out what seemed to be a forest filled with trees further out, too.

"Are there dangerous creatures living in places like that?"

"Yeah. There's some intelligent monsters in there, but most of them are vicious and can't communicate, so it's pretty dangerous"

"I see. So there's a lot of rough places in this world too, huh? Well then, how about we head to the village? You haven't seen your family in a long while, right?"

"Yep. This way, Mister!"

Ann held my hand and walked with a fast pace. We ended up on a simple hardened soil road as she guided me away from the stairway. When I looked back at the Saredo Great Rift, I managed to catch a glimpse of a simple bridge made out of rope and planks of wood that looked like it'd struggle to even give pass to a single carriage. Did Ann fall from that? Upon further inspection, I saw traces which indicated that it was repaired recently.

Ann continued to guide me along the road to the east for nearly an hour. Along the way, I saw some fields here and there. I wondered if there was a clan of giants that pulled dead trees from their roots in those far off fields. They seem to be at least three meters tall, or maybe my depth perception was out of whack. The fields in the immediate vicinity were, to put it bluntly, very dry. There were lots of stones in them, and the dirt seemed coarse and dehydrated compared to the rich black soil back at the ravine. They lived in a pioneering village, maybe that was related to why the soil was rather sterile.

"Ann, is life at the village difficult?"

"Yeah. My Auntie said it would take ten years for us to get a good harvest. There's not really any rich people back in my village."

Yeah, it might be because it was still just a pioneering village, but it seemed life was hard even in a world like this.

"Then you guys will be having lots of tasty crops in a decade? I hope it works out."

They may be mere words of consolation, but that kind of thing was important when facing hard times.

It was a bit of an old story, but I tried out the marriage feature in an online game once. It was supposed to be like a fun way to display that you married someone else's avatar using an event item called 'Wedding Ring.' On paper it seemed like a good idea, at least... But some players who married their friends ended up becoming mentally unhinged, and desired to monopolize their partners. In due time, they leveled up and changed class from online stalkers to real stalkers.

I remembered this one time I was being ambushed in front of my house, and I ran away to a childhood friend's house without thinking.

"It's okay now."

I could never forget the feeling of security those mere words of consolation gave me.

"Yeah, me too. Everyone's doing their best to make it happen!"

Ann's smile as she nodded at my words was simply dazzling.

"A-Auntie! Auntie!"

When we approached what looked like a village with a bunch of tiny buildings, Ann started running towards one of the fields all of a sudden. Right ahead of her there was a... dog-faced creature with a dumbfounded expression on her face. And I say 'she' because there was an unusually large swell in her bust area, so I figured it was safe to assume they were female.

"Ann? Is it really you!?"

Ann ran to hug her even though her clothes were covered in dirt and dust. The kobolds that were hard at their farm work started to gather around them when they heard the commotion.

"Well if it isn't Ann!"

"You're alive!?"

The surrounding kobolds started a bit of an uproar. Yeah, the same way we Asians couldn't tell Caucasians apart from each other, and vice versa for them, I couldn't really tell apart one kobold from another, among the flock that started to gathered. The only real differentiating feature was their height, and Ann, because she was wearing a pretty dress.

The kobolds seemed to differ in their coats of fur. There were some that look like Shiba Inus, some with black or white spots, different colored eyes and arms, and so on. I was pretty sure I wouldn't be able to tell one apart from the other if they looked kind of the same and you shuffled them around, though.

"So Ann is back? Now that's something! I'm sorry, but I'd like to hear all about it in detail. Would you mind coming over to my house? Jenny, Ann, you girls come as well."

A huge minotaur wielding a hoe arrived after hearing the commotion. It seemed like he was the mayor of this pioneering village... In the end, I was guided to the mayor's residence together with Ann and her aunt.

The mayor looked rather old, and had some wrinkles on his face. He also had a kind of calm demeanor to him; but between his stern face and his large build—that seemed more than capable of folding a human in two with just one hand—I almost wanted to back down on reflex. It was hard for me to keep a straight face while Ann walked alongside him as if it was the most normal thing in the world. There weren't any kids who would be happy about you getting scared by their friends, I guess. The humans that have been born in this world might be used to this sort of thing, but my culture shock had started to kick in pretty hard.

The village I was guided to was structured in a radial manner, where roads and fields spread outwards, and the houses were built towards the center. Speaking of which, all of the houses are pretty simple buildings. The walls were made out of dry hardened earth blocks and tree bark, while the roofs were made out of straw and simple wooden planks.

If you made a house like this in Japan, it would get blown away by a typhoon or a small earthquake. I wondered if there were even any of those around this region. Eventually we arrived at a house which appeared to be particularly large compared to the others. Apparently this one belonged to the mayor. Rather than being bigger just because he was the mayor, I figured it was just a house tailored to his rather large stature. I mean, really, the guy was well over two meters tall.

"Oho... Who would have thought there would be a labyrinth of the Great Dark Lord down the Great Saredo Rift. "

While I told him about my job as labyrinth manager, the mayor poured me tea in a cup as big as a helmet from the human world.

"At any rate, the fact that Ann was saved after falling down the bridge is of most importance. I would like to extend my thanks to you, Mister Aoi. These days, Jenny, Sarah, and all of Ann's acquaintances were quite depressed because of the incident, you see."

I talked about the whole story regarding how I ended up taking care of Ann. He seemed pleasantly surprised, and pleased she was safe this whole time. He may have looked all macho and scary, but he very much seemed like a simple and mellow person on the inside.

"I'm really glad I saved her as well. It would have been painful for such a nice and healthy girl to die so young."

I went in 'working adult' mode for the first time in a long while. I also figured I would have to greet the villagers, so I thought it would be good to put on my suit's tie and coat as well.

"Thank you so very much. Ann's like a keepsake from my sister. Whenever I thought she wouldn't ever come back I... (sniff)"

Ann's aunt, Jenny-san, cried while hugging her.

—Jenny-san... Ah, it's kind of weird to reference her the same way I would someone back at home, huh? Force of habit, really.

"Here, a handkerchief. Please be happy Ann came back safe."

I offered a linen handkerchief to Jenny. The fact I hesitated back then to give Ann the medicine mouth-to-mouth because of her cute doggy face sent pangs of guilt through my soul—like a thorn right into my heart.

"I can't believe such a nice person saved you... FNNNRK..."

Was that no good? It seemed to cause the opposite effect. I'd dealt with these kinds of situations a lot in dating sims, but when it came to real familial interactions, I had no idea what options there were.

"Umm... Mayor Hopper, I have about one month left until my labyrinth manager apprenticeship period is over. Would you allow me to trade in this village? There is no one but me in the labyrinth, and I have a few things that could be considered special products, so I think it would be beneficial to able to purchase and exchange things in the village."

"We welcome you with open arms. Our village is rather poor, as you see, so peddlers only come occasionally. It's really good news there'll be new business, however small," he replied, while nodding.

—Alright, I can finally say goodbye to the daily pumpkins!

"Oh yeah, can you use this currency? I use it to buy and sell stuff with the other managers."

I took out a silver 5000 DL coin I had in my pocket.

"It's quite alright. That's the same currency that's widely used across all of the domains of the Great Dark Lord. There are certain local currencies issued by regional lords themselves, but regular currency like this is better to use."

It was good to hear that I could use the coins here. If I combined that with the delivery box from the labyrinth, I really might be able to become kind of a merchant. Tundra was always short in the fresh food department, after all.

"Though, I have to say, your coat looks way glossier than before,

Ann. You look like you filled up quite nicely as well. You look so fancy now that I almost didn't recognize you."

—So kobolds add hair glossiness to their appearance assessment? I'll keep that in mind.

"Yep, the food back at his place is really tasty. He lets me eat until I'm full, too!"

Despite Ann's cheery tone, all we had most of the time was that insipid pumpkin that didn't improve one bit, no matter how much salt or sugar you'd sprinkle on top. She talked about the food with so much joy, even though the most we ever really had outside of pumpkins were the occasional beef jerky, or dried fruit from Tundra. Her joy made me feel a complex mix of happiness and guilt. I wondered if it was the difference between a child raised in a pioneering village where life is difficult, versus a Japanese that got to eat as much as they wanted.

"You really took care of Ann so well..."

Jenny continued crying while holding Ann close. Aunts and uncles who took children under their wing were usually pretty cold to them in stories and fairy tales. It was basically a cliché, but Ann seemed to be really loved.

"Aoi, what do you plan on doing from now on?"

"Since I'm still a labyrinth manager, I guess I have to go back there and actually manage things."

Although it might be presumptuous of me to call that ravine with a cabin, some trees, and the stairs going up to the surface a labyrinth, but I was at least a labyrinth manager in name.

"I see. Please, feel free to come to the village at any time. The village market opens up every ten days. Let's see... The next one should be in eight days, and it lasts from early in the morning until noon. You're welcome to participate, if you wish."

"Thank you very much. Ann, thank you for helping me out so much... Well, then—"

I got up and almost fell over as I tried to leave after stroking Ann's head. Her hands were firmly holding the cuff of my slacks.

"What's wrong, Ann?"

—Oh, there's big tears coming out of the corners of her eyes. Did I set off some weird event flag!?

"I don't want you to go... Aoi... I want you to be with me."

—I class changed from Mister!?

Wait, no. I was happy about that, but it wasn't the problem here.

"Oh man, that's a little difficult for me. I may be an apprentice, but I'm still a labyrinth apprentice. I can't stay in the village forever."

I was kinda cheated into it, but it was still more or less my job. I patted her fluffy head while the tears started pooling in her eyes. It looked like she felt more than relaxed around me now. Maybe this was how she felt deep inside. She probably had put on a brave face this whole time after getting separated from her family.

"Then I'll go with you..."

She held onto my pants tightly with both hands.

—Y-Yeah, what a bind...

Both the mayor and Jenny were looking at us, but all they could manage was a forced smile. I was at a loss myself. My communications skills weren't high enough to manage to read the face of a dog or a cow, so it wasn't like I could say for certain, but I still felt the atmosphere had gotten kinda heavy, somehow.

"Hmm... Mayor Hopper, Miss Jenny. It may be somewhat of a wild idea, but would you mind hearing me out? I'm kind of short on hands around the labyrinth, and I'm, as you see, just an apprentice. Perhaps I may not have the most stable of income, but I'm certain I can hire a single kobold easily enough."

I was really happy Ann was able to reunite with her family, but I would honestly feel alone without her back in the bottom of the ravine, should she stay here. It would be a damn shame to lose my body pillow after getting used to her for over one month already.

"Hahaha..."

Mayor Hopper looked somewhat baffled.

"Do you wanna live with me, Ann? Being a labyrinth manager helper isn't easy, you know?"

"Yes!"

"Wait a minute, I'm happy you're happy about it, but you have to confirm this with Miss Jenny."

"Auntie, I can, right? I want to be with Aoi."

"Well, Mister Aoi. If it's not an inconvenience, can I ask you to take her with you? I think she can lead a better life under your care in the labyrinth, rather than barely getting by here in the village, and not even knowing if she'll eat or not. She's still a growing girl, after all. I might be a little lonely, though."

She said while staring straight into my eyes, and holding Ann tight.

"But of course, leave it all to me. Well, I say that, but Ann helps me a whole lot too. Let's keep doing our best, okay?"

"Thank you, Aoi! I'll do my best!"

Ann's childish response was really charming.

"Please give me one hour. I have to get her things ready—her clothes and the like."

Jenny took Ann with her and together they left the mayor's residence. I guess they went back home to pack her things.

"Mayor Hopper, would you care to tell me about this country's situation while we wait? I came out of the bottom of that ravine just today, so I'm not really informed about what's going on in the world right now."

"If you would like to hear what the mayor of a humble countryside village has to say, it'll be my pleasure."

And that's how I came to learn of this country's situation and culture.

The mayor's house stood at the center of the village, and there were several houses made out of hardened earth and straw roofs scattered around the fields. The house in which Jenny and Ann lived was among those. While she finally came back to it after several months away, it took her no more than ten minutes to pack all her things. It wasn't like Ann was wealthy to begin with. Excluding some rags she apparently used for farm work and picking up edible plants, all of Ann's belongings fit in a tiny handbag.

They may fall under the 'Economic Class' according to the Tundra listings, but the dress Ann wore now, without any sign of wear or patchwork repair, would be considered above average for the village she was from.

"Ann, you have enough spare clothes at Aoi's place, right?"

"Yeah, I have five dresses just like the one I'm wearing now, and I have two pairs of clothes to wear while working."

She hadn't brought anything more than some underwear, a few metal trinkets, and a wooden trunk that seemed to be a keepsake from her parents, among her luggage.

"Ann, sit there."

Jenny placed a thin cushion on the house's wooden boards and sat down, then motioned for Ann to sit in front of her. Jenny's eyes were still red from crying so much earlier, but she had a very serious-looking expression on her face.

"Okay..."

Upon seeing Jenny's unusually serious expression, Ann also sat on the thin, patched-up cushion that didn't do much to lessen the hardness of the floor.

"Answer me even if it makes you embarrassed or afraid. How does Aoi treat you normally? What do you think of him?"

"What do I think...? Let's see. He always pats my head, and he praises me when I do my best. He also always lets me eat lots of tasty stuff, and is super kind to me. Ah, he also told me before that I was like his little sister!"

Ann's answer made Jenny sigh in relief. She didn't think Aoi was a bad person, judging from the conversations they've had so far, but he was still someone she met just today. He may have seemed good at first glance, but he might have been treating Ann badly in reality. Although they were only aunt and niece, she worried about Ann as a girl on the cusp of adulthood—one of marriageable age.

"It really looks like Aoi's a nice person. Do you like him a lot?"

“Yep, I love him lots!”

Ann’s heartfelt smile dispelled Jenny’s worries completely.

“Say, Ann. Do you want to stay together with him forever? Would you hate to get separated from him?”

“Yes, I want to stay with him.”

“But, you know? You’re almost at that age... You have to start thinking about becoming a bride soon, and if you marry someone, you won’t be able to see Aoi that easily anymore.”

In these fantasy worlds, and especially in rural areas like these, the marriageable age came awfully fast. It was normal for girls to get married off as soon as they started developing their secondary sex characteristics, to a certain extent... Or simply put: As soon as they could give birth. Although the growth rate of kobolds and half-kobolds was different to humans, marrying when they were about 13 years old was normal, and 18 years old was seen as lagging behind.

“Eh? No, I don’t want that. I want to be with him!”

“I see, then there’s a good method for that. The hurdle to become Aoi’s wife might be a little... high, but you can become his mistress. You can stay together forever if you do that.”

Half-kobolds had a longer lifespan and matured slower than a purebred like Jenny, but Ann was way too pure compared to others her age. As far as Jenny was concerned... Ann’s slight unfamiliarity with the subtleties between man and woman worried her. Even if she managed to wed her with a kobold with a gentle personality, Ann would end up looking more like she was playing house, rather than a housewife. But despite abruptly entering a marital situation, Ann was still a fast learner, so it would be fine. Jenny initially thought she would start acting accordingly in due time, but ever since Ann returned, Jenny’s thoughts changed completely.

She felt respite after thinking Ann was dead this whole time, and she was also in debt to Aoi for saving her. But above all, Aoi represented an unbelievable asset that they wouldn’t have been able to find in any of the neighboring villages, or even the frontier cities. He may have been an apprentice, but being a manager of a labyrinth under the direct control of the Great Dark Lord meant he was leagues above any of the farmers living in the village. To put it in earthly terms, it would be like a high-ranking government bureaucrat being appointed to some rural village where there was barely phone signal.

“Mistress? Umm... So something like his wife?”

“Yes, it’s just a little different. Would you want to be together with him, even if you’re not his wife?”

It was completely different, but Jenny dismissed the small details entirely and declared it was basically the same.

“Okay, I’ll become his mistress if we can stay together like that!”

As the guardian of a girl that was about to reach marriageable age, Jenny smiled from deep within her heart. Interspecies marriages usually had to deal with the hurdles of differences in physiques and sensations, but luckily Ann was half-kobold and half-human, so she could get over the race gap easily. The fact Ann was already wearing way better clothes than she had when she lived back in the village, improved her complexion, and also had a newfound gloss in her fur were testament enough of how high Aoi’s standard of living was compared to theirs. He also had good enough sense to not lay his hands on a completely healthy and pretty girl like her, even though they were completely alone this whole time. Not to mention his character didn’t seem bad from what Ann had claimed.

And more importantly, Ann seemed to have taken a liking to Aoi, and he cherished her as a sister. Generally speaking, the pioneering villages tended to marry off boys and girls almost as easily as a person would spontaneously adopt a kitten, only to release it the next day. They could have tried to marry off Ann at least six times by now, but hadn’t done so. Jenny, who considered Ann like her own daughter, would rather not force Ann to meet some stranger and marry them off right away. She’d like for Ann to meet someone she came to love of her own volition. Aoi was a perfect match economically, practically, and emotionally for her. There was no reason to let such a good man get away.

“You’re such a good girl, Ann. I’ll teach you something very important now, then. Let’s see... Try to imagine this: What if Aoi let you go and was only kind to other people in the village? What would you think?”

“Ehhh? I’d hate it! I don’t want that. I don’t really know why, but I want him to be kind to me, too!”

Ann raised her voice after imagining the sight of what her Aunt said.

It evoked an unknown, confusing feeling inside of her. It felt like a cold sensation had spread all over her chest.

“I see, then you'll do what I'm about to tell you, no matter what. You can't doubt it, even if it's a little embarrassing. What you imagined just now might happen for real if you don't.”

“O-Okay! Please teach me, Auntie. What should I do!?”

“First of all, this evening you will...”

And so, Jenny taught Ann all the tips and tricks in the arsenal of a blossoming woman to seduce their man, for nearly an hour.

“I see, so the peace between the boundaries of this country and the neighboring human country, represented by the Polaris Fortress, have been maintained for the past hundred years. But bandits sometimes pass through the navy's vigilant watch and plunder around, so it's dangerous, right?”

“Even then, we're somehow able to go on living thanks to the Great Dark Lord and the Demon Lords. We're certainly grateful for that.”

—Ah, the existence of Great Dark Lord and Demon Lords has been on my mind for a while.

“Great Dark Lord? I know I'm a labyrinth manager, which makes me one of his subordinates, but what is the difference between the Great Dark Lord and a Demon Lord?”

“Difference, you say...? Both of them are way above us, so we don't really think too much about that kind of thing.”

Mayor Hopper folded his arms and sonorously blew air through his nose. A very cow-ish reaction.

“The Demon Lord is more like a king for us. If there is something troubling the village, he or his subordinates will lend us their help. We're really thankful that The Great Dark Lord and the Demon Lord help us in times of need. We're tasked with constructing the labyrinth for the sake of the Demon Lord, although we see ourselves helped as well, indirectly, because of it.”

Right, so was just like I thought before. The Demon Lord acted like a governor of sorts, and the Great Dark Lord was more like the president.

"By the way, Aoi, you've been rubbing yourself for a while now, is something the matter?"

"No, I just feel kinda chilly for some reason."

It wasn't the kind of chill you felt when a cold was coming. If I were to put it in game terms, it was kind of the chill you felt when a good player was aiming at you from a distance.

"I relaxed a lot after completing the stairs to the surface back at the labyrinth, so this might just be all the piled up fatigue. I'll try to go sleep early today."

"That's good. You must take time to sleep when you're truly tired."

While waiting for Ann to finish packing up, Mayor Hopper told me about the situation of the other villages, their special products, and about the other labyrinths. I couldn't complain about the idle talk. Intelligence gathering was the most basic foundation in all game genres, you couldn't miss it. And for a total ignorant to the world like me, even the minimal information received from the mayor of a town in the boonies like this was a fountain of wisdom. Ann might be a smart girl, but the amount of information she could give me, compared to the mayor leading a whole village, was overwhelmingly different.

"Sorry for the wait."

Jenny opened the door and Ann was holding a wooden trunk behind of her.

"S-Sorry for the wait..."

I wondered why was Ann hiding behind Jenny. I had the feeling she was more embarrassed than turned off by something, but I couldn't tell why, exactly.

"Thank you very much for talking to me, Mayor Hopper," I said while standing up. "Ann, wanna go back home before it gets dark?"

"Yes!"

I held out my hand and Ann happily jumped to grab it. By the time we descend the stairs at the Great Saredo Rift and found ourselves back at Labyrinth #228, it was already getting dark. We stayed longer than I'd thought back at Milt Village.

On my way back, I passed by the trees I'd planted before and took some firewood and water bags from them, then continued on towards the cabin. I opened Tundra's catalog after firing up the stone kiln I had built in front of the cabin, and set the pumpkin for today's dinner.

"You're gonna buy something?"

She stuck to my back and looked at the catalog from behind. We had been looking at the shopping window together ever since I gave her admin permissions to purchase from the Tundra catalog herself.

"I was thinking of making something, like a special product of sorts."

"A special product?"

"Yeah, we finally managed to connect with Milt Village, right? We've been stuffing nothing but stones in the delivery box so far, but we can buy and sell in the village now. We could use the currency we have, but I still want something I can sell or exchange in the village. Stone would be hard to carry, and I don't think there's anyone that can even buy it up there, don't you think?"

"Ohh, the polished stones are really pretty, so I think there would be people that want them, but I doubt there's anyone that would exchange them for crops," Ann replied.

They didn't seem to be well off enough to allow themselves expensive hobbies, for sure.

"We can just carry whatever goods we buy from Tundra there. Ann, can you choose some daily necessity stuff, and whatever the people back at the village might need?"

"Yup, got it. But... I think that thing would probably be the most popular item."

"Which?"

Ann pointed to the hoe that was set against the cabin, the same one I'd created using the <Dungeon Management Tool>.

"The men working on the fields always told me how much they wanted quality tools like the hoes and sickles that are sold in bigger towns. The ones in the village are all old and rusty. Even the edges are made of wood."

"I see. I couldn't sell it with the delivery box, so it kinda was just there this whole time. Good thinking, Ann."

I pet her fluffy head.

"Mmmm..."

Ann made a really cute sound when I had done so. It made me wonder if it was because my technique had gotten better, or maybe she had gotten used to being pet.

The pickaxes and hoes I created with the <Dungeon Management Tool> turned into light particles and disappeared as soon as their durability ran out, but you could keep using them as normal until then.

"The problem will be whether or not I can take them out of the labyrinth. I guess I'll have to try that tomorrow... Hmm?"

A window opened near my hand.

<WARNING> All items created by the <Dungeon Management Tool> will disappear within half a year's time when removed from of the labyrinth.

"Oh, there's actually a warning about that, huh? Looks like they'll disappear in half a year, but I think it'll sit poorly with the villagers if we treated it like a rental system of sorts."

I had to put a disclaimer for this when selling them. It was a bit of a pain, but on the other hand, if I just spammed these and flooded the market, the price would tank, and every blacksmith would be put out of business.

"We have to capitalize on the environment here. The vegetation in the ravine is totally different from that of the surface's. There may even be medicinal plants around there. Ann, is there a doctor in the village?"

"Doctor? No. If you go to the city, there's doctors that can cure you with magic or make medicine, but there's nothing like that in the village."

"So there are doctors that specialize in normal medicine or magic? Interesting."

"Then there must be a demand for medical supplies."

I search through Tundra's book category... and something that looked promising.

Practical Medicinal Herb Studies
~Wetlands / Waterside Edition~ (JPN) == 588000 DL
Seller: Manager, Labyrinth #7

Rating: ★★★★★
Reviewer: Manager, Labyrinth #201
- a really rad book, it explains everything about the medicinal plants that grow in the wetlands and waterside environments, how to pick and storage them as well. it even holds your hand through the processing methods to make medicine too. very very nice book. on the other side the pricing can go **** itself, that said, I don't regret the purchase.

Rating: ★☆☆☆☆
Reviewer: Manager, Labyrinth #16
- Entry-level piece of trash. Can't use it as anything but a reference book. The contents it covers may be vast, but this level of study is still too green. I recommend you to buy "Make Your Own Potions - Aquatic Plants Edition" instead, written by yours truly, of course.

It was pretty expensive, and it seemed like it had haters among some people in the trade, but well, maybe it had good stuff too.

My funds went well over 10 million DL thanks to the stone we sold from digging up the stairs, so this kind of expense wouldn't hurt that much. Although, while 10 million may seem like a huge personal gain, considering the cost of the expansion and maintenance of the labyrinth, it was an amount that would easily melt away when used to pay for construction work. I was still far away from buying expensive fresh food from Tundra and saying goodbye to the pumpkin diet. I may have grown fond of living in this rundown cabin after two months, but the constant expenses from repairs and rebuilding were unending. I needed to keep a good amount of savings just in case.

My wallet and head hurt from the mere thought of the price of wood for construction, transportation charges, hiring villagers that could do carpentry work, various employment expenses, and the cost of meals.

Since one stone was typically 802 DL, then the stone we delivered through the box should have given us 100 million DL. I wondered if shipping so much in such a short amount of time had some kind of impact, because after we made it to 10 million in sales, a receipt came out of the pig, along with a message card that read "Payment will be processed after inventory is sold".

We couldn't reasonably expect the stone to keep carrying us all the way, so we had to think of a new method to raise money. And I had almost forgotten due so many things going on, but I was still in my trial period. There was the possibility I would get rejected as well. If that happened, then everything would have been for nothing, even if I started renewing the cabin, so I would have to make do with what we had on hand right now. I was worried about what to do about Ann if that happened, too. I had to discuss it with Karumi-san when the time came.

I ordered the practical herbalism book and put six 100000 DL coins into the piggy bank. I started reading the book as soon as it arrived, and did so all the way until nighttime. The blue light enveloping the ravine after sunset was as magical as ever, but it wasn't really bright enough to read a book. There was a magic light crystal which illuminated about as much as a fluorescent light for sale on Tundra. It consumed Willpower and emitted a bright light, but it was a popular item, so it sold out right way. I wanted one of those, someday.

In the end, I ate more of the sugared pumpkin Ann had made, as well as a tennis ball-sized grape-ish fruit, and we finally retired to bed for the night.

I couldn't really make sense of the events that transpired. The faint and mysterious light of the glowing moss shined into the room from the window, and a beautiful girl laid down on top of me.

The girl looked right at me with her big amber eyes. Eyes filled with uneasiness, or was it expectation...? The complex mix of emotions in her eyes gave off a rather mysterious vibe. Her matching amber locks of long hair were incredibly beautiful as well. My gaze followed the line of her hair and landed on the oversized white shirt she was wearing. My eyes became glued to her exposed skin. It took all of my willpower to not continue further.

She seemed dangerous, yet bewitching. I was overcome with an immoral feeling of corrupting a girl that hadn't yet reached maturity. With her touch, the girl broke me down and made me feel this undeniable attraction to the opposite sex.

Her feminine, frail figure that incited you to restrain; a smile that made you feel a deep, fiery passion, together with the need to protect, numbed my brain and reasoning like sweet, sweet alcohol. So I slowly took my hand to the girl's head, as if it was the most natural thing in the world...

—Wait... What happened? What's going on right now!?

I stopped the hand that was going towards her shoulder mid-way.

—My hand seemed naturally guided to the girl's head, but wasn't there something off about this!?

I was at a loss of what to even think.

—I went to sleep like usual, right!? How many years has it been since I felt this confused?

Let me try to break down what went on. Rather, let us disconnect for a second and think over everything that happened leading up to this. It was a good thing I had trained really hard as a gamer to not lose my cool no matter what. It was a really useful skill...!

—Well, then... I think it'll be okay if I recall about 30 minutes, let's do that:

1) *I put the leftover water in a pan and used the embers from dinner to warm it up a little bit before going to sleep like always.*
2) *I dipped in a cloth and used it to clean Ann's body first, then she went to bed like always.*
3) *I clean myself a little with the warm water as well.*
4) *I go and lay down on the bed, and a beautiful, half-naked girl is laying on top of me and hugging me.*
5) *No good. The skin contact in places I've never felt before is making me lose my mind (We're here right now.)*

"........"

That was weird. What kind of event goes off after going to bed for the day? That was way too sudden.

—Umm... What's happening here? Am I having a dirty dream? I'm so confused that I'm literally speechless. Although we're working all the time, Ann's always close to me from the second we wake up until we go to sleep. I can't quite put my finger on it, but I can't process my lust as a man...

I remained silent. But an uneasy expression took over the strangely familiar, beautiful girl in front of me.

"Is... my body... weird? Does it make you feel bad?"

"Huh? Ann?"

"Yes."

I was shocked, but the memory I'd discarded as a mistake jolted back into my mind. I see, this was the Ann I saw when I met her for the first time. Where did the fluffy doggy girl go? I also had the feeling she grew a few centimeters as well.

"No, it's not weird. I think you're pretty cute, but... your body's changed so much,"

"This is my real body. I usually use my kobold form because I can use kobold abilities with it. Auntie told me to stay like that normally."

"I see... so that's what being a half-kobold means."

So her appearance by default was that of a human girls', and she gained a kobold's abilities by changing into that form... How unexpected. Her sitting on top of me, naked, with only a white shirt was wearing away at my self-control. Wasn't that the shirt I gave her so that she could sleep? Since she normally didn't really need pajamas to sleep in her kobold form. I thought of it like a cat or dog feeling safer if they had something that belonged to their owner. Something familiar like a shirt or a towel. That's why I gave her my shirt, but I realized just how much of a destructive weapon it really was. I couldn't tell you what kind of effect this weapon had on me with a clean conscience, though.

"Yeah. My dad was a human and my mom a Kobold, that's why."

So that was what she meant by half-kobold. Could Ann's father be from the Earth? This place had all kinds of races and clans, so it wasn't exactly a place where one would need to be a 'specialized fetish' like in Japan, but it was still doubtful. Kobolds were indeed cute, but the hurdle to take one as a partner, not to mention procreation, seemed quite high.

—No, that's not the problem right now!

"Hngh… She told me it wouldn't be the same, but it really feels way different to hug you while in this form. It's making my heart beat so fast."

I lose myself in her enraptured eyes as she continued to cover my whole body with her embrace. This was bad, really bad.

Men across the world would start counting prime numbers or repeating mantras inside their heads, but in my case, I remembered the battles against hard bosses from a Japanese MMORPG tournament I'd participated in with my old party, to get my mind in order.

I recalled being in a town attack as a bow horsemen. The image of me above a swinging horse, focusing to hit another archer on top of the bell tower, helped relax my mind. I could remember the trajectory of the arrow flying to its target as I shot; the concentration I needed as a bow horseman… Phew, I calmed down a little bit.

"Wait a second, Ann, who told you that?"

"Huh? My auntie."

—JENNYYYYYYY! What are you teaching to your niece!?

"My face feels hot, and there's a tingling feeling inside my chest. I wonder why…"

—She's close. Too close. Way too close!

"Hyah!"

The abrupt warm feeling in my throat was so sudden it made me moan unexpectedly.

"A-Ann, what are you doing?"

The whole situation made me stutter. I was having a hard time processing all of this.

“(lick) I don’t know why, but I feel like licking you. Oh? My heart is beating even harder.”

“Ann? Umm... Do you know what you’re doing?”

The angels in my heart spoke out in unison...

—“Go for it, lucky dog!”

They said with smiling faces and a thumbs up! I know I want to, but this wasn’t right!

“Hm...? We’re just being with each other and sleeping together, right?”

Her face was totally red, but she gave me a pure and innocent answer. She didn’t understand this situation at all!

“Umm... And then I have to hug you real tight.”

Well, I did feel happy in more than one sense when she hugged me so strongly...!

“And, well... Help me take care of this feeling inside of me, please, Aoi,” she whispered.

The words she whispered into my ear were like a bomb to my self-control. Wasn’t that a little too much!? How was I supposed to take care of it!? I’d like to know! My mind was on the verge of going blank from the situation. Ann’s smile, and her desire to entrust herself to me, didn’t help in holding it back.

“I-I see... Y-You’re probably just tired. S-So just hug me. Let’s put the blanket over us and sleep... Okay?”

I put the blanket around the both of us and used the technique that worked whenever she had trouble sleeping because of muscular pain, or missing her family throughout these last two months; I pat her head with everything I had to make her fall asleep...!

“Hmm... I’m sleepy... you... know... I talked with... Auntie... Mmm... She told me I could... become your... If I... did, I... could... stay with you... forever... A... Aoi... I... love you...”

She fell asleep... To be honest, those last words were a far bigger weapon than the direct contact of skin, or her feminine smell creeping its way into my brain. My heart was pounding so hard

I thought it would burst from my chest. Jenny's trap was really powerful. Terrifying, even... I may have wanted to follow the primal desires of my heart, but my situation as manager here was unstable. If I laid my hands on her as my trial period ended, and I couldn't come back for some reason, I'd end up hurting Ann deeply.

Also, I wanted to thank my brothers that helped me get to the finals of that MMORPG tournament, and for giving me the memories I needed to stay sane just now. I wanted to thank that other archer; remembering the moment both of us tensed the bow with our dominant arm and let the arrow fly at the very same time, and the way he turned the tables by cutting it up with a dagger, then charging at me head on. Your high tension, murderous intent, and passion-packed swords dance were the only things that kept me in check. Were you the angel named conscience? I wanted to boo the other ones that were giving me a thumbs up, with lascivious smiles. I really wanted to know if there were different angels in my heart, and my conscience.

If I was a character in an otome game, I would push me over the limit and just hug the heroine, and fall asleep just like that. But that was impossible, I couldn't do it. It took me a good while to slip out of the bed and the cabin without waking up Ann in the process, and then about 30 minutes to straighten out and calm down my heart.

I couldn't do anything about it, I was a healthy man. There was no way I could sleep hugging Ann as if nothing had happened, after she opened up her heart to me like that, unless you castrated me or something...!

The next day, Ann paid a visit to Jenny's once again.

"Ann, did it go well?"

"Well... We slept together, but it was just like always."

"That's weird. You told him the line I taught you, right?"

"Yes. I turned into my real form, hugged him real hard, and whispered into his ear just like you told me to. But he covered us with a blanket and patted my head. It felt so good I fell asleep."

"Tch... Seems Aoi's one step ahead of us."

Aoi's strategy made the veteran Jenny click her tongue, with a villainous look on her face.

“A-Auntie, your face looks kinda scary.”

“Say, Ann. Do you remember Aoi’s face last night? Did he look annoyed? Disgusted? Pained? Which one was it?”

“Umm... Yes. He looked surprised at first, then troubled, and he looked pretty pained by the end. Hey, Auntie. He looked like he was in a lot of pain, did I do something bad to him? Will he hate me?”

“Hahahah. It’s fine, don’t worry. He really loves you, that pained face is all the proof you need.”

“R-Really?”

“That’s right. When boys can’t contain themselves, they do something pretty violent to girls. Well, if you love the person you’re doing it with, there’s nothing more blissful as a woman.”

“Hmm... Is that so? I was really excited, but he seemed to be in so much pain. I feel kinda sorry.”

“That’s how I know he loves you. Men make that face when they want to treasure the girl they love.”

“I-I see. So he does love me.”

Although some of Jenny’s words were rather skewed, her experience added a lot to her persuasiveness, which makes Ann show a big, sincere smile.

“Well then, what will out next plan be...?”

“Auntie, let’s try something not too painful for him, okay!?”

Ann recalled how Aoi looked last night as she mustered up the courage to murmur those words right into his ear.

“Then you’ll be doing a sneaking visit tonight.”

As a mother trying with all her might to tie Ann and Aoi together, Jenny decided to double-down on her efforts.

“A... Sneaking visit?”

Sadly, the girl that was in no position to stop her Aunt's tyranny, as she knew far too little about her means. If only she knew, she would at least have room for doubt about stopping or not, but alas.

"First of all, keep everything as normal for a while. Oh yeah, make sure you're dressed lightly, or even naked when you sleep together. Since you two will be in the labyrinth of the Great Dark Lord, try to get out of the kobold form as much as possible when together with him. You'll have to try and live with it to get closer to him. Okay?

At this point it would be like a critical hit to Aoi, but Jenny was determined to take this as far as koboldly possible.

"Yes, my heart starts beating really fast when I'm with him in my real form, but I'll do my best."

"It'll be good if you keep it up for about two weeks, okay? He should get used to sleeping together with you naked by then. That's when he gets careless."

"Yes, yes! And then what?"

"Then you do the sneaking visit. If he's determined enough by then, you'll finally become his mistress."

"Huh? Are sneaking visits that awesome?"

"You see, the deed will be done by the time he wakes up."

Jenny's next plan was to overwhelm him with her feminine charm and appeal to the fire of his youth, but it could backfire, causing him to distrust women if it didn't go well.

"Done... deed?"

"It'll be kinda hard to explain without an example..."

The figure of a lone boy came into Jenny's view as she wracked her brain thinking of a way to explain.

"Oooh, well if it isn't our nice neighbor, Boboru. You're right on time."

"Huh? Umm... Good day, Miss Jenny. Wh-Why are you holding my shoulders?"

The youth Jenny was about to assault was a kobold that was about two years younger than Ann... Although strangely enough, he was older than her in kobold years. He was named Boboru, a timid young kobold that lived in one of the neighboring farmhouses.

“I’m sorry to bother you, but I need to teach Ann something. Would you mind becoming my teaching material for a little bit?”

When the young boy saw Jenny’s wry smile as she licked her own lips, his instinctive sense of preservation kicked in. The fear and the shivers went down his spine beckoning him to run away, but Jenny’s grip on his shoulders said otherwise, as she slowly dragged him into the house.

“Eeek! You’re kinda scary today, Miss Jenny, I’m scared...”

“There, there, you’re a man too, Boboru. It’s no big deal, I promise.”

“I’m scared! Help! Anyone!”

Boboru’s hand stretched out in terror, trying to seek help. He barely reached the outside entrance to the house before the door slammed shut, preventing his shrieks from echoing out to the village. That day, the single boy became...

“Teaching material.”

As he climbed one step on the stairs of adulthood, Ann learned one thing about the subtlety of adults with Jenny’s practical field trip: the race of kobolds wasn’t a particularly strong one within this world. However, the women living here at the border had a level of strength that went above and beyond regular kobolds.

After Ann left for Jenny’s house early in the morning, I spent a good while sitting on the chair in front of the cabin, just thinking for a long while. I wondered how long it had been since the last time I did *that*. Fortunately, Ann left early in the morning. I could still feel her touch from last night even after we woke up and had breakfast together, so it was a bit difficult looking her straight in the eye. I’m glad I had some time to calm down and sort out my feelings.

Just then, someone happened to visit the cabin.

“Nice to meet you, I’m Sara from Milt Village,” she bowed.

The girl that introduced herself seemed to be around the same age as Ann.

She had bright blonde hair and deep blue eyes. She wore a seemingly very well-made apron dress, with simple colors that suited her very well. She seemed pretty light-skinned and tidy compared to the other villagers. She was pretty cute in a different way than Ann. It seemed almost otherworldly, like looking at a doll. She had a very lady-like air to her.

“Nice to meet you, I’m the apprentice labyrinth manager. My name’s Aoi.”

Staring for long was rude. It was common sense for adults to return with a polite greeting when given one.

I served some of the water I was drinking to Sara while I introduced myself carefully. I happened to be out of tea leaves already, but the water around here was far more delicious than mere tea. Buying a tea capable of matching the taste of this water would cost some good money.

“Milt Village… Do you happen to be one of Ann’s friends?”

“Yes, I’m Ann’s best friend.”

—Oh, one rank higher than a simple friend, huh?

“I’ve heard about you from Ann before. She seems really happy about working out here with you.”

I see, so she heard from her. I wondered where she knew me from.

“Is that so? What brings you here, Sara?”

“I have a request to make.”

“Request? Would you mind telling me what is it about?”

What in the world? As her best friend, she might want me to send Ann back to the village. But I had hopes of Ann staying here with me, and it seemed that was what she wished for as well.

“I also heard she showed you her true form. Ann was really happy you didn’t dislike her.”

So she knows about her true form. The best friend title was not just for show, then.

"If... you're planning to do something awful to Ann... Then please stop it! I'll take her place, I'll do anything you say... So please..."

"Huh...!? (cough) Excuse me! (cough)"

She declared that with a face that was like the concept of determination itself. I was surprised I didn't end up spouting out the water I choked on just now.

—Last night, and today as well!?

Holding back the part of me that wanted to nod at the proposal from a cute girl telling me she'd "do anything I say" was hard! Besides, aren't I the one being awful here? After it took so much effort to not do anything to her yesterday...!?

"Please wait a moment."

I took a deep breath to regain my composure. Nothing good could come from getting emotional in front of someone this serious.

I'd only played it because it was being talked about, but there was this romance simulation game in which you suddenly had 108 sister-in-laws and little sisters, and each and every single one of them loved you. The promotional line was something like "I can't believe this harem is legal!", and it was called "Pole☆Sisters", if I remembered correctly. Compared to that, this wasn't all too illogical of a development. Yeah, this was nothing. If you chose any of them, the remaining ones would go crazy and try to make you break up as hard as they could. This was more real than a pointlessly brutal scenario like that.

It had a phrase that went "Can you make it to the ending!?" and all. And you can bet I repeated the game over 20 times, but right after talking about breaking up with the 98th sister, the 99th came and stabbed me. Needlessly to say, I got a pretty bad ending and became unable to keep playing afterwards.

"I did hire Ann, but I'm not planning to do anything cruel to her like you say, Sara."

"Huh...? But Ann says you're always sleeping together."

"The house isn't that big, and we just have one bed, you see. It's kinda embarrassing, but I didn't know much outside of the human race, so I thought Ann was younger from how she looked, and figured it would be kinda lonely for her to sleep alone..."

—Yes, that's what I thought until last night! Really...!

But buying another bed now would be difficult. I think Ann would just cry if I suggested it.

"Ah, Ann's always talking about how kind you are to her!"

"She's a pretty cute girl, after all. She often reminds me of my sister that I just want to pamper and stuff."

It was a shame my real little sister back in Japan wasn't as cute or innocent as Ann.

"Are you sure you're not trying to do something indecent to her, and then dump her right after?"

I understood very well just how strong Sara's imagination was right then.

"If I was that kind of person, don't you think I would have sent her home already?"

"Huh!? Wait... What!?"

Seemed like Sara had noticed the words that came out of her mouth when she let her imagination run wild. She covered her completely flushed face with both hands and hung her head. Cornering her like that was kinda harsh, so silently I refilled her cup of water, waiting for her to settle down.

"I want to ask you one thing—why did you say you would take her place?"

When she finally calmed down, I decided to raise a question of my own.

"Because I'm her best friend."

Why would that be a reason to take her place? I didn't get it.

"Ann is really, really happy whenever she's talking about you. I never saw her smile like that before."

As far as smiles go, I remembered her making a really sweet-looking smile sometimes. Ann was pretty cute when she did.

"Ann's my most important friend... That's why if there's something that might make her smile disappear, I'll take her place. I can't do anything but that for her," she said with a bitter tone, as she clenched her fist.

—So she's that important of a friend to her...

I felt as if I understood something new about Ann, but it also made me kinda jealous. I'd had many rivals before, but never a close friend that thought about my well being like this..

"Then I can't do anything bad to you, Sara. Ann would be completely heartbroken if I did anything to hurt her best friend."

To be honest, my tone might have been quiet, but 90% of me was putting up with it and grinning.

I'd been holding back for one whole month. That incredibly provocative event last night almost sent me over the edge. And if a girl like Sara came and told me I could do anything to her, then of course it would end up hitting me where it hurts. My desire was telling me to do so many awful things right now... I wanted to cry.

"I won't... I won't lose! I've been the closest one to Ann ever since we were little, after all...!"

Looked like I chose the right answer. Sara declared herself as my rival as she glared at me with regret and sadness mixed in her eyes.

"Okay, I accept the challenge. No matter which one wins, I'm sure Ann will keep on smiling, so let's do our best, okay?"

"O-Okay...!"

Alright, I scored the first point. She got flustered when I accepted the challenge head on with a smile on my face... Not very adult of me, if I do say so myself.

"Let me walk you back to the village. We can talk more about Ann if you want on the way. It's up to you."

"Uhhh... I guess I don't mind."

According to what she told me before arriving to the village, Sara was the only girl from a family that was relatively well-off when compared to the other villagers. It seemed like her body wasn't very strong, so she never could run around and play with the other children. But she never was lonely because Ann was her talking buddy.

She had become unbearably sad when she heard Ann fell off the bridge in the Great Saredo Rift. It seemed when she heard the story about her being alive, but then leaving right away because she got employed, made her think the worst and act rashly. Was it my imagination, or did she immediately think that Ann was doing the most sinful things possible?

◇

"That was way calmer than I thought it would be. He's a good adult."

Sara muttered as she closed the door of her room. She and Aoi parted ways at the village's entrance. Sara had already pictured the kind of person he was, but Aoi was way different from the lascivious and corrupted adult she imagined. He turned out to be a pretty calm and polite adult.

"It's a good thing he wasn't a bad person... Right? Oh Dark Lord...!"

After confirming Ann was alright, the embarrassment of her actions, and the outrageous things she had said finally hit her all of a sudden. Her whole face turned as red as a tomato.

"What should I say to Ann...? That I went to the place of her beloved Aoi and had a fight with him? Well, it wasn't a fight, but I can't tell her I talked about something like that."

That said, it was really difficult to just go and apologize.

"What should I do... Eek!"

As she walked around her room while thinking, Sara staggered and fell to her knees.

"Huh...?"

She felt like she was being crushed under the weight of a giant hand, and collapsed onto the ground with a thud. There had been many times where she had collapsed before due to her weak constitution, but rarely did they occur to the extent of being unable to do anything.

"Sara's home! Hey, Sara, Auntie told me to give these to yo— Ah! What's wrong!? Sara!"

Fortunately, Ann found Sara collapsed on the floor after being sent by her aunt to deliver something. She fell unconscious seconds later.

"Up you go... Now to get some help!"

Ann carried Sara, laid her on top of her bed, and went to call her parents, or any adult, right away. Since her body had always been frail to begin with, her collapsing wasn't that unusual, but after spending so much time together, there was something about Ann that made Sara's parents react with urgency every time it happened. The adults gathered right away and started deliberating. Ann couldn't do anything but watch from the sidelines. She understood what was happening, but there wasn't much input she could herself.

"This is the first cursed cold of the year."

"If only we had some medicine..."

Ann suddenly raised her head after listening what the smart elf of the village murmured when she was finally done examining Sara.

There were no doctors in the pioneering village. Although, there were cases where the villages were poor, and most doctors only knew medical treatment for about one or two races.

There were races that were similar, like humans and elves, but with different tribes and clans, the medical science differed greatly. There weren't many doctors that studied medical treatments for various races. The ones that did only lived in big cities where they got as many clients as they could possibly want. The chronic shortage of doctors was one of the evils of a multi-ethnic nation like this.

Ann only had one clue: Aoi holding a difficult-looking book in one hand and saying...

"I'll try making medicine today."

From before she left for Jenny's house this morning.

"Depending on her luck... it'll last about two or three days."

Upon listening to the grave words of the elderly elf woman, Ann ran all the way to see the beloved labyrinth manager that saved her as well.

After I'd escorted Sara back to the village, I decided to watch the plants growing near the cabin with my copy of "Practical Medicinal Herb Studies ~Wetlands / Waterside Edition~" in hand.

It was written on a coarse, bad quality paper, but the actual contents of the book were rather complex. It had everything from descriptions of the plants, to sketches by the author. It was awfully convenient to have.

What surprised me the most was that it wasn't printed. Everything from the descriptions to the sketches were made by hand. I couldn't do anything but nod at the high price after realizing that. As I expected, the ravine in which the labyrinth was located was a really special location, because the plants the book referred to as "Legendary plants that have very limited habitats and are hard to come by naturally", were growing here like weeds. You could say I was blessed in that regard.

Let's see… there was bluelight moss growing here and there. If I dried it out then boiled it, I could make a stamina tonic, and it was tasty enough that you could use it as a tea. If I ground it together with pure water, I could even make a vitality potion, and then…

I took some in my hand, but It looked just like moss to me.

"The clover-ish thingies growing by the sandbank are supposedly called 'phosphor buds.' If I grind them up and dilute it in water, I can make a stamina potion. And if I boil that down, it'll turn into a healing potion."

While they may have looked a weed to me, the leaves were exactly the same as depicted in the book's sketch.

—It lists them as precious and limited potion materials, but I don't think I'll ever run out when there's this much around here.

So there was 'medicine'; disinfectants to prevent festering, pain relieving effects, et cetera.

And then there was 'simple medicine,' which was a medicinal plant that was uncommon around the village—similar to finding Aloe

Vera plants in the middle of the street. The difference was those had medicinal effects that were easy to understand in a modern setting...

Finally there were 'magical potions'... They had an irrational effect when compared to modern Earth science, like recovering lost stamina directly, or restoring damaged organs. The book said that the rarity value rose when it came to raw potion materials, and that scarcity had a direct effect on the price of potions as well.

"Ah, they're supposed to be scarce, at least."

I prepared a basket for the plants and rocks I'd collected, and a glass bottle for the moss, then spent a while examining the surrounding area of the cabin with my book in hand. I found herbs growing all over like weeds, and as much moss I could ever need stuck to stones in the ground and all sorts of other places, like the cabin walls. Seemed like I could make as many magic potions as I wanted.

According to the book, the streams and ponds I was so used to by now were "The bodies of water in which bluelight moss can appear and propagate are few and so far in between they're considered almost a miracle; magical potions can be concocted in such a place." I'd been drinking this ever since I arrived here. Would it be okay? I was kinda nervous now. This ravine was where a large-scale engineering process was supposed to occur in order to build a labyrinth fit for people to go in and out in hordes. Things became even more complicated when the possibility of destroying such a valuable environment in the process was uncovered there.

—If I started selling these in the village, it would be more like an emergency first aid kit rather than something for regular use, so I think it would be better to reduce the number and make more types of medicine.

It was way different in the sense of easily buying medicine and taking it when you had a cold, back in Japan. In a poor pioneering village like theirs, they wouldn't rely on medicine unless the symptoms were too much to bear. That meant they'd go for medicine when they were practically in the worst situation possible, so I'd like to raise the quality as much as I could.

—Vitality, stamina, and healing potions. Those three are my main objectives right now.

It was kinda pointless to use a basket when they were growing right in front of me, so I tossed the medicinal herbs into the iron pot I normally used for cooking, then sorted them all by kind over the table. It didn't take me even one hour to gather a mountain of material.

I used the <Appraisal> skill from time to time just to make sure none of the wrong herbs slipped in.

—Simple sorting work like this isn't that bad, huh? It reminds me of that realistic alchemy simulation game called "Atelier Meimei".

Since the book said I should grind and mix with water, I drew some water out of the pod in front of me with a mortar I'd bought from Tundra. I threw some moss inside, and started grinding away with the pestle.

I didn't hate this kind of simple trial and error work. The game I was thinking of was a real life-oriented PC simulation game made by a little indie company; but they made you grind a pebble against the mortar for eight hours straight while mixing in about three types of herbs and five types of minerals, with a set timer in the tutorial to make a salve. It was literally aimed at experts specifically—perhaps excessively so. The amount of game time required was so overwhelming that I didn't play much of it, but I had a friend that overcame the hellish difficulty and spent a whole month of real time in the game to farm gold. He was praised by the other players as a god... Well, he got hospitalized and almost turned into a real god after playing for a month straight. Man, those were the days.

I kept moving the porcelain pestle until the liquid gained some consistency and a green tea-like color. After grinding away mindlessly for a while, I noticed the liquid was suddenly a mysterious cobalt blue color.

—So my technique was too good... Nah. Maybe the materials are too good?

It went from a green to a transparent cobalt blue when I mixed the green moss and the water. It was kinda hard to disregard nature when something turned into a color it shouldn't have, but I guess this was completed... Right? I thought to put it in a container for now... That was no good, I had to get a container for this thing first. Unlike with games, there wasn't a convenient mechanism that put the potion in a bottle right as it came out of the pot.

I opened the Tundra window, ordered some glass bottles for potions, and opened the cardboard box right away. Since Tundra always used cardboard boxes or manila envelopes to deliver things,

I'd made a habit of carrying around both a knife and a paper knife to open them.

—I don't know if the level of technology is low, or if the quality of material is bad out where the labyrinth's placed in the desert, but they're cheap and functional, so I guess I don't care. It's really affordable. I wonder if they taught the glass manufacturing technology to nearby villages, then outsourced it all to mass produce them.

I took one of the diamond shaped containers and poured the cobalt blue liquid from the mortar into it.

I was using a large mortar; I could make about 100 milliliters of potion every time, and the bottles were kinda like, erm... Tiny energy drink bottles? I managed to fill up eleven of them with the cobalt blue liquid I'd prepared.

"Execute Appraisal."

I put the stylish lid it came with over the glass bottle and tried examining it as a finished product.

Name: Grade 6 Vitality Potion (Quality+)
Description: High quality medicine that replenishes Vitality greatly. Restores 2000 points of Vitality in 1 minute. Effect decreases 25% when applied to an open wound; performs the equivalent effect of a Grade 7 revive potion. Recovery time is sharply shortened due to the Quality+ effect.

—How much Vitality is 2000?

I mean, it was good that it pointed out the effect accurately, but the unit of measurement was so alien to me, it was kinda hard to understand. I checked my 'Labyrinth Manager Status' screen again and confirmed my Vitality was just 120 right now. So this would bring me right back from death if I had a fatal wound. Is that how powerful it was?

—I think the effect's kinda overkill for a rural village emergency first aid kit.

These legendary rare materials sure were something... So this was what the book meant. And that was only using the moss that grew all over this ravine. It was so powerful that even an amateur like me could make something 'Quality+.' Well, I didn't think the effect being too much could ever be a problem. This was when the delivery box came in handy. You could count on it to assess things reliably. I put in one of the potions I'd made inside the box and closed the lid. When I opened it again after listening to the usual sound of coins clinking inside the box... there were a few 100000 DL coins mixed in the bunch.

"Hmm... Looks like there's 480000 DL here. It fetched a better price than I imagined."

Excluding the glass container that cost around 9000 DL, it was still nearly 480000 DL in profit. I had mixed feelings about this being more profitable than working day and night digging up stone this whole time, but never mind that.

Wasn't this price a little out of reach for a remote pioneering village?

Villages that get their main income from agriculture and stock farming wouldn't have that much cash. If all I wanted was cash now, I could just sell it to the delivery box. I guess I could bring some to Mayor Hopper and consult him about it.

—Should I exchange it for other goods, or ask for a loan, or something? What a pain.

After that I tried making stamina and recovery potions. I used both the mortar and the pot for the recovery potion, but I felt kinda unsatisfied with the result.

"I managed to make the stamina potion well, so what's the problem here, huh?"

I looked at the bright green stamina recovery potion bottle sitting right next to a clear deep dark green bottle that was supposed to be the recovery potion. I put my hand on my chin and thought. The UI's semi-transparent appraisal window in front of me displayed 'Grade 5 Stamina Potion (Quality++)' and 'Grade 9 Recovery Potion (Quality+)', respectively.

—That's probably enough, as far as medicine goes. But it's kinda underwhelming compared to the vitality and stamina potions.

When I actually made it, the recovery potion got a lower rank than the other two types of potion somehow—Grade 9 quality.

There were many standards for grading magic potions that I didn't know anything about. After looking at the Tundra review page and comparing the recovery potion classifications, I noticed that the Grade 10 potions were more like a cinnamon infusion, and were used more often than not as prophylactic medicine to fend off diseases before they could set in. The Grade 9 potions were used more like vaccines or antibiotics because of the weak effect. I was interested in what effects the more advanced potions had, but the problem was that despite using overwhelmingly high quality material, I couldn't manage to do anything but the most basic things, still.

—It's times like these that made me wish I had something that displayed my skill levels. If I was told the quality dropped because I tried taking on a high-level recipe with almost no skill, I'd at least be able to understand why.

I took another look at my 'Labyrinth Manager Status' screen, but the translucent window only displayed the usual three stats: Vitality, Stamina, and Willpower. It almost made me regret my minimalistic UI love. Have I been too corrupted by MMORPG games after playing them for so long?

—If I'm not being limited by a skill tree or anything, then it's simply technique in the end. I guess the materials and the mortar alone can only carry me so far.

I looked at the fresh ingredients and the mortar on the table. Even in that realistic alchemy simulator I was talking about earlier, simply mixing wasn't enough even in the tutorial. I didn't think that game's potion making was all that similar to this world's method, but it couldn't hurt to use it as reference.

—But I didn't make any errors making the actual medicine, did I? Then it must be the conditions and the utensils.

For example, the materials were one variable; like the way they were picked up, the degree of freshness, whether they were dried in the shade or the sun—maybe they were even boiled. Then there were cases in which ingredients were seeped in chemicals, with their properties extracted and such. There were more ways to produce potions outside of grinding with a mortar; there was filtration, high temperature and pressure heating, stirring, separation, et cetera. A lot of methods came to mind all of a sudden.

—I would really like a recipe now... I didn't think having only legendary rare materials would backfire like this.

I ordered a small pamphlet-sized book from Tundra called "Do It Yourself! Vitality Potions for Dummies!" that happened to have more information on the actual manufacturing process. There were various ways and materials to make vitality potions. All the different methods were described down to the last detail, like boiling down medicinal plants and heating up mineral ore to extract its components. Then it really was a problem of material and manufacturing techniques? This book confirmed my worries.

However, the book actually listed about 20 kinds of materials to create various grades of vitality potions; even then, I couldn't figure out how to process the materials I could get from the ravine. I bought another book from the same series called "Do It Yourself! Recovery Potions for Dummies!" as well. But just like last time, all I managed to figure out was that you could make them out of various materials, and there were various ways of making them depending on that.

—No one's selling recipes to make potions out of legendary class materials, huh...? Figures.

I sighed as I browsed through the 'Pharmaceutical Literature' section of the Tundra catalog. The regular ingredients were way more popular and user friendly. That seemingly obvious truth was incredibly underwhelming and painful.

—Well, this is fun if you think of it like a game. Fumbling around for recipes is what makes an alchemy game entertaining... I guess I'll take a break for now...

There were many games that centered around alchemy as a theme, but there weren't that many games that tortured you with recipe gathering as well. The difficulty curve was so high that they were hard to sell. I decided to take a break to pull myself together while I thought about how nice it would be to play a game like that instead.

I'd been warming up the water from the spring I usually drew water from. Drinking hot water was kind of my current obsession. I didn't know what was causing it, but the water smelled kinda nice when you warmed it up.

Do It Yourself! Vitality Potions for Dummies! == 300000 DL
Seller: Manager, Labyrinth #315

Rating: ★★★★☆
Reviewer: Manager, Labyrinth #601
- A introductory book on potion making, couldn't be easier to use! This is the first alchemy book of the series. It explains the process of making vitality potions with different materials in an easy but thorough manner. The great amount of illustrations that come with the explanations makes me really happy. This is one book I can't recommend enough for those looking to step in the world of alchemy.

Rating: ★★★☆☆
Reviewer: Manager, Labyrinth #552
- i heard you could squeeze potions out of rocks but it turns out you need an special ore to do it. i was surprised to discovers theres ways to make potions that dont have anything to do with medicinal plants. unfortunately we dont have any of that ore near my house but i reckon the challenge is nice!

Do It Yourself! Recovery Potions for Dummies! == 620000 DL
Seller: Manager, Labyrinth #315

Rating: ★★★☆☆
Reviewer: Manager, Labyrinth #601
- Finally, I've been waiting so long for the new one! My only gripe is that difficulty level this time is kinda... As usual the instructions are detailed and the illustrations are always appreciated. But making recovery potions is so hard I ended giving up anyway. It might be difficult to handle if you're a beginner, despite what the title says.

Rating: ★★★★☆
Reviewer: Manager, Labyrinth #172
- I'm always looking for new books as a potion maker, potions are always priceless as a bargaining tool outside the labyrinth. Purchase it so you can help fight off the eternal stock shortage! The production can't catch up. There's men collapsing because of overwork, this is no laughing matter people! Let's all make more potions!

"Aoi! Aoi!"

I sat on a chair and basked in the sunshine while watching over the greenery and the moss spreading across the ravine, while sipping on my warm water elegantly, when Ann jumped up, calling for me excitedly.

"Hey there... Ann, calm down first."

I rushed to hug Ann and patted her head to help her calm down.

For a second the options flashed inside my mind... 1) "What happened!?" 2) "Help her calm down first."

So I chose the second option. I found that I was now rather used to the excessive skinship with Ann... She must have had a good reason to get riled up like that, so it'd be better to calm down first instead of getting worked up over it together. After a while of patting her head, she gradually calmed down.

"Aoi! Sara is... Sara is... Ah! Sara's my best friend."

After she'd finally stabilized, I carefully listen to Ann while I tried to soothe her, as the tears pooled in her eyes. It seemed like Sara had fallen ill and collapsed.

Apparently it wasn't that unusual for her to fall ill because of her weak constitution, but it seemed she caught something really bad this time. According to the elder elf that worked as the mayor's counselor diagnosis, the sickness Sara had was called 'cursed cold' or 'thinning disease', and it specifically targeted humans; kids, and people with frail constitutions, got it more often.

It wasn't really infectious, as it didn't infect other species, and it only attacked once. But it was still a serious disease that killed one in every five people it did infect, and it seemed like Sara would be in a dire situation if her fever didn't break within two or three days.

"Ever since I fell here, she hasn't been sleeping well, Aoi... Please save her! I'll do anything if you do it!"

—The second offer to do anything I say today...!

Calm down, black beast of mine. Please make my self-control stay in place. So both of them would do anything for their best friend, I was really jealous now. I understood how Sara felt a little better.

Well then... Ann seemed to think she was partly responsible for this. I didn't think so, though.

"Yeah, let me see if I can do anything for her. Can we use medicine to cure that?"

"Thank you, Aoi!"

—Umm... Ann... It's pretty serious when you glue to me like that...!

"Erm... It really would be great if we had a doctor, but maybe we can make a special medicine for this particular disease. Oh, right. A Grade 7 potion..."

I did have a few recovery potions on me, but making a Grade 7 would be... challenging.

"Let's check out Tundra together, Ann."

"Okay!"

I searched for 'cursed cold medicine' on the Tundra catalog and... it was sold out. Looking at the reviews, it seemed the materials used to make it were sensitive to the season and couldn't be harvested all the time. On top of being scarce, it was rare for there to be stock in the first place. I doubt there would be a restock anytime soon.

If the recovery potion we needed was Grade 9, then I had enough of those. But the quality of this one seemed to be way higher than the ones I made, since the potions out of stock were Grade 8 and above. The price was high as well, but since these potions were so versatile, the supply couldn't meet the demand.

"Now this is a problem. Looks like we won't have much luck with Tundra."

"What about the medicine you said you were gonna make?"

"Sorry, I couldn't make anything higher than Grade 9 recovery potions."

"What can we do...?"

"Ann, it's too soon to give up. I taught you that the first time we played games, right? You can always regret things, so let's try doing everything we can right now."

I handed over a bag with eight bottles of dark green liquid I'd made to the crestfallen Ann.

"Deliver these to Sara's home. They're far from a Grade 7 potion, but it's way better than no medicine at all. Tell them to give it to her if she looks in pain. Can you give these to the person that's taking care of her and come back?"

"This many? Even though they may not work?"

Ann raised her head. I could clearly see the worry in her eyes.

"It's okay. Truth is, I became Sara's friend as well today. Of course I'd want to save your best friend, and my friend, right?"

Well, we were more like rivals for Ann rather than friends, and we just met today. And thinking calmly about it, I really didn't have any reason to go this far for her, but I couldn't help but do anything but try to help. I wanted to save her, too... Oh yeah, if I could manage to cure her, I'm sure the expression on Sara's face when she found out would be priceless. With something as fun as that on the line, there was no way I couldn't get over a bit of a hard event like this.

"Thank you so much! What should I do when I deliver these?"

"It might be a little tiring to run back and forth so much, but can you help me make the medicine when you come back? I wanna try making a Grade 7 recovery potion."

"Yup, got it!"

Ann leapt out of the cabin, potion bag in hand, and I begin clashing with the potion making.

"Let's confirm first... Will I always get the same quality with the same procedure?"

I did it just like last time, and slowly ground the phosphor buds for the potion in the mortar. The sound of the pestle grinding against the mortar echoed across the ravine. It was unusually loud without Ann around.

—It's like a fairy tale... A sweet little girl collapses, and the medicine I make might save her life.

The one that collapsed was my rival instead of a heroine, though, if I may add.

—Normally I would be so frightened by the pressure I'd want to just run away from here, but I promised.

"This is not a game. This isn't an NPC in some quest. This is a real person. A real life on the line."

I grumbled to myself about it for a while.

"Man, I hate this kind of thing. You can kill any NPC like it's nothing in regular games, can't you? Oh well... No point in getting worked up about it. It's just business as usual."

Some people might get angry I was comparing games with reality, but I didn't really like it when games took reality too lightly to begin with. Of course I won't spout some garbage about how I wasn't not scared because I had done this in games before. I was worried about Sara, and Ann as well, after seeing her so sad because of her friend.

The thought of not being able to make the medicine came to mind. The anxiousness, frustration, and panic of not knowing if the medicine would even work were wreaking havoc on my mental state, but my pride as a gamer wouldn't let me even think about escaping a trial like this. People usually talked about how life was just like a game. Well, then, people had to do their best with this game called Life.

When I'd finished grinding with the pestle, I mixed what I had on the mortar with water, poured it into the pot, and set up the fire to boil it down. I let the green liquid boil until it gained the consistency of matcha, and its green color darkened. Then I took it off the fire, let it cool, and filled one the bottles with it.

"Execute Appraisal... 'Grade 9 Recovery Potion (Quality+)'. So it's the same..."

I had a faint hope, but the quality didn't change. It might be useful for something, so I filled some glasses with it.

"I'm back! I'm gonna help you now!"

Ann had returned.

"Welcome back. I put some mats with medicinal herbs around the cabin, can you bring them here?"

"Sure!"

The only thing that could be heard in the room was the sound of medicinal plants boiling on the pot below the stove we used inside the cabin. The moss started lighting up the ravine as day turned to night, and everything was painted blue except the blazing orange of the stove taking over the inside of the cabin. As night drew on, I got to my fourth attempt ever since Ann arrived. It'd only been a few hours, but apparently letting them dry was the right answer, though

the highest quality I'd managed to get so far was Grade 8.

After giving it her all gathering phosphor buds and firewood, Ann had wrapped herself up in a blanket and used my lap as pillow. She looked so comfortable. We were way past bedtime, so I understood why she was so tired. She went back and forth between here and the village two times today, and she worked really hard up until a moment ago.

"Good grief... Is there even anything bad about you?"

When I looked at Ann's sleeping face, the way she entrusted herself to me made me want to keep doing my best. It was a burst of energy more than even a thousand cracks of a whip to my back could have mustered.

"Ah... Mm... Zzz..."

It made me feel like a fool that was being led around by the nose, so to calm down some I patted her hair. She seemed to enjoy it as she had let out some cute noises. It was kinda scary how naturally cute she was...

"Execute Appraisal... So increasing the boiling time or the amount of material doesn't help, huh?"

After my fourth failure... I took a deep, long sigh while I stuffed the bottles full of 'Grade 8 Recovery Potions (Quality+++)'. The wall between Grade 8 and Grade 7 was larger than I had expected. It wasn't something you could force yourself to improve upon in a day or two. It took time and experience, both of which I didn't have the luxury of right now.

"Whoa, there... Looks like I'm tired, too. I've gotten so used to sleeping as soon as it gets dark these last two months. Guess I can't do much about that."

I ground some more phosphor buds in the mortar in preparation of another attempt, when I was suddenly struck with a bout of drowsiness, and noticed the thing that was pouring into the mortar wasn't water. I ended up mixing in a stamina potion instead. I didn't want to wreck my sweet little vocal cords or wake up Ann, so I gave up on trying to exclaim my displeasure. Suddenly, I noticed something.

—Haven't I done something like this before?

I was reminded of something when I saw the phosphor bud green paste blend with the bright green colored stamina potion.

"Yeah, it was in one that indie game. It was called 'El-11 SIU-M,' right?"

It was released around a certain big event that happened every summer. It was regarded by a select few as one of the best classic games, made by a group of veterans under a studio called SilverAge Games.

You played the role of the manager of a little classic bar, and you could increase the warehouse capacity by becoming a subcontractor of a larger company, or by making your very own brand, and carving your way out in the world until you hit a niche market. For an indie game, it gave you a great amount of freedom, and had a ton of depth. That was why it was lauded as one of the go-to classic gems of PC gaming.

Among all the real types of alcohol you could brew in the game, there was a certain one that was composed of just of rice and water. But, if you used alcohol instead of water, then the mixture would react differently, and the result had special properties.

—I've been mixing it with water before boiling up until now, but if I used a potion instead... What would happen?

I had nothing better to do besides try out new things; thankfully, the night was still young.

"Execute Appraisal... Wow, I did it."

The small bottle in my hand was filled with a mysterious emerald green liquid that emitted a faint glow. The translucent appraisal window stated 'Grade 6 Recovery Potion (Quality++).'

Morning had started to creep in as I looked out the window. I ended up pulling another all-nighter, huh? At least I had results. I'd tried several experiments after coming up with the replacing water with potion idea, but just mixing up the stamina potion normally seemed to give effective results.

"Ann, wake up. It's morning already."

It pained me to wake her up when she was sleeping so peacefully, but I had to.

"Hmm... Good morning."

Ann slowly opened her eyes, got up a little, and hugged me while still half-asleep. She may still be halfway in dream land, but her charm really did a number on me...! Laugh at me all you want for getting flustered about her hugging and jumping on me, but I still have yet to become overtaken by my desire. Still, I also didn't feel like running away from this happy feeling.

"Ann, Ann. Wake up. The medicine's ready."

"Huh... Really!?"

She perked right up and relinquished her hug. Now that she had finally let go of me, I really missed the feeling of her being glued to me. I really did...

"Yeah, I made a Grade 6 recovery potion. I wanna get it to her right away, wanna come with me?"

"Yes, let's go!"

And so we headed off to deliver the potion to the village as dawn broke.

◇

"Ngh... Oh? What is this? What happened?"

Sara awoke from her own bed, confused by the situation that surrounded her. She only faintly remembered she had gotten sick from something and was bedridden. It was a sensation Sara had been used to ever since she was a child, but her body felt surprisingly light this time. There were no lasting effects that indicated she had even fallen ill. On top of that, Aoi was leaning on the side of her bed, totally asleep. His head was resting defenseless beside her lap. Ann was sitting in a nearby chair with a jealous look on her face—watching Sara get worked up over what was happening was quite the sight.

"Ah, Sara, you're finally up! Are you okay? Does it hurt anywhere?"

"Huh? No... Hey, Ann, can you tell me what's happening?"

Still confused, Sara listened to the whole story from Ann. She told her about how she had collapsed and apparently caught some dangerous disease called 'cursed cold.' She also told her about how

Aoi stayed up all night making medicine for her when he found out. When he gave her the medicine, ascertained that her complexion improved and her breath stabilized, he fell asleep like a rock on the spot.

"Uuuh, then I can't be angry at you... If I move you out of the way, I'll even seem ungrateful."

Sara said with mixed feelings tinging her words as she put Aoi's head back on her lap.

"That's not fair, I want to do it too!" Ann said, filled with playful jealousy.

She jumped up into the same position as Aoi and put her head over Sara's lap as well.

"Ehehe. I'm so glad you're feeling."

"Say, Ann, why do you think Aoi helped me?" Sara asked, puzzled, as she pet Ann's head, which was perfectly lined up with Aoi's.

"He nodded right away after I asked him to save you! He said he would help because you're his friend, too."

Ann looked at Sara with a curious look on her face that said "What's wrong with that?"

"What should I do? This rival is tougher than I thought..."

Ann looked up at Sara's troubled expression, as she laughed embarrassingly.

It was noon the next day, on a moss lawn around the cabin... Originally it was just a stone walkway we had built to move the cart back and forth while we worked on the staircase. Soon after we finished working, the soft moss took over and turned it into a makeshift lawn. Today, Sara was visiting, and she was using Ann as a lap pillow.

"I brought something to prove my gratitude, but don't expect me to bow down and thank you."

She said as she handed me a basket filled with mushrooms and wild plants, while looking straight into my eyes.

"Ann told me she wanted me to use her as a lap pillow."

"And you didn't want to?"

Yeah, I know very well what Sara really wanted to say.

"Ann looked really pleased when I put my head on her lap, but she lost to the sunlight and fell asleep. I've been under the sunlight with her like this for over 30 minutes now, isn't that praiseworthy?"

The sun was kinda strong today; good weather all around.

"Why does Ann even want you to use her as a lap pillow, anyway?"

"I don't know, but I just couldn't refuse when she told me 'I can do it but you can't?'"

I couldn't make fun of her when she said it with such a melancholic face. There was no way I could object to something so dreamlike as watching two girls being so cute. It was like a man's dream.

"Uuh..."

Now this was an awkward mood. After delivering the medicine and confirming it worked, I fell asleep on her lap after passing out because of the exhaustion. I'd rather not even mention the fact, though, for our peace of mind.

"You know, I won't give up being Ann's first place, but I'll accept Ann leaving the village to come live here."

"Thanks, hearing that from Ann's best friend makes me really happy."

"That said, please promise me one thing. You have to protect Ann no matter what happens."

—"Ain't that a bit too headstrong!?" Was what I was about to say, but I couldn't form the words in my mouth.

"I can't say I can with complete certainty that I can do that, but I can promise to do as best I can to protect her."

"I think it's good that you don't take it lightly, but that's unfair..."

"Are you gonna start nagging me for that?"

I thought an innocent promise like protecting a girl no matter what was more fitting for a 16 year old boy.

“What should we do to make the promise official? People lock their pinkies together, back where I come from.”

“That’s for promises between married couples. Normal people here use these for promises.”

And then she presented her ring finger to me. It was interesting how the fingers used for promises changed depending on whether you were married to the person or not.

“Then, it’s a promise.”

“I promise.”

I locked my ring finger with hers and swore. The fact we had a peaceful exchange made me so happy that I couldn’t even imagine Ann and Sara were suffering so much until not so long ago. It may not look like that much of an achievement, but I was satisfied with the reward I got for completing the potion making ‘event,’ so to speak… I’m glad I did my best.

Saving Sara and making up with her didn’t really change our daily lives much. I was still in my trial period. But in the meantime, I was devoting myself to prepare for the next village market fair, and looking for products that may have a demand.

I figured that being able to make so many types of potions was enough, but I had no real variety outside of that. I didn’t even know how much value the potions would have inside the village. I understood the process, so I tried making more recovery potions when everything settled down, and managed to make more Grade 6 products with the a ‘Quality+’ property.

“The color is really pretty, and they seem to be in demand… but I can’t say for sure yet.”

I put the little bottle with the emerald colored liquid against the light and tried to appraise it, but I still couldn’t tell what exactly it did for someone. The translucent window that came out said “Cures most illnesses and relieves the symptoms of severe illnesses to some extent.”

I guess I wouldn't know until I tried it out.

I tried making special products that made use of what I had in the labyrinth, besides potions. I tried using the wire net I'd bought from Tundra to reinforce a glass, making a makeshift candle lamp. Then I placed a piece of bluelight moss and poured some water inside to make a lamp that didn't require any fuel.

The moss wouldn't spread if it didn't have a lot of clean water around, but since it could keep shining on without withering even with no water, it was still usable. It might not be as bright as an oil lamp or a normal candle, but it made for a good source of light still, because it required no maintenance, nor consumed any fuel.

"I'm not too sure about this... Execute Appraisal."

Name: Bluelight Moss Lamp
Description: A lamp that emits a pale light in the absence of sunlight. The intensity of the light will be constant as long as it's properly watered. While not requiring any fuel, its brightness pales in comparison to lamps that employ fire.

Yes, looked like it turned into a lamp just like I wanted. Its nature might be a little different from what I intended at first, but the appraisal was useful enough. I wondered how it determined the kinds of the things I made. It seemed to be able to distinguish failures, at least. I made about ten lamps and put them inside a leather bag I'd made for the occasion, along with the potions. I also began making some more hoes and sickles with the <Dungeon Management Tool>.

Things were awfully quiet around here since Ann went to visit Sara. Even if she lived here in the labyrinth, I'm sure she'd like to cherish the bonds with her best friend and family. Despite that, and even though I'd gotten kinda distracted because of the whole deal with Sara and her illness, I was still amazed by Ann's real form.

I knew Ann was a half-kobold from the first day I appraised her, but I didn't know she could transform into a kobold form to get their abilities. Her true form was literally the same as a normal human girl. I couldn't rely on appearances to guess her age because our races were different, but nothing could beat the impact of the beautiful girl I found in her the first time around. No matter if she had a doggy or human form, she was Ann on the inside, so my way of treating her wouldn't change much. But if she kept up the skinship level we've had so far while in pretty girl mode... Then my mind would snap at some point.

It seemed her form changed due to the shock of the fall when I first found her, but then I asked about why she was in kobold form back when we met, to which Jenny gave me another answer. She said it was because of self-defense. Apparently it was easier to get targeted by demons or other things if your appearance was of a human's.

I may be speculating a little bit here, but there might be multiple human clans out there, and it must be easier for the other races to judge beauty among humans. But when it came to kobold faces, it must be hard to differentiate a pretty kobold from a normal one, unless you were a kobold yourself. "She's like a little sister to me, so I can't see her as a woman" is a line I'd heard more times in games than I could count, but I really couldn't keep that up if that happened again.

My view of Ann had already shifted from somewhere along the lines of a little sister and a pet, to a pretty girl that was somewhat like my little sister. I'd like to put various things about that on hold until the end of my training... but Ann's way too powerful.

I wondered if they sold some sort of 'calming tea' in Tundra... I had Tundra open on one side, while I chugged down willpower potions, and kept making hoes and sickles with the <Dungeon Management Tool>.

That night we played Ann's favorite game.

We played the tabletop game while I recalled all the games I'd played back on Earth. I called it "Labyrinths and Dragon's Feast." After we were done playing, Ann called out to me after we had cleaned ourselves and headed to bed for the night.

"Hey, can we talk a little bit before going to bed?"

I doubted I would be able to calm down if Ann and I slept together in that tiny bed under the same blankets, while she wore nothing but my white shirt just like before. When I heard Ann's voice though, one full of trust in me, I could feel my heart calming down a bit.

"Sure, what's wrong?"

"What's a sneaking visit?"

"H-Huh...!? (cough) (cough)"

I was caught so off guard that I started to have a little bit of a coughing fit. The calm sea that was my heart went back to the choppy waves it was riding just a moment ago.

"A-Ann, who told you about that?"

"My auntie. She taught me a lot of things, but I forgot to ask about that word."

—You started plotting the next attack already, Jenny…!?

"I see. Hmm… It's kinda hard to explain as a man. I think it'll be easier to understand if you just ask Jenny about it."

"I see. I am, umm… sorry, that I bothered you before. I did, didn't I? You looked in so much pain and all…"

—She looks so apologetic and cute, I'm the one starting to feel sorry…

"You had a reason for it, right?"

We had been together for two months now, and I knew how much of a pure and caring girl Ann really was. It worried me at times.

—If I really looked like I was in pain, I'm sure Ann would stop even if she trusts Jenny's wisdom.

"Yes. I want to stay with you forever, but Auntie told me the time we can stay together like this isn't so long unless we… marry."

"I see…"

Ann was still a child… No, thinking about it now that she has changed forms, I could see she was growing, but her honest and cute character made me embrace a younger impression of her. I'd also almost forgotten I was in a medieval fantasy world, after spending so much time peacefully stuck at the bottom of this ravine. Sara was treading between life and death after getting a little sick. Death was always looming around the corner; lifespans weren't that long, and the mortality rate of babies was too great also. I knew marriage and childbirth started at an earlier stage of life here, compared to those of modern Earth, but I didn't fully understand or realize it yet.

It was a blind spot for me. Even though I knew there were differences between our cultures, we were still from separate worlds. Of course their set of values and customs would be completely different from mine.

“That’s why Auntie told me that if I do this ‘sneaking visit’ thing, we can be together forever.”

A chill ran down my spine when I’d finally realized what Jenny’s next scheme was. There’s no way I could tell Ann any of that, though. Not when she was opening her heart to me and choosing her words so carefully.

“Hey, can we really stay together forever? It won’t make you hate me, right…?” she asked.

The anxiety-tinged words leaking out of Ann’s mouth hit me like a truck. I felt like they were pushing me down, as if the gravity was turned up. Ann was being pretty bold, but it was obvious she was pretty worried and anxious about this. What could I do? I’d be hard-pressed to simply resolve the situation by saying…

—"We can be together forever."

I didn’t want to make a promise that involved the future when mine was so unclear due to the trial period. That said, I didn’t want to reject Ann here either.

Rather than spouting words of acceptance irresponsibly, it would be better to reject by carefully wording things as to not hurt her; that would be the best. That was my judgment call as an adult… But I hated it. If I hurt her with heartless adult words, words with no feelings behind them, it would truly be the worst assessment of my life.

—Think… You have tons of experience overcoming difficult moments like this, don’t you? A way to not hurt Ann and not take responsibility…

One such way rose to the top of my head as I thought as hard and fast as I could.

“You’re so smart, but you miss the mark so much sometimes, Ann.”

“H-Huh…?”

The uneasiness made her curl up a little bit, and I hugged her as gently as possible.

“If I hated you, there’s no way we’d be this close together. Even though you have so many doubts and fears, there's no need to worry. I could never hate you, don't you think so too?"

"Do you really mean it...?"

"Yes, because I feel the same way about you. You can stay here as much as you want."

"Really?"

"Yeah, but... can you wait a little bit for me to reply on whether or not we can truly stay together forever? You know, I'm still just an apprentice labyrinth manager, right?"

"Yes..."

"It'll be decided if I stop being an apprentice or not in a month or so. That's why we should make a promise."

"A promise?"

"Yeah. If I stop being an apprentice in one month, can you ask me the same thing? I'll answer then."

"Yes, I got it... I promise. I'll ask no matter what, okay?"

Ann rested her head on my arm and began sleeping quietly. I wondered if it was because she felt safe now. Man... I was fortunate that I wasn't picky with visual novels. This option wouldn't have come out as smoothly if I didn't have so much experience with those. I was thankful for being a gamer from the bottom of my heart. Nonetheless, the option I used as reference was one that tied you to the ending of one of the heroines, if I remembered correctly. I just postponed it.

—Didn't I pretty much accept her just now, though?

Maybe I was too hasty. The doubts started to swirl inside my heart, and were promptly melted away as soon as I saw Ann's peaceful sleeping face as she used my arm as pillow. A bitter smile formed on my face, and a feeling of resignation mixed in my heart as a small laugh escaped my lips. She was super soft and fluffy in kobold form, but with this form, her hair type changed from fluffy to smooth; not that it stopped me from patting her head like always. I fell asleep as the bittersweet flavor of the herb spread across my mouth.

I managed to sleep together with her and stay sane today thanks to the herb I'd bought from Tundra today after dinner.

Samathi Herb (Dry; 8 pc. set, 15 g) == 1,800DL
Seller: Manager, Labyrinth #201

Rating: ★★★★☆
Reviewer: Manager, Labyrinth #48
- Useful herb for analgesic/pain killer purposes. It's dry, but it comes back to life as soon as you add some water, it's useful since you can put it over scratches or open wounds given they're not too deep. I'm glad it's safe to use for children as well.

Rating: ★★★★★
Reviewer: Manager, Labyrinth #16
- A handy herb for when you need to pull all-nighters. Boil the dry leaves with hot water and you'll get a relaxing bitter-sweet tea. It has a really calming effect for the nerves when you're staying up all night. I tried analyzing the components and ran some tests, but I didn't find any addictive agents or side effects. The problem it's that its nature changes when you extract its components, so it's not really fit for mass production.

Strongest Gamer
Let's Play in Another World

Chapter 3

Milt Village's square was crowded with people on the morning of the market day. For the most part, it looked like a place where people bartered with money. Those that had goods spread them out on a cloth on the ground and lined them up like street vendors, and those who weren't selling visited the stalls and negotiated.

"There really are a lot of races living in Daemon, aren't there?"

There were small kobolds with the same physique as Ann gathered in the square, but there were also minotaurs like the mayor, beast men with tiger heads, and even one-eyed giants with horns coming out of their foreheads.

It was very interesting to see humans and people with pointy ears—that I supposed were elves—living so peacefully among these giants and demon-looking, monster-like creatures. It feels like it was just commonplace around here.

The tiny kobold pups and the ashen-skinned, goblin-like children ran about and played together. The elf running the vegetable stall, and the lizardman dealing with vegetables and pelts, looked at them with smiles on their faces.

"Ann, are there normally this many kinds of races living together in normal villages?"

"Not really. Villages usually have one or two races living together, at most. The only places where there's this many races are pioneering villages like this, or big cities. I think my granny was from a village where kobolds and humans lived together."

That made sense. Races whose body structures were close to each other might be able to have children, but finding a marriage partner which you could even do so with must have been difficult when there were so many races like this.

You might be able to produce offspring even among races that looked totally different in this world, but then there would be a different type of problem. Like, the anatomy of the child might be far too warped to fit in anywhere. If you showed me a picture of one of these cyclops in a swimsuit, I wouldn't really understand the sex appeal, at least. If it was like a town or a village that didn't have much variety of residents, it would be convenient to have multiple races doing business in hard labor or farming work, but it would be kinda difficult in terms of ensuring the perpetuation of one's species.

I was carrying the hoes and sickles made with the <Dungeon Management Tool> on my back while Ann carried the bag with the potions and lamps inside. I could feel a lot of strange glances coming my way. Ann wasn't too out of place, but I was a new face around here; they must be on guard.

"Mayor Hopper, good morning."

I found the mayor spreading out an old rag right in the center of the square.

Next to him there was a stake sticking out of the ground, with a rope attached. On the other end of that rope was... a six-legged lizard that seemed to be about 50 centimeters long, tied by the head. Maybe he was selling it as a cooking ingredient?

"Oh my, if it isn't Mister Aoi. Well met."

Mayor Hopper's happy bovine countenance couldn't have been more heartwarming as he proceeded to raise the lizard and snap its neck as if it was a pair of chopsticks, to which he handed over to a female goblin, which I assumed was a housewife from her appearance. She handed a corn-like thing in exchange. The whole encounter left me unsure what to feel.

—So it was an ingredient after all...

"I'd like to participate in the village's market. I was wondering if you would allow me. Also, where would the peddlers happen to be?"

"Oh, goodness. It's not that big of a deal. You're very welcome here. The peddler's festival is a little ways from the square. Just head for the village's northern exit."

"Thank you very much. Ann, what are you looking at?"

Ann, who turned into her kobold form as soon as we left the ravine, was now looking intently at the mayor's lizards.

"Ah, it's nothing. It's been so long since the last time I saw normal meat."

That was because we've been eating nothing but pumpkin and beef jerky... I wanted to do my best selling this stuff so I could get Ann's favorite foods as well.

I thanked the mayor once again for giving me permission to participate, and proceeded to set up my stall in a corner of the square.

"Alright, Ann. I don't know the prices of things in the village, so I'll leave things to you. Exchange the hoes and sickles for vegetables and meat we can eat, and don't forget to mention they have durability and can only be used for half a year."

I lined up the hoes and sickles on top of the cloth and delegated the pricing and negotiations to Ann.

"Huh? You want me to do that all by myself?"

Her fur visibly stood on end due to the surprise of me dumping the work on her all of a sudden.

"Listen now, Ann. It's true I may be more of an adult, but I don't know anything about this world outside of the labyrinth. Which means you—hell, even the kids of the village know way more than me. I don't know how much tools and food are worth in the village. Rather than listing the price too high or too low, I'd rather rely on you."

I may have been able to sell items to Tundra and get their assessment, but in a fantasy world where a normalized distribution system wouldn't get developed without trading in person, I couldn't really use Tundra's price assessments and references for commodities in relation to localized farming villages and urban areas. That's why I decided to leave it all in Ann's hands.

Since it was a countryside village, chances were most of them knew Ann, so they wouldn't be wary of her. And the adults would keep their prices accordingly if Ann was the one running the business as well. Quite the bulletproof plan. I might have a bit of a weakness by just acting as figurehead, but I could bear with that...

"I got it, Aoi! I'll do my best. I'll do business so we can have meat and vegetables for dinner tonight!"

Ann clenched her paw and accepted the challenge.

I hoped she could get ingredients that could get cooked up later. If she was given a live lizard as an ingredient, well... yeah. Let's ask Jenny for help if that happens. If I was in a realistic survival game where we had to deal with securing food in a solitary island or in an extremely cold region, I'd know a little about it. But here, I didn't have even the slightest idea about food making or ingredients. It'd be fine if wasn't tasty, but we'd have a problem on our hands if I came around something poisonous because of my ignorance.

"Mister Gald, I have good stuff. Take a look!"

The man Ann called was like a mountain of muscle roughly two meters high and covered in clothes that were patched up all over. A pair of big tusks extruded from his mouth. He must be what people called an ogre. He looked capable of pulling off a pretty mean face, but he really seemed gentle when he was in a good mood. I could tell that the opposite expression of his face wouldn't be for the faint of heart.

"Oho, well if it isn't Ann. I was worried ever since I heard you got employed, but you look quite well. Your complexion looks pretty nice. Have you gotten fatter?"

"Hey! You have to tell a girl that her fur looks glossy, and her figure looks better!"

Although the exchange between him and Ann was as pleasant as the weather, I couldn't help but feel a chill down my spine as his tusks moved around as he spoke..

"You're her employer, mate? How's this little cute thing behaving? She's a good 'ittle working girl, ain't she?"

"Yeah, she's smart and works hard. Are all the children of this village the same?"

“Gwahaha, not a chance! Ann’s a pretty special lass, y’see. My kids have been so lonely since their cute and smart big sister has left.”

“Now that’s a problem, I don’t want all the children mad at me because I stole their beloved big sister away from them.”

The talkative ogre named Gald gave me a hearty laugh. While he certainly looked rather rough around the edges, he was still a nice guy, nonetheless.

“Geez! You have to go behind me and just look, Aoi. You too, Mister! Rather than talking, how about looking at the wares? We have hoes with iron blades here. You told me you needed some before, right?”

Ann looked more peppy than usual. I wondered if it was because she was around so many familiar faces.

“A hoe with an iron blade, you say? I certainly need one, that’s for sure. Must be pricey, though...”

He lifted the tool and checked the handle and the blade to make sure.

“Now this is quality. The handle is solid and pretty well done. The blade is as pretty nice piece of art as well. But... the price must be steep, eh? I don’t think someone as poor as me could afford it.”

“It’s not that expensive since it’s a little different from a normal tool. It’ll break after half a year, so it’s cheaper than the ones the blacksmith sells!”

“It’ll break after half a year? So this here’s a magical tool? How much are you asking for, then?”

So things like this could be accepted as magical items in villages like these? The popularity of magic here seemed way higher than back on Earth.

“You’re cultivating demi corn back at your place, right?”

“Yeah, I somehow managed to haul a harvest big enough to fill 20 sacks, so I won’t have to worry about food for now. The taste is a bit iffy, but I want my kids to sleep with their bellies full.”

“Hmm... Demi corn is easy to make, but the harvest is over if it dries up. In that case... let’s see. Yes, how about one hoe for two sacks?

Ann extended her soft paw towards the ogre with a speed that denoted her enthusiasm.

When she changed to girl form, her hands became like those of a human's, but it was kind of a shame those cute soft paws were lost in the process.

"Hmmmm. I do want the hoe, but 2 whole bags is..."

The ogre folded his arms, perhaps in thought as to whether Ann's price was appropriate or not. Those gigantic and burly arms seemed as big as Ann's waist.

Leaving it to Ann was the right choice. She might have be negotiating on a bag-to-bag basis instead of weight, but I didn't know the first thing about how much any of it was worth. Raw currency really was great. I wanted to know how big those sacks were when we headed back to the cabin. I'd be more of a pushover if I didn't know that much by the next time we traded.

"Then how... about a normal sack and two little ones. It's a special offer just for you!"

"Y-You're on! I'll get it in that case. Can I bring the sacks in later?"

"Yes! But please do it early, okay?"

Seemed like the deal was sealed. And so, the ogre man took one of the ten hoes I'd prepared for today.

"Aoi, I sold a hoe. And I got some sacks of dry demi corn for it, too! Even if we only eat that every day from now on, it'll last us a whole month!"

"You did your best, Ann. Good girl."

"Awoo! I'll keep at it, okay!?"

I patted her head, as a cold sweat ran down my spine. I had to do a market and price investigation as soon as possible. I'd also have to rely on Jenny to teach me about the ingredients and food recipes.

The intuition I'd built after spending so many years playing spoke to me. If I stopped putting in any effort here, then my future of depending on Ann for everything, like a gigolo, was almost certain. Although I did have some kind of admiration for that kind of life, what kind of example would I be setting for her? I couldn't do something like that...!

"Phew. They're all sold, huh?"

"Are farming tools really this profitable?"

It had been barely two hours since Ann took over the negotiations and the bartering, and we already sold all of the 15 sickles and 10 hoes we'd brought with us this morning. There was a jute bag filled with dry corn, with grains so big they looked like little potatoes, which sat on top of the cloth where the tools were lined up not so long ago. There was also a big bacon-like salted block of meat that weighed about 20 kilograms. And also, one of the lizards from the mayor's stall, which was already dead. It had just finished dripping blood out of its head, thankfully.

Apparently the poor lizard was unable to escape its fate. The ones from the mayor's stall seemed particularly big, but I saw plenty of other villagers selling them as well. I thought they might be somewhat of a parallel to chickens on Earth.

"Yes, everyone uses tools nonstop around here, so everyone working out in the fields wants good tools. The one you make turn into light and disappear when you use them too much, but they rarely get chipped or rust, so I wonder if they'll get really popular."

While I looked at Ann's radiant smile, an uncomfortable feeling started swirling inside of me as I surveyed the mountain of goods the sales had reaped.

"Ann, is Mister Gald an ogre? Is he as strong as he looks?"

"Yes, people from the ogre race like him are really strong!"

"Then why does he need farm tools? With that much force he could... use a stone hoe or something, or uproot a tree out of the ground and till the soil with it."

"Huh...? Yes, I guess he could."

She tilted her head to the side in confusion, and looked at me with a curious face.

"Then why are there so many people that want an iron hoe? I might understand if it was a weak elf or a kobold, but we had some people from the giant race buy some, too."

"U-Umm. Well, that's because it's easier with an iron tool?"

I understood that it was easier, but the odd feeling still didn't subside.

"Ann, you think Mister Gald will be done with his work faster thanks to that hoe, right? What do you think he'll do with his free time?"

"Let's see. He really loves children, so I think he would play with them... Or teach them to fish in the river that's a bit far away from the village... Maybe?"

Using your free time to do the things you liked, I could understand that as well. That was the same reason why this village's position seemed odd to me.

"Ann, we got a lot of corn and vegetables from selling the tools, right?"

"Yes, we wouldn't have trouble eating for around half a year with all this!"

"I don't want to say it too loud, but this village isn't that rich, huh? Then why did they give you this much?"

"Well... these sell for very cheap if you go to a town; they're not really popular."

"That's odd. How come?"

"You can make a whole lot in a village... but it isn't tasty at all. It's not very nutritious, either."

Ann said sorrowfully as she looked at the mountain of produce in front of us. I see, cultivating in the wastelands could yield a good amount of harvest, thus they didn't starve. However, they wouldn't gain weight since the nutritional value was so low, and since they sold for so low, you wouldn't get rich anytime soon trying to cash it in.

"You know a lot, huh, Ann? Is it difficult to raise crops that'll sell for much in the city?"

"Yes, to grow those, the soil needs to be better. We'd also need a lot of water, and it seems the field upkeep costs would rise as well."

"You're quite the bundle of knowledge, aren't you?"

"Awoo. You said you were 'ignorant,' so I just want to help you."

While I praised Ann and patted her head, I came to the realization of the weird feeling I had. That being... living in this pioneering village, filled with countless types of people and races, yet still managed to be peaceful. No, if I took into account that this was also a countryside village, then they were too peaceful...

Even though the villagers only wore patched up rags and had no hope of living any better in the near future, they weren't desperate or bitter—they just lived peacefully. They only bartered and exchanged between each other for goods at good rates. I had yet to hear about an unfair trade even once around here. Even though they were basically living in poverty, they could avoid the danger of starvation due to the amount of variety of produce they could get cultivating the wasteland, and accepted their status of poverty because of it.

I didn't see any desire to break free from poverty anywhere around. But I also didn't feel like there was something sinister behind it. They might be living in poverty, but it seemed that they led peaceful and fulfilling lives in spite of being impoverished. It wouldn't be an exaggeration to say this was some kind of paradise. It was a scene so moving that it'd put a religious person, who said that a modest and honorable life of poverty was the way to live, into tears. However, for someone like me who took pride in their gaming abilities, this was far from paradise.

If I used my beloved games as a metaphor, it would be like if you kept playing, the difficulty curve would drop off to stupefying levels. Playing the game was like a double-edged sword.

That was the very same reason I felt annoyed by this paradise, while at the same time I thought it was charming. It was distasteful to try and force someone to change their playstyle, but when you saw players that weren't taking the game seriously, you'd feel the need to set them straight. Because of my life with Ann, I knew that the villagers—including Ann—all accepted poverty with open arms. But I was sure they also still had dreams and aspirations, too. I gave the villagers tools to make their livelihoods easier, just like I gave Ann a job and some income. Giving them something to aim for could change the village's outlook on things. However, I didn't have enough time to really make an impactful change for them. I had less than a month left. Before I even noticed, the sense of loss and frustration overcame the relief, as I recalled that my time left here was almost up.

"Hey, can we hold hands?"

Ann presented her paw to me after she was done packing everything, and had the bags up on her back.

"Sure, something the matter?"

A warm and fluffy feeling enveloped my hand as I held hers.

"You looked pretty sad just now."

"I see... Thanks. You're so kind, Ann."

Right. If I only thought about the fact the ending was closing in, I'd end up squandering what precious time I had left.

The bag on my back was pretty heavy with all the corn and meat stuffed inside; not to mention the headless lizard that hung from it. And so, we headed to the place where the peddlers were.

I found the peddler the mayor told me about right away. It was a cart with a curtain attached to it you wouldn't find anywhere else around the village. The goods were lined up on the ground near the cart's roof rack. It was to be expected, but the variety and amount of products was really different from the rest of villagers. But I guess that's what sold the most around here. New jute bags, iron hoes and axes, plain colored cloths and everyday appliances—nothing too showy all in all.

Seemed like the villagers made their rounds through here today already. The cart was filled with jute bags of various produce and live lizards.

"Nice to meet you. Can you show me the goods?"

Perhaps the peddler had gotten enough customers for the day. He was relaxing and smoking a pipe that let out a sweet mint-like scent, when I called out to him.

"Oooh? I don't recognize you... Are you a new villager, boy?"

His physique was way more rugged and wild than a normal kobold. The male wolf-faced merchant took the pipe out of his mouth and responded. He seemed to be a canine type, but not exactly the very same as a kobold.

—Maybe he really was a wolf, or a human beast, or something?

He had a pretty big scar across his left eye that looked like it was caused by a sharp object—it was quite striking. The rough tone of his voice gave me the impression he was no youngster either.

"Yeah, the name's Aoi. I'm kind of a hermit that lives close to the village. Nice to meet you."

I was a labyrinth manager, but I couldn't recall that set of stairs leading down to a shabby cabin inside of a ravine labyrinth without feeling embarrassed.

I didn't live quite the life of a farmer, so I couldn't come up with anything besides hermit. This wolf man looked sharp though, like nothing amiss would get by his watch. The atmosphere about him was akin to encountering a worthy rival in a game tournament.

"Hmm. Kwaharharhar, what's with that? Well, you wouldn't have been too convincing if you told me you're a villager with that getup anyway. I'm a peddler, Fez's the name. Nice to meet you, Mister Hermit."

I shook hands with Fez and noticed the strength of his muscular arm. The palm of his paw had a pad just like Ann, but his was rather rough, and kinda painful to touch.

"Fez, can I use DL to do business with you?"

"Getting paid with money is really appreciated. Oh, so that's why you came to me?"

"Yeah, every deal with the villagers involves goods, so using currency is a bit hard. But you accept money, right?"

The hoes and sickles were insanely valuable in the village. It was kind of hard to ask them to pay them in cash. Even if we bartered, exchanging large quantities of fragile expensive goods like leafy vegetables or eggs would be difficult. However, once something got into a peddler's cart, it should have a set price tag, so I was expecting there to be no problem with just paying with money upfront. My hunch looked to be true.

"Ann, choose what we need to get by for a while with a budget of around 30000 DL. Don't worry if it goes over that buying iron cookware or things we really need, okay?"

"Yes, leave it to me!"

Ann dropped her bag and headed to look at Fez's lineup, with a serious expression on her face. I was in trusting 'Ann Mode' once again. She seemed really happy that I trusted her, but trusting everything to her made me feel kinda bad, too.

"Digging into the matters of the village is a little odd, to say the least. You're an odd one, man. You seem kind of uninformed if you don't even know if you can pay with money, but you don't seem that odd. I'd believe you if you told me you're a noble that got kicked out his mansion, or something."

It might feel kind of wrong coming from Earth, but in a meritocracy where nobles rose in power depending on their physical strength or wisdom one after the other, family lineage awareness was still something to keep in mind, huh?

"You look pretty sure of your skill as a peddler, Fez. Have your worked as mercenary or something like that?"

The rift I could feel between me and Fez was less like that of a merchant feud and more like... of a gamer standing in front of another player in a match.

"Heh, you've got quite the eye, don't you? I did work as a mercenary for a while, enough for my name to spread a little, at least. I was called Fez, Berkud Frontier's Red Spear..."

"So you run your business alone because you're confident in your strength, huh? Why become a peddler if your name was so famous anyway?"

"Ah. Well, that's a long story."

That looked to be a touchy topic for Fez, but I wondered about where he got that scar on his face.

"You see, I was kind of having some fun with a widow working in the peddler business, and the daughter of a merchant... And both of them got pregnant at the same time..."

Well, that was as valid of a reason to retire from the mercenary work as taking an arrow to the knee was...

"I don't really know what to say, but... do your best."

I couldn't do anything but place my hands on the shoulders of the crestfallen Fez as he told his story with a gloomy tone. This wasn't a battle he could win with his mercenary experience alone. He was probably told to stop pursing that line of dangerous work as soon as he had children.

"Oh yeah, I have some rare items on me, wanna take a look?"

I took out a bluelight moss lamp out of the bag Ann had carried all the way here to shake off the heavy mood.

"What's this blue light you've got there?"

I brought the lamp closer to Fez. Since it got bathed in sunlight from being taken out, it didn't take long for it to return to its normal state.

"It's not that bright, but it's a lamp that lets off a blue light in the dark. It'll work as long as you keep it watered, so it's good for saving oil."

"Now that's something I've never seen before. I haven't seen a lamp that doesn't need oil even in the big cities."

"It's something that needs a really valuable material. I have ten of these. I'll sell them to you for cheap, so how about trying to sell them to the villagers, eh?"

"I don't really mind, but why don't you do it yourse— Ah, I see. They're expensive, huh?"

"Yeah, I use a glass container for it, so it's kinda difficult to exchange for meat or vegetables. One of these is worth 120000 DL, but since it's an unfamiliar item, I can sell 'em to you for 30000 DL. That'll be 300000 DL for all of them."

"The offer is quite nice, but it's still pretty expensive. The fact it doesn't need oil is pretty good, but a clay oil lamp is still cheaper than this."

I checked the price of lighting equipment in the Tundra catalog beforehand, but it was just like Fez had said. A simple oil lamp made out of pottery and cloth went for as low as 1500 DL on Tundra. And if you used fish or tallow it was kinda smelly, but cheap.

"Right... Then how about I hand them to you so you can try and sell them? I don't mind if you sell them for cheaper, and we can decide on a final price later. How about half and half?"

"Those are some pretty nice conditions. I don't mind them, but are you sure?"

"Yeah. I need a little bit of advice, could you help me with that? See it as a consultation fee."

"That's fine by me, but I won't help you with problems about money or women."

—Hey, why did you look at Ann when you said that?

"No, it's not that! I just came here recently, so I want to fit in with the village quickly."

I couldn't slack on my social relationships with the locals if I wanted to pursue about the expansion of the labyrinth, and employment of manpower for it.

"Well this is a pioneering village, so you have a bit of luck there, but even then it takes time to fit in."

"Being helpful around here is the best way to fit in, right? So, that's why I made this."

I took a potion out of my bag and handed it over to Fez.

"Ohohoho, a potion... No, a magical potion. So you're a hermit that knows about alchemy as well, huh? What does this little guy do?"

"That's a Grade 6 recovery potion."

"Bwah!?"

—Hey, there. Now that's a puff.

A big round, white cloud of smoke came out from the tip of Fez's pipe as the surprise made him blow unexpectedly.

"I... (cough)"

"Are you okay, Fez?"

He choked over that pretty badly, but he was so small I didn't wanna overdo it by patting his back.

"Are you stupid? It's hard to come by these even in big cities. A Grade 6 recovery potion can sell for way higher than any jewel!"

Hmm, so it was that rare, huh? It did sell for 1.5 million DL when I put it in the delivery box; it also sold out as soon as I took a look at the catalog afterwards.

"Figures... I was thinking of selling it to the mayor, but I don't think he could just buy it off me since it's so valuable."

"Well, you've got the right of it... Do you have more stuff?"

"I have Grade 6 vitality potions and Grade 5 stamina potions as well."

"The whole village would get wrung dry if they bought this from you."

"That's why I wanted your advice. I'm not really looking to make a profit, but it would be bad to just give it over for free, wouldn't it?"

"Of course. Oh man, now that's a harder consultation than I thought."

Fez was so confused he couldn't help but scratch his head.

"It would be better to talk it out with the mayor. Everyone's gonna close up shop by noon, can you wait till then?"

"Yeah, I sure can," I told him. "Hey, Ann, are you ready?"

"Yes, I managed to spend around 20000 DL or so."

She chose some porcelain cutlery, jute and wool cloths, a cord to hang laundry, and a frying pan. She also got daily goods, like some eggs, leafy veggies, and pickled vegetables to cook. Pretty practical choices overall.

"Hey, Fez. You wouldn't happen to have cute accessories for girls around here, would you?"

"I don't have much in the way of variety, but how about this?"

Fez took out a beautiful silver ring passed through a leather strap.

"A necklace? Is this silver?"

"Yeah, a real silver ring. Finger rings get in the way of work in a village like this, y'see, so there's a lot of folks that put a strap to it and hang it on their necks. Just put it around the girl's neck if you chose her. Since we're doing business now, how about we leave it at 40000 DL?"

"Not a bad deal. I'll take it."

I took my wallet out of the bag and handed over four 10000 DL coins.

"You don't have any small coins? You're pretty stacked for real, huh?"

Fez put all the things Ann chose inside the bag. We ended up making it even heavier. Well, Ann had gotten strangely strong as of late, so there probably wouldn't be any trouble.

"This is for you, Ann. You're always doing your best, so here's a little something."

I handed the silver ring necklace to Ann.

"Oh... Umm. Thank you!"

She seemed a little confused at first, but it didn't take long for a radiant smile to take over her face.

—Ann's really a girl, huh? I suppose accessories would make any girl happy, though.

"So I put on like this... How does it look?"

She put it around her neck right away.

"It really suits you. You look like a princess."

"Ehehe~"

I think I exaggerated a little, but she seemed happy, so whatever.

"Hah!"

Fez was a married man, and a peddler at that. How about complimenting clients a little more?

Around noon, I visited Mayor Hopper's house along with Fez after he was done wrapping up his stall.

“I see... A magic potion would be a great help, but it is pricey, indeed...”

The Mayor’s face lightened up when he heard vitality potions could heal wounded people and recovery potions could cure most diseases, but as expected...

“If you were to sell this in a town...”

And his mood deflated as soon as he heard the price.

“But missing this chance is indeed a shame.”

What Fez proposed was to make a potion deposit in the mayor’s place for use in an emergency. I’d have to come around every six months or every year to refill the potions, check that they haven’t deteriorated, or replace them outright if they couldn’t be used anymore. As payment, the village would have to keep giving me a periodic supply of crops and meat even if I didn’t need it. It was very close to the way medicine was sold in Japan a long time ago. I was surprised Fez could come up with something like that, but it seemed this kind of arrangement was quite common when a doctor settled in a remote village where medicinal plants could be gathered to cover their life expenses.

“Hey, Fez, I really have a lot of vitality potions, so how about showing the effect?”

The remuneration was specifically to deliver food to me every three days. At present, they’d just be giving enough for Ann and me, but the deal included them giving us enough food for up to eight people if our numbers increased. With the current state of the village, feeding only two of us was still quite a hit.

I proposed trying the potion out when I noticed the mayor was doubtful of the proposal. While the fact the number of people could increase was written in the contract, it still seemed kinda bad that he was thinking so hard about it.

“So we need someone that’s injured, huh...? Little Gen injured his forearm a while ago.”

When we asked whether there was a person like that in the village right now, he guided us to a young man from the giant race living in a corner of the village.

I thought 'Little Gen' was a cute nickname for a giant of about 3 meters, but it looked like he was still a little rascal in the mayor's eyes. Interspecies social relationships in another world were difficult.

"Is it just an arm injury or a broken bone?"

"I was looking for plants and rock fell. My left arm is swollen and hard to move."

The young giant spoke with the same accent as the mayor's, and had a very particular speech pattern as he said his arm was swollen. It was obvious that the wound itself was deep, so assuming it was a bone fracture was pretty reasonable. Yet the only thing he complained about was that he couldn't move it anymore? Was this the power of a giant's genetics?

"Is there a cloth around? I'll pour half of the bottle on the wound. It might sting a little, but do your best to endure it. You'll have to drink the other half of it as well."

As soon as he applied half of it to the wound, and drank the rest, the wound started to heal. The caved in flesh started to fill out, and a minute later there wasn't not even a hint of a scar.

"This is amazing... So this is how the Grade 6 ones work!"

Both the mayor and Fez were visibly impressed, but my impression after seeing the actual healing up close was that it was kinda grotesque, honestly.

I knew it was something common in fantasy settings, but actually watching it was way too raw. Maybe it was because games fooled you with sparkly effects...

"I can't believe it. You could ask for food delivery every single day with this kind of thing."

Seemingly impressed by the potion's effect, the mayor accepted the contract immediately. Now there would always be a vitality, stamina, and recovery potion in his custody.

"Say, I'm kind of short on cash right now, but I'll bring the real deal next time. Would you mind selling me some of those then?" asked Fez.

"I can't hand over that much, but I guess five of each would be okay."

I also decided to sell them to Fez to thank him for mediating the contract. My favorite item was the lamp, though...

I said goodbye to Fez in the mayor's house and headed off to take cooking lessons at Jenny's place. I took the ingredients I got from exchanging this morning with me. I was really pleased we got more to eat than we could even ask for. Jenny taught me all about them, and different ways to cook them as well.

In other news, even though I disliked the idea of salt-seasoned lizard, it turned out to be quite tasty. It tasted like bird thigh, although it had a certain elasticity to it. The tasty smell of the lizard cooking up in its own juices made me eat two of them in the end. It seemed Ann was also starved for meat, because she completely forgot her table manners and was eating with her hands alongside me.

"Well then, now this is a problem... It doesn't taste like anything, but this is how it really is?"

"Yeah, it was always like this when I ate it back at the village."

A problem arose when we tried out the ingredients we got from exchanging with the villagers in the market. Since the lizard meat turned out to be so tasty, I was expecting something along the same lines out of the crops and corn, but that didn't seem to be the case. I tried having a taste of the ingredients with a simple method of boiling the cabbage-like leafy crop and the demi corn I'd gotten from the ogre with water, but they weren't tasty at all. It honestly surprised me.

It wasn't so awful that I didn't want to eat it, but I wouldn't go out of my way to eat it either. At the very least, I didn't think I would be enjoying a meal of it anytime soon. It was difficult to express my disappointment, but...

"My day is ruined."

Would be the most accurate way to put it, I think.

The cabbage-like thing looked tender at first, but the fibery texture was so dense I was appalled at first. No matter how much I chewed on it, the thing was still hard to swallow. It also smelled a lot like grass, but nothing of that was reflected in the flavor—it was so damn insipid.

Then we moved on to the demi corn. To sum it up in three words: Hard to eat.

It got so soft it started falling apart when you boiled it, and despite looking like corn, the individual kernels were so huge it looked more like oversized rice. The texture when you popped it in your mouth was extremely dry, like munching on an unpeeled potato. It spread all over my mouth so quickly that I had to reach out for water. It also had no taste like the cabbage thing. It had a slight tinge of sweetness, but you wouldn't even notice if you weren't looking for it.

"I see. So less nutrition means less taste too, huh?"

Surely they would do great as a diet food back on Earth, but it was really troubling to think they ate something so devoid of nutrition in a pioneering village, where they busted their backs working every day in the fields.

"I've heard the vegetables they sell out in towns are way tastier! But... everyone back at the village eats this kind of stuff."

So she's used to this kind of thing. Now I knew why she loved the pumpkin so much even though it was kinda crappy. It wasn't that different from the corn and vegetables of the village. I'd rather have the pumpkin. At least I could stomach that with salt and pepper while munching on some jerky, or whatever.

"I understand why they would be cheap if you took them to any town now. It may be a bit of a luxury, but I would really like to eat tasty stuff after all."

"Yeah..."

Ann also took a bite of the boiled demi corn on her plate, but it didn't look like she was enjoying it at all.

"But this sure is a problem. There's no way I can just ask Fez to get us vegetables from town when we have a farming village right in front of us with more than enough stock to go around."

About half of our food storage was taken over by the pumpkins, but even after giving Jenny some of the ingredients we exchanged back at the village's market, we still had enough to eat for about two months.

“Ann, do you know if there’s any way to make these tasty?”

“If you want something tastier, it’s pretty pricey in towns...” Ann replied with a sad tone.

I guess she was right.

I didn’t think it was proper for a gamer like me to give up in this kind of situation. It wasn’t like I lived a luxurious life before all of this, but I was still raised in Japan. I wanted to at least eat tasty food, even that was a bit overkill in a fantasy world like this.

“Anyhow, I’ll do my best so we can eat something at least a little bit tasty.”

And so, we lined up the ingredients and all our cookware in front of the cabin, and set to work to prepare them in such a way to make it tasty.

“Yes, I’ll do my best too!”

Given her achievements so far, I couldn’t really expect her to be much use in the kitchen, but she seemed like she was eager to help. I guess she was really interested in tasty stuff after all.

“First we have to try the corn and the vegetables one at a time.”

“Uhh, so the demi corn and the white bana? Can you really make these tasty?”

“I don’t know... the odds aren’t looking too good, to be honest. But it doesn’t hurt to try, does it?”

So we had the demi corn and the white bana; I still thought it looked like a cabbage, though. It seemed like they were quite accustomed to these two back in the village. If I managed to improve them, it’d be good for everyone, because I had the feeling I was gonna be seeing a lot of them from now on.

“Well then... How do we cook these?”

I did have a lot of experience cooking in realistic survival games, but unsurprisingly enough, it was my first time trying to cook ingredients I didn’t know anything about.

All the cooking methods Jenny had taught me were rather common. At the very least, my cooking knowledge from Earth came in handy. Though it was necessary to remember the parts you couldn't eat from the lizard, it didn't differ all that much from the typical ways of preparing a normal chicken. Well, besides the obvious difference in appearance.

"Let's think about the demi corn first. I would be able to try a few things if I had flour, but I guess it won't be so easy for now."

"Flour? What's that?"

"You don't know? Isn't there bread or... Well, it's corn, so it would be more like tortillas? You don't know about any of those?"

To make flour out of the corn I would need a measuring cup, or something like that. They're quite pricey on Tundra, and with my current budget, I didn't think it'd hurt my pocket too much. My aim right now wasn't that, though. I wanted to figure out a recipe that would let me make as much as I wanted, using stuff from the village.

"Ann, is there anyone that likes the dryness of the corn?"

The feeling of it draining the water out of my mouth was way worse than the nonexistent flavor.

"Well... I don't think so. I've heard that tasty demi corn isn't so dry."

Looked like my biggest fear wouldn't be a problem. I'd be seriously concerned if anyone actually liked this stuff...

Japanese at large say foreign rice was way too dry and not tasty at all, but people from different regions would say the Japanese rice was way too sticky and not tasty at all as well. So I had to consider the difference in preference.

"Then let's turn it into something we both like. We'll start with the texture."

I opened Tundra's catalog, deep in thought, while I boiled some of the corn in hot water. I searched in the 'Food > Flour' category and buy a product called 'Fake Starch'...

Fake Starch (1 kg) == 3500 DL
Seller: Manager, Labyrinth #201

Rating: ★★★★☆
Reviewer: Manager, Labyrinth #112
- High quality starch. But I wonder what the fake is about... It dissolves well in water and it doesn't add any weird flavors either. I was impressed that I was able to make a bowl of rice just like the ones back home as much as I wanted, sticky and tasty just like I like it! I think it's good enough to be called normal starch, but I feel a bit squicky about the fake part.

I could use starch as flour just like I was aiming to, but the 'fake' part made me a little nervous.

"Well, how about that... There's a lot of Japanese seasonings in this category, huh?"

When I tried taking a look at the 'Seasonings' category, there was surprisingly a whole 'Soy Sauce' section. Lots of brands ranging from the dark and thick soy bean-based sauce that Japanese were so used to, to more mild ones. There was even fish paste in here.

I heard before that anywhere around the globe that Japanese people went, they brought soy sauce and miso with them. But the Japanese that came to a whole different world here still took the time and effort to make soy sauce and miso as well.

—If I ever have the time, I'd like to try making some kind of seasoning like soy sauce out of the ravine's moss.

This time I chose the fish paste and ordered it. The fact that they were cheaper and the supply was more stable than soy bean-based sauces was a good thing, but the fish paste also had a nice flavor, and was a pretty simple way to enhance the flavor of something. I heard about it a lot from the clerks in the 'Side Dishes' corner back at the supermarket I always used to go to. Although what I really loved from there were the croquettes, but I digress.

<u>**Fish Paste (Pottery Made - 1 L) == 5200 DL**</u>
Brand: Small Fry Concert
Seller: Manager, Labyrinth #370

Rating: ★★★★★
Reviewer: Manager, Labyrinth #421
- A magnificent harmony of the blessings of the sea and earth~ The strong smell was a little bit of a problem at first, but I forgot all about that as soon as I got a taste of it, it's excellent! It blends really well with the crops we grow over here. It goes well with stewed and boiled dishes, this is amazing~

Rating: ★★★☆☆
Reviewer: Manager, Labyrinth #28
- Extremely tasty, but it isn't so popular with children that aren't so used to it. I thought it was really delicious, but children that aren't used to fish paste or soy sauce will have a little bit of a hard time with it. They told me it has a fishy smell. Even though it's so tasty and all...

Nonetheless, compared to a liter of soy sauce that went for over 10000 DL, I was surprised something this good cost only 5000 DL for a liter, and was well stocked to boot.

It said the supplier was Labyrinth #370. Hm, yeah. I was always buying salt from this labyrinth, it seemed. If he was putting up salt and fish paste for sale, then it must mean the labyrinth was near a beach of some kind. He probably had a salt pan or something nearby, too. I was kinda jealous of how well he used his resources.

I ordered and paid the fee—it arrived as fast as ever. I wanted this delivery speed back on Earth as well.

"Thank you very much~ This is a fragile product, so be careful."

Perhaps it was because of the pot used to hold the fish paste, but the box was strangely sturdier than usual, and had a sticker that read "Handle with care!" on it. I guess it was better to keep that in mind and be careful when there was a sticky note that said "Handle with care!" and "This side up."

"Ann, can you open the package, please?"

"Sure!"

Since she was in human form, Ann didn't have her tail right now, but if she did, it would probably be wagging from right to left. That was how happy she was to help.

"First, let's peel the demi corn and smash it a little bit."

I took off the skin of the demi corn, which was about the size of a man's fist, and crumpled it inside the pot.

"Now we add the starch and mix—there. If this goes well, I think we won't have too many problems with the dryness."

But what I did just now made me think of something. There was this one realistic zombie survival game called "Last Days, Last Life" that had you choose your race first thing in the character creator. If you chose Japanese and set your affinity to 'tough,' you'd need less food to survive compared to a Caucasian character, and you could fill up your hunger meter faster than normal if you mixed starch with normal rice.

I'd wondered why they would sneak in something that affected Japanese characters exclusively like that. It was a mystery to this day. Well, the knowledge came in handy, so whatever...

"Ann, can you open that pot?"

"Yes!"

I took the pot Ann held out to me and sprinkled some of the fish paste into it. This should compensate for the lack of flavor.

"Ann, can you put the frying pan on the fire?"

I asked Ann while kneading the now cold demi corn inside of the pot. Having someone around to help me with the cooking was really nice.

"Yes~ Ready!"

Ann moved the pan over and placed it onto the fire. At first I was a little afraid, but now I could leave easy cooking to her no problem. Seeing Ann grow little by little made me really happy.

I finished kneading the now sticky demi corn and shaped it into a pretty ball, before flattening it and pressing it against the now warm frying pan. Truth was, I wanted to put even more oil and fry it to make something similar a to croquette, but I didn't have any way of making oil, and it was pretty expensive to buy. I also wanted to make a recipe that was easy to reproduce in the village, so I held off for now.

"It smells really good..."

It ended up looking somewhat like a hamburger. It roasted on top of the frying pan until it had a light brown color. Ann stared at the cooking demi corn in awe. The nice smell must have been enticing her. I flipped it over and let it set until the other side was completely cooked as well...

"Alright then, it's complete. Ann, I don't mind if you wanna try it first. It's hot, so be careful."

I put it on a plate right in front of her, and Ann stabbed it with her fork almost instantaneously.

"Hot! Hot! Got! So tasty! This is delicious! Sho hoooooot!"

It wasn't all that surprising that she put something that was still steaming right into her mouth, but it was worthwhile seeing Ann's happy smile as she ate it.

I got a mouthful for myself as well. The dryness of the demi corn was completely erased by the fake starch. It didn't taste all that doughy, and its consistency was miles better than before. The smell and taste of the fish paste made it even more appetizing. This was the biggest hit since roasted lizard, truly tasty. It was kind of like a sweet potato mochi—to compare it to something from Earth.

"Can I... have more?"

—It'd be nice if someone could teach me a technique to resist the urge to protect and pamper her when she looked at me with those upturned eyes...

In the end. over half of the demi corn dough ended up in Ann's belly. She was still growing. so it was okay, though I had to be careful not to let her get too fat.

Cooking the white bana turned out to be incredibly easy as well. I just took some, chopped it up and stuffed it inside a jar to preserve, alongside some leftover fish paste and water. Then I ordered an item called a 'fermentation mushroom' from Tundra that was said to be a carrier of something like a lactic acid bacteria, which supposedly to sped up the fermentation process. I stuffed it in together with everything else. It would have been way too hard to get rid of the fibery texture with any single method.

Zaua Pirutz (100 g of Fermentation Mushrooms) == 1800 DL
Seller: Manager, Labyrinth #16

Rating: ★★★★★
Reviewer: Manager, Labyrinth #112
- Easy way to make pickled products. All you have to do is chop whatever vegetable you wanna use and you can make something that really feels like slightly pickled vegetables. It's good that it doesn't have a strange flavor, but people that really like pickled products might find themselves a little dissatisfied? It smells, so make sure you ferment in a well ventilated place, have fun pickling it up!

Rating: ★★★★☆
Reviewer: Manager, Labyrinth #7
- A very interesting material to be sure. It seems to be a mushroom that has a symbiotic relationship with a microorganism similar to lactic acid. The mushroom itself houses them, and the mushroom's secretions accelerate fermentation greatly thanks to it. It's one of the ideal examples of fungus having symbiotic relationships with microorganisms. Also who was the fool that came up with that stupid brand name?

Three days later I took the fermented white bana out of the pot. They had a similar texture to pickled bamboo shoots. I made a bet to see if the fermentation process softened up some of the fiber, and it seemed I was right as rain this time.

"(munch) This ish tashty!"

"I get it, but quit talking with your mouth full, okay?"

I thought it was obvious that the taste had improved from the way Ann stuffed her mouth with the pickled white bana.

I took a bite as well. The taste of the fish paste, with an added mild acidity, spread across my mouth. It was so Japanese it made me want a bowl of rice. It was good news that Ann took a liking to the taste of fish paste. It was better if we had similar tastes if we planned on living together.

When I thought about it, even though there were different races living in Daemon's towns and pioneering villages, their food preferences didn't vary? It was kinda convenient, but it still worried me all the same.

"Well then, Ann, now that we know how to make things tasty, how about we both practice?"

"Yes, I'll do my best!"

Our next goal was to make even more of these until the next village market day. Since the food didn't require any delicate temperature managing or flavor adjustments, it wasn't that hard to repeat once you memorized the process. I guess anyone would be able to do it if they remembered the recipe at least a little.

We started preparing for the next market filled with satisfaction after creating something delicious.

Thankfully Ann didn't share the 'no good at cooking' attribute that visual novel heroines usually had. She made a lot of beginner mistakes at first, but she managed to still make edible dishes, even if she was limited only to these two ingredients.

◇

This would be the second market day we'd participate in. Ann and I were occupied in front of the kitchen counter all day yesterday.

The day of the market, we decided to hand gift some for all the people of the village that were worried when Ann fell down the ravine. The gifts themselves were rather simple: a piece of baked demi corn Ann made herself, and a set of pickled white bana.

It took us a whole day to make 200 servings and wrap them inside a bactericidal container they used to preserve food in the village, in sets of four. That was pretty tiring, to be honest. We might have been doing this to celebrate Ann's safe return to the village, but there was a reason for all this.

—To teach them that they can take their drab everyday meals and turn them into something tasty, with just a little bit a work and some money!

That was it.

Before, I felt admiration for the peace they achieved here, but I was upset at the same time. This was my first step towards changing the minds of the villagers, while still keeping the peace.

The fish from Labyrinth #370 was pretty tasty and budget friendly, but if I just brought them to the village as they were without thinking about the costs of transportation and selling labor, it probably wouldn't end well.

They weren't acquainted at all with fish paste in the village, and I guess they didn't use more salt to cook than what was absolutely required just to get by. They weren't used to the luxury that seasonings provided in the first place, let alone use them.

What would happen if they knew that the things they consumed everyday could drastically change with some effort?

I'd changed my views of new features not too long ago. This should work.

For example, it was like when the world was filled with monochrome TVs, and people all over the world were introduced to color TVs. It was hard to go back once you had an improvement like that.

This time, our stall was pretty modest.

Our main attraction today was the pumpkins, because the surplus of them was threatening to explode the warehouse. That, along with some economical packs of fake starch and fermenting mushrooms I'd gotten from Tundra; plus salt for seasoning, sugar, and fish paste. No hoes or sickles this time around. They didn't need that many of them in such a tiny village. If I'd brought those every single time, all the people that needed them would have been covered, and there wouldn't be any demand.

"The delicious food from before has this thing inside it? It smells pretty fishy, doesn't it?"

"Starch? It has such a curious name, but it's so white and pretty. Will it really give it that kind of texture?"

"This thingie? So the pot goes for 8000 DL? Hmm... it would be hard on my husband's wallet..."

Just like I'd planned... the crowd gathering around the stall this time was different. Now it was the wives instead of the husbands who were eagerly looking at the items.

It was a good idea to have Ann hand out the demi corn... cakes and the pickled white bana around. It'd be nice if no one noticed the fish paste price tag was a little higher than what was listed on Tundra. I figured it would be fine to sell it for as much to the village, but it'd end up being a huge deficit due to the 'shipping' charges of bringing it from the labyrinth to here if the demand increased.

The housewives ranged from humans, elves, dwarves, to even kobolds like Ann. Hell, there were even orcs, minotaurs, and giants among the crowd. The spectacle was amazing, to say the least. I could somewhat manage to discern a male dwarf from a female one, but I still had a little bit of trouble figuring out a kobold's appearance and sex. I guess I just had to get used to the increased difficulty of making out individual differences.

There was a reason as to why there were so many people gathered around here. Aside from giving out the gifts that Ann and I had prepared, I started giving out samples to all the wives that had heard the rumors and came by within the first hour of opening.

The first ones to eat the samples were the men and children at first, but they gave up due to the sheer enthusiasm of the housewives, and disappeared before long.

There were a lot of wives asking all sorts of questions in front of the stall. I guess there weren't many people with that much pocket money in a village like this, since not many people were actually buying.

Even if it didn't sell this time, people would at least know it existed. I guess I could also leave the selling to Fez next time as well. And right as that thought crossed my mind...

"I'll have one of those fish paste thingamabobs, please!"

An elf, maybe? Her ears were kinda pointy. The wife that spoke up was a pretty well-built lady, and led a vanguard of five other housewives with a money-filled bag in her hands.

"Just one, right? Thank you for your purchase."

I gave the pot to her and she embraced it as if she just picked up a rare treasure, with a big warm smile on her face. The housewives accompanying her were quick to express their delight.

Fish paste was sold in one liter pots, but it seemed they'd decided to rally their money together with their fellow housewives as they heard my explanation about how one pot was more than enough to make a hundred dishes with the demi corn.

Barely an hour had gone by before the housewife that had made a fuss and bought the fish paste came back after trying it out with her cooking...

“Try this!”

She passed them around quickly among the others. I was truly impressed by her speed, and the depth of the relationships between all of them, that allowed her to give it out without any hint of selfishness.

She gave one to me as well. The taste was sweeter and smelled more like seafood. Perhaps she used too much fish paste, but even then, it was still delicious. Soon enough, there were more housewives rallying together saying “Let’s raise money together!” I ended up selling a total of six fish paste pots that morning.

“Bring more of these for the next market, please!” implored the housewives that didn’t manage to buy a pot this time.

They kept urging me to bring more with unbelievable insistence.

“Looks like you had a good day... You doing okay, buddy?”

I arrived at Fez’s cart as he was already closing shop and picking everything up. His hair looked kind of messed up, and he seemed absolutely exhausted with a mountain of vegetable and corn bags all over him.

“Do I look okay to you? It’s the first time I’ve had so many clients in this village.”

The tired Fez breathed a heavy sigh, then crossed his legs and took out his smoking pipe.

“Sorry about that. I didn’t expect the people to come rushing to your place, but it really was more than I expected.”

Since I was selling the fish paste for money instead of exchanging for goods, the wives that didn’t have enough money rushed to Fez’s cart in hopes of cashing out their corn and vegetables with him.

“I did hear about that. You turned out to be quite the schemer, eh, hermit? You’re surprisingly sharp.”

Fez stuffed the tip of his pipe with some kind of fragrant grass and inhaled deeply. The usual smell of mint started wafting along.

“Mister Fez, what do you mean? Aoi was just teaching everyone to make tasty food.” said Ann.

"He didn't just teach them to make tasty food. It costs money if you want to eat something tasty. He's training their stomachs to make them say 'I'll work harder so I earn more money to eat more tasty stuff.' Simple enough, but the result is still rather... strong."

"Um... What's so bad about that? Everyone in the village gets to eat tastier things, and I think it's good that they have a reason to work harder. It helps your business too, doesn't it, Mister Fez?" replied Ann, tiling her head in confusing.

"I'm ticked off because he got the upper hand today. It's not cute at all when he's so good..."

"H-Huh...?"

Ann looked more and more worried by the second. Yeah, I'd like it if Ann could stay this innocent forever.

"If you hate it that much, then all you gotta do is step up your game, right?"

A long while ago, the AI in simulation games were more of a pushover; but as the advent of multiplayer came to the simulator genre, it became more difficult to survive, let alone win, against your opponent when you couldn't do much.

"As a merchant, I have no choice to. So, what's your endgame?"

Fez's expression was as grim as a dog's face could be, and his words feel like sharp blades.

"My... endgame?"

—That's actually a very good question. What even is my goal here?

"Yeah, you drew your hand and kindled a fire among the villagers. What do you intend to do with this situation? If you're planning to disturb a place like this village... I hope you're prepared."

Fez gave me a powerful smile, baring his sharp canines.

"But of course."

A situation in which the villagers got the seasoning bug and wanted money. Well, if I was a merchant, I would also be skeptical about this kind of thing. Money lending and high risk, high reward seed-selling were not to be taken lightly.

"I have no endgame. This situation itself is it. Don't you think it's better to see them all filled with energy like this?"

"...Huh?"

His expression was rather comical now.

"See, while the village was always calm and serene, I wanted it to be more lively, you know? Today's market was so bustling it looked like a real town."

"Hold it right there. You're telling me that all of this was just to make the village look more lively?"

I wondered why Fez looked so surprised. Then again, we were in an environment where it was easy to do bad things, should you desire.

"Yeah. Is that so bad?"

"What in the world are you trying to get out of this!?"

I see. That was a concern fitting for a merchant.

"Nothing at all. It's not interesting just to think about loss or gain, is it...? Oh, maybe you want to protect this simple village from my evil influence?"

"I'm the fool here for thinking about it seriously!"

Fez's almost tearful response could have made it all the way to the sky. Perhaps I had hit the bullseye just now.

"So, do you have anything else up your sleeve, hermit? I'm pretty beat myself, if it ain't obvious already."

Fez went into full sulking mode, and his eyes looked incredibly tired.

"I wanted to ask you something. The housewives looked really happy, but none of the men seemed into it at all. The whole mood was kinda heavy for some reason. Did something happen?"

"You're quite sharp when it comes to these sorts of things, aren't you? Something did happen—it was the day after the last market. About two or three days of travel west from here, a village was attacked by the human clan. They made a pretty mean mess out of the whole place."

The human clan... Did he mean the human-only country that opposed Daemon?

“West... Wasn’t there a fortress or something in that direction? Didn’t they suppress the invasion?”

“The fortress has a tight grip on the land, that’s why those rats snuck in small troops via boat. The feudal lord and the Demon Lord’s navy did their best, but the damage was done already... And, well...”

Now that he mentioned it, I heard something like that from the mayor as well.

“What happened to that village, then?”

“The villagers ran away and somehow made it all the way to the city. It seems the feudal lord’s troops made it to the village after they made their escape. Thanks to that, I’m wary wherever I am. I hired an escort and everything to accompany me for about a week as well and all.”

Corsairs that arrived from the shores... Were they authorized to do that by their country, or were they paid to do so?

“I don’t think they’ll come all the way to my house, but I’ll be more careful from now on as well. Thanks for telling me, it really helps.”

“This is just service for a good money-paying customer. Do me a favor and buy something off me, would you?”

“If I find something nice, sure.”

It was nice to have someone to make some small talk and exchange jokes with. I would say that Fez was the closest thing to a friend I’d made since I came to this world. I window-shopped a little while chatting with him, although I ended up going home without buying anything.

After the seasoning sampling and market rush, life didn’t change all that much.

“Lunch’s ready!”

“Okay~ I’m coming!”

"Oh, yes~ I was getting hungry~"

I announced lunch time with the frying pan in one hand and both of them answered in kind.

One was the ever cheerful and cute Ann, and the other was a relaxed adult woman.

"Whoa! It looks positively tasty today as well~"

I placed the meat and potato stew-like dishes on top of the wooden table that had ranked up from the pile of rocks I lined up from before. Ann was quick to display her joy with an "Awoo!" The woman besides her had impossibly long, droopy ears and locks of bright green hair that swayed as she walked. You couldn't get hair like that in Japan unless you used a lot of dye. She had a sculpture-like appearance and a relaxed air about her, which was apparent enough by the relaxed tone in her voice.

Once every few days, she would come to deliver food from the village according to my contract with the mayor. Her name was Deneb, and she was apparently around the same age as me, and she joined Ann and I at the table.

She was supposedly a blood relative of the mayor, but I would have never imagined that imposing cow-faced mayor could even be related to a pretty elf like Deneb. Interspecies relations truly were complex.

"Good morning to you, Mister Aoi~"

"Good morning, Miss Deneb. Thank you for the delivery."

As usual, she arrived around the time I was preparing breakfast with a basket full of food. We hadn't really agreed on a set time to deliver the food, but she always arrived early in the morning.

"Uncle Hopper—I mean, the mayor—sends his regards~ Someone got hurt from falling off a tree while they were working to chop it down, you see, and he got better right away thanks to your medicine~"

"The fact it's useful is more important than anything else. I'll go refill it next time I come through the village."

"Thank you very much~ Ah, that smells wonderful~"

Deneb usually got so close that it felt like we would end up touching if she moved even a little bit. It seemed she wasn't just trying to flatter me when she said something smelled nice; if her enraptured face was anything to go by, that is. It was pretty erotic when she was like that, to be honest...

"I'm preparing breakfast, after all."

"It smells heavenly~"

She moved in so close that our shoulders and hips started touching. The soft feeling made the hand I was holding the frying pan with shiver.

"Yeah, well..."

"It smells sooooooo good~"

She was literally glued to me by this point.

—No wait, this is all messed up! I can't explain why, but this is too much...!

"........."

"It smells absolutely... delicious~"

Deneb placed her head on my shoulder and traced circles with her fingertip on my side. I wanted someone to praise me for hanging on so desperately. No doubt I would lose it the moment I opened my mouth.

"W-Would... you like to have breakfast with us?"

"Whoa, are you sure~?"

She suddenly separated from me, put her hands together, and faced me with a smile stronger than a thousand suns.

In the end, I just ended up smiling back in defeat before the pretty—and strangely erotic—lady.

Although she may have been a pretty good trickster, her sex appeal status was on a different level from the usual extreme cuteness I got from Ann on a daily basis. From that day henceforth, Deneb ate with us every time she came around to bring food. I got a little curious, so I asked Ann about what she thought of Deneb...

"Pretty relaxed, but she's a really kind lady."

Were her impressions. The desire to eat tasty food sure was terrifying. It turned a laid-back lady into a weapon of sexualized destruction...

"Mister Aoi, when will you be cooking the meat I brought today~?"

"Oh... That's the one I asked you for before, right? I was thinking of skewering and roasting it today."

"Huh? A spit-roast? Whoa!"

Ann was positively ecstatic about it. She was just so lovely all the time. Deneb felt kinda closer than usual. There was so much body contact it was kind of overwhelming. But, it did have its side benefits, so it was kinda complicated.

"So you're having a spit-roast tonight~ I'm so glad I procured a lamp just in case~"

"Wha...!?"

I unintentionally gulped down air when I saw Deneb take an oil lamp from the basket.

—Don't tell me... She came prepared to have dinner here as well!?

"Say, Mister Aoi~ It's been a while since the last time I spoke with Ann. Do you mind if I do~?"

She asked while sticking as close as a wet shirt to me.

"A-Ah... Y-Yeah. Sure."

"Hmm?"

—Ann, would you please notice how I'm suffering here instead of looking confused!? I might be able to get away from her if you forced your way in between...! Please!

"Whoa, it's positively delicious~ Meat with sauce is so tasty~"

In the end, Deneb ended up staying all the way until dinner. I don't know if there was a god in this world or not, but: God, can I let loose and give in to the temptation already...?

Strongest Gamer
Let's Play in Another World

Chapter 4

The ever dwindling days left of training slowly passed by.

Since there were so few days left, I didn't really bother doing something hasty. If I did anything else and it went poorly, then at worse I'd leave something half-baked behind. I didn't know what would become of the labyrinth, but it would still be good to have a budget. I made something of a treasury for all the DL coins under the cabin, and collected all the materials that might be overabundant, along with the potions and lamps I'd made, and sold them all to Tundra.

Ann diligently polished the stone before placing it in the delivery box.

We wouldn't get any cash until the inventory cleared out with the normal stone, but the polished stone was listed separately so it didn't count alongside the typical variant. Though, it was kind of a shame that the amount of work didn't change the price that much.

Some time ago, one of the dolls we'd made out of stone and metal to play tabletop games with fell apart, and so we decided to start making palm-sized stone figurines that day instead. We went at it for about two or three days and managed to create something worthy of selling, despite being complete amateurs. Even if Ann was only a half-kobold, she was really skilled at it. I thought all those laid-back days of minimal work would slowly diminish my tempered body from carving out the stairs, but...

Aoi Kousaka
<Apprentice Labyrinth Manager>
Vitality: 128/128 **Stamina**: 882/882 **Willpower**: 152/152
Skill(s): <Dungeon Management Tool> <Appraisal>

I checked the translucent window just to make sure, but it didn't seem like my Vitality or Stamina decreased after being raised. I found it a little strange that my body didn't get even a little bit muscular despite my stats going up. Since bodybuilding every day wasn't really my hobby, I guess it was convenient enough still, all things considered. I wondered if my Willpower going up was thanks to the potion making... That would be good news to me since I was kinda self-conscious about min-maxing in Stamina.

The moss, which was a highly valuable material for potion making, fortunately spread around and grew about as fast as normal vegetation. It only took about three days to come back after I had harvested some of it. I took my time to make potions, and made sure to store them properly. I also tried to create new potions with the guide book in hand from time to time. I really enjoyed the easygoing slow life of an alchemist and a doctor.

Thanks to the various kinds of potions I'd left in the mayor's residence, Deneb kept delivering fresh vegetables and meat. The flavoring and nutritional value was somewhat of a problem still, but I was happy enough to have something different to put on the table other than the endless stream of pumpkin.

The countdown I kept scratching into nearby stone was down to ten days, assuming a month equaled 30 days in this world. Roughly every ten days, Fez would come around for the village market. Ann had left for the village earlier in the morning. She told me she wanted to eat meat and eggs last night, so I gave her money so she could buy some from Fez's shop.

It was right about time to harvest leafy vegetables—like white bana—in the village, so there would a lot of corn, vegetable, and pumpkin cooking. I figured a growing girl like Ann would want to eat meat dishes as much as she could.

I read about a way to brew moss tea in one of the herbalism books, so I gathered some and lined them up to dry on top of a cloth in the shade... It was bright by day, but at the bottom of the ravine where nothing but sunlight refracting off the stone walls would reach, I could still manage to dry them out... After I was done with that, I headed to the village market to window-shop for a bit. I didn't really have anything else to do there, but staying cooped inside the bottom of the ravine wasn't healthy for anyone.

I noticed something wasn't right as I walked towards the village. It seemed there was smoke rising off in the distance. Not white smoke, as if they had an open-air fire, but black smoke, as if something was burning.

A bad feeling had overcome me, so I quickened my pace towards the village. When I reached the small hill where I could take a look at the whole village, I manage to catch some buildings in the center of the village that were broken down, and one of them was on fire.

"What's going on down there...?"

I could clearly see from on top the hill that there was some kind of giant standing in the middle of the village square. It was way bigger than a single-story building. I calculated that it must have been about ten meters tall, and made of scrap and round cogwheels. There were three of those metal giants standing in the center of the village.

"Hermit, mate! They'll see you like that, get down! Come over here!"

I heard a familiar voice while I stared off at the warped shape of the giants. Instinctively, I crouched down and headed towards the voice. I found Fez apparently hiding inside a tiny thicket sitting on the wasteland.

"So you made it fine? Hey, do you have a potion on you?"

I noticed as he said it. Fez was holding onto his side, which seemed to be injured. His clothes were torn apart and there was blood coming out of his wound under his paw.

"Yeah, give me a sec. I brought a vitality potion with me."

These days I made it a habit to carry a pouch with a potion or two inside, similar to carrying a first aid kit for emergencies. I was happy that I'd started the habit.

"Fez, put half of this on the wound and drink the rest."

I rolled up a green dyed cloth and marked the potion so he knew how much to pour out, then handed it to Fez.

"Thanks, I made a mistake... Guh..."

It must have hurt to pour the potion on such a gash. He grimaced and downed the potion afterwards.

"As effective as ever, huh? I was prepared to bleed out to death out here, you know?"

When he took his hand off the wound, the gash that peeked out of his torn out clothes disappeared and was soon replaced by fur, as if nothing ever happened.

"What happened in the village, Fez?"

"The village got attacked by that Human clan. It was probably a party that came to plunder via a ship."

There were humans in the village, but they were part of the population of Daemon, along with all the other races. These must have humans that come from the country that existed west of the Polaris Channel.

"Raiders? Then they must be after anything remotely valuable they can find. What about the villagers?"

"The villagers are as good as merchandise to them... They might be taken in as slaves. I think the ones that don't resist will be safe. As safe as a slave could be, at least."

The word 'slavery' didn't conjure any sort of positive image in my mind. All of a sudden the deadlock inside my head unraveled with a click, like the percussion hammer of a gun clicking everything in place, and my mind was set in motion. That was how I got into the right mindset. Filled with tension, on the verge of stepping into the final stage, with all eyes on me. Right now I was a 22 year old apprentice, nothing else. Aoi Kousaka, a gamer that refused to give up until the bitter end, against all odds.

If their objective was slave trading, they wouldn't haphazardly spill blood. Since Ann was always in kobold form outside of the ravine, she should be fine, even if their plundering involved raping the women...

"Phew..."

—Now... Let's think. What can I do?

"A raid party, huh...? What are those metal giants?"

“That’s the ‘Extended Knight Armor,’ I reckon. The main force those humans use to fight—giants made out of metal and gears.”

“So there’s a person inside of that?”

A stark contrast from the knights that wore armor and rode horses.

“Yeah, humans have their limits, but they have the power of those metal things. There should be people riding them. Even if they didn’t have those, there’s still over 30 armed soldiers. I don’t think the villagers could resist, even if they wanted to.”

“Even though it’s a village of 200 Daemon people?”

“Yeah, there might be some folks that are more powerful and sturdier than the raiders among them, but they’re as good as dummies with no training. When you compare them to soldiers armed to the teeth, the difference is just too great.”

So even if they looked like demons, they weren’t all that strong. That counted double for villagers who were used to living in peace.

“But you were hurt, too. Did you fight them off?”

“No, I noticed the difference in power was too Great to fight back. I was running away to a neighboring town to ask for help, but I guess they were expecting just that. I got ambushed by a human soldier on the road north of Milt Village that connects with the closest town; that’s how I ended up like this. Well… I did get lucky to meet with you here after running away.”

I had really mixed feelings about just leaving Ann in the village controlled by that raid party, but Fez’s judgment was correct. No matter how much of a talented ex-mercenary he was, we were outmatched in number and equipment. Rather than resisting in a situation where many villagers wouldn’t be of much use, it was better to seek out help.

“I see. I’m glad you managed to escape, at least.”

“Are you sure? I left Ann and the villagers behind and ran away. I was prepared to take a blow to the muzzle in exchange for the potion…”

“And you did so because your experience as a mercenary told you to, right? I think you were right… Don’t worry, I’ll charge you the price of the potion with something else. Your wallet will feel lighter, so you better be ready."

"That hurts more than this wound did..."

Knowing the price of a Grade 6 vitality potion, it wasn't a surprise that Fez was all but pleased with my consolation.

"Haha... So you'll profit as long as I'm alive, huh? I'll avoid the road I got ambushed on and head to town to call for help. You have a house outside of the city, right? It's better if you hide."

Fez rose up a little bit. I wasn't entirely sure what to do myself. There should have been stuff besides swords and lances in Tundra's 'Military Resources' page, like the guardian golems and such.

As my mind started to wander I heard a sound, like a bullet cutting through the air. An arrow suddenly landed near the thicket we were hiding in.

"Drats... They found us!"

When I looked at the direction that Fez had turned to, I saw two ironclad men holding gigantic bows, and an armored man on horseback wielding a spear, running in our direction.

"Mate! I'll run north, you go the other way! It's better than getting taken out together!"

Fez rushed behind me and jumped out of the bush. I lunged out in the opposite direction and started to run as well. I knew that if I lost even a second to doubt in this battle event that I'd end up with a first-class ticket to a dead end...!

I ran through the wasteland. There wasn't really much vegetation to speak of, just stones and boulders sprinkled here and there. I felt a stinging pain on my upper left arm due to an arrow that grazed it the second I came out of the bush. Blood spilled out in a stream, but there was no way I could stop running. Perhaps I'd gotten unlucky while Fez got lucky. The fact was that the cavalry soldier was still in pursuit of me. My body felt awfully light all of a sudden. Maybe those three months of work weren't just for show, but the speed of a human was not the same as a horse's in the end.

The horse seemed to be having somewhat of a hard time running across the wasteland, and I was trying my best, but the distance between us gradually narrowed.

"HAH!"

I put both feet forward and slowed myself down with a slide to lower my speed. The lance of the cavalryman behind me passed right over my head and brushed against my hair. This was about the fourth or fifth time I'd avoided the lance trying to impale me. At first the soldier looked bewildered, but soon enough he started setting up the next attack immediately after I evaded. Perhaps he had gotten used to it.

He seemed like a skilled rider, but that didn't do me any favors!

"(pant) So… (pant) This is hard mode, huh…?"

Words that I'd almost forgotten about slurred from my mouth as I caught my breath and prepared for the next attack. I didn't have anything on hand to make a weapon. All I had was my business suit that barely fit from all the running and workouts I'd done, and a bunch of potions. There was no way I could weaponize them. The big gash on my arm still bled quite a bit too, and my Stamina to keep me running was depleting rapidly.

Even if I gave up and fell to my knees, I couldn't complain about it later. If this was a game, a normal player would have just thrown the controller against the nearest wall by now, but there was no reset button for reality. There were no extra lives if I met my end here.

—Is this what instinctive fear feels like?

The shiver that ran across my left arm made my right arm feel heavier for some reason. Panic had started to set in and my body tensed up, but the joy and focus that surged from deep inside caused me to return to my senses.

I wasn't getting off on my own suffering, but I was definitely one of those weirdos that got more and more excited the harder something became—I had the heart of a gamer.

"Life may be a game, but you shouldn't underestimate the power of life."

The horseman held his lance steady and dashed full speed towards me, ready to attack.

"I'll say it now and I'll say it again. I'm a hardcore gamer! Pft, look down on life? Don't make me laugh. I play for keeps no matter what it is!"

I ran towards a tall bush behind me.

"Yeah, this is a hard level, but it's not that big of a deal! There's always a gimmick or two!"

I timed the horseman racing behind me with his lance ready, and jumped horizontally. The sharp spearhead pierced the base of my neck all the way to the tip of my collar. Luckily it was a shallow wound... but it hurt like hell! There were no games out there that could reproduce the feeling of pain yet, so this was new for me.

"Ngh...!"

I rolled over onto the hard rock-filled ground and listened to the sharp neigh of the horse. He'd gotten thrown into a bush with thorns as thick as the spearhead that had pierced me just now.

"So... The archers didn't chase me, eh? I like rises in difficulty, but that would have been a little too much."

I got up off the ground. As the dirt and pebbles fell off my face, I looked around me and sighed in relief. There were no archers here. Seemed like the horseman was out of commission. I took a vitality potion out of my pouch and poured half of it on my wounds, and drank the rest.

"The glass didn't break at all even after all that running? The desert labyrinth... Umm... Labyrinth #35, was it? They're my favorite glass seller from now on."

A sharp pain ran through my body when I poured the potion over my wounds, but it faded away as the wounds themselves closed up. I tucked away the empty bottle back into the pouch. The thorny bush shook slightly—perhaps the horseman and the horse were on their last legs. I decided not to stick around long enough to find out and headed off to the labyrinth.

◇

"Phew... I'm finally back."

After reaching the cabin, I got some water with my usual pitcher and drank it up. I sat down to catch my breath on top of a wooden chair whose legs were a bit corroded by the moss from leaving it outside.

“What can I do? I can’t do much to liberate the villagers on my own. Even saving Ann alone would be difficult, especially with how I am now.”

Running away from a single horseman alone was hard enough, and there were still at least 30 more of them, according to Fez. Not to mention the three sets of ‘Extended Knight Armor’ out in the middle of the village.

Storming in upfront was out of the question. Even coming up with a plan to sneak in and help Ann at the very least would be extremely hard as well. If I did it by night, the difficulty would be lower, but I had no guarantee Ann or the other villagers would not be taken away today.

“Hmm? Did Ann forget this?”

While I looked around trying to think of a plan, I found something on top of the table outside the cabin. A simple necklace made out of a strap and a silver ring, just like the one I’d bought for Ann.

“It’s wrapped up with a parchment... Heh. Hahahah... Ann, that’s not fair.”

I spread out the parchment that the necklace was inside of, and a bitter laugh spilled out of my mouth. There were letters from this world written on it. Their shapes were somewhat different, but Daemon writing was roughly the same as Japanese.

> To Aoi,
>
> This is a present to celebrate the end of your apprenticeship. I had to cry for Mister Fez to drive down the price, and I managed to buy a ring just like the one you got me in the end! There’s so many things you don’t know about this world yet, and I’m always worried about you! This ring matches mine, so make sure you put it on, okay!?
>
> - Ann.

I held the ring tightly... Yeah, it didn’t bend even when I put a bunch of force on it. Guess this really wasn’t pure silver. Fez, you dirty dog, I paid you at least 10000 DL when I bought Ann’s! I supposed it was expected of a merchant to be as tricky as possible, though.

“Ann, visual novel heroines use a little more roundabout methods these days, you know? Don't tell me you're the heroine of an otome game... Heh..."

An amused laugh leaked out of my mouth. While laughing, I felt a certain something, accompanied by an uncontrollable heat overflowing from deep inside my heart.

—That sneaky little girl.

This sort of heartbreaking twist wasn't popular nowadays. Was she trying to become a tragic heroine despite all I'd done? I couldn't help but laugh at myself for thinking about lowering the risks as much as possible.

"Well done."

I continued to laugh after finding my answer. I may have been able to find an ideal way if I'd gathered information and thought about it calmly, but I'd already decided I would save Ann...

"Right now."

Yes, that was what I promised Sara.

Taking the funds I'd gathered from three months of work, plus my healthy body, and the high risk of me losing my life, into account... My range of options vastly expanded.

—So what if there's a power difference so large that I can't overturn it with a single sword or spear? Gamers live to turn around handicapped situations!

But yeah, I'd like to avoid taking the wrong guess here. It wasn't like gamers at large, including myself, had no fears at all. It'd be more accurate to say we were one of the world's most cowardly beings. Even now, while a hot something stirred my body and heart into action, there was still a slight shiver that ran down my spine. That was the very same reason we would do trial and error, all to prepare ourselves to take on hardship in all its forms.

And so we stood up to fear, wielding the joy to overcome adversity, which burned bright, like a raging fire that consumed everything in its path. If I could wield that with both hands, then I had nothing to fear anymore.

Shall we take this game of life seriously now? I guess it was about time.

As I got up, ready to take action, I heard a very familiar sound of a door creaking open behind me... One I hadn't heard in over three months. And when the door closed with a sonorous slam, the scenery around me changed in an instant.

The sound of cars coming and going could be heard from outside of the window where the sunlight rays poured into the room, along with usual train and busy town noises. Instead of the feeling of my slightly crooked chair, it was the feeling of a springy cheap cushioned sofa that supported my weight. The pure, clean air of the bottom of the ravine was replaced by the characteristic cheap scent of instant coffee. I was back at that monotonous office building where everything started.

"It's been a while, Kousaka-san."

"It really has... Karumi-san..."

The words were kind of stuck in my throat. The sudden change of scenery was a bit of a shock to me.

"Your performance was outstanding. To put it briefly—well done! Even among all those that received training in the past, you achieved the highest ranking in terms of production and facility expansion."

I could barely pay any attention to the congratulatory words being thrown at me. I looked over the room and spotted a business newspaper on the table. My heart was filled with relief by the date. Two months have passed from when I'd first started—we were in the end of August now.

At the sight of this nostalgic, peaceful scene, I was filled with a sense of loss rather than relief from returning from another world.

The three months I'd spent in that old shabby cabin, with the mayor, Jenny, Fez, and most importantly... Ann, felt like some kind of fever dream now. It was like a sort of phantom hallucination had hit me all at once.

"Karumi-san. I have a lot of things I want to ask you, and I'd like you to answer me, but first of all... was 'that place' real?"

My suit still had the marks from the arrow and lance that had pierced it. Those wouldn't come out no matter how much I'd scrub, and more importantly, I was still holding the silver ring—I wouldn't be able to think about anything else if I didn't ask for confirmation.

"Yes, it wasn't a staged trick or a dream. It was real beyond any shadow of a doubt. It is a bit different from our world, though."

"Thank you very much."

My heart felt at ease by the confirmation.

Those last words about the world being different ticked my interest as a gamer, but they didn't seem to have ill intent behind them, so I let it slide for now.

"First, allow me to apologize for causing you so much trouble. It was inexcusable. I was supposed to send you to a facility with enough personnel to advise and guide you, along with enough supplies to last you three months without having to do anything, but I ended up sending you off to a barren place due to defective documentation."

Yeah, so that initial situation was irregular as I'd suspected. The difficulty wasn't that bad thanks to the delivery box inside of the cabin and the Tundra , but someone that wasn't used to games would've had a harder time for sure. Perhaps they would even starve or freeze to death from being unable to figure the system out.

"One week after I sent you there, I noticed the mistake in the documents and verified it in a hurry. But by then, you were already living normally, so I was allowed to just monitor your progress."

What was I doing one week after I got there again? I must have been planting the waterdry trees, harvesting pumpkins, and eating jerky. Wasn't that when I'd finally put together a decent bed and Ann fell from the sky...? Yeah, you could say I was living normally.

"Did I get called back here because the results of my training came out?"

"Yes. If you wish to resign, these three months of training will be taken into account and you'll be remunerated for your work. In the case you want to become a full time employee, you'll be officially starting your new job as appointed manager of the Labyrinth #228 in a week's time."

"Why is there a week period in between?"

"A human invasion is currently endangering the vicinity of the labyrinth. We concluded it's impossible to secure the safety of the manager due to the lack of defensive measures in the facility. We're considering a period of one week for the danger to subside in the surrounding area so that safety can be assured."

Enough time for Fez to get to the town and drive away the humans with Daemon's armed forces? Or enough time for the human raid party to leave after ransacking the whole place?

—So I'd be safe if I spent a week back here on Earth?

"The surrounding environment has to be put in order, and the rebuilding of the pioneering village isn't that complicated. The movement of people to rebuild the village and bring in the most immediate supplies for community life will take about two weeks. The estimated time until it becomes a proper village will be about one month."

That was a rather sound judgment. Yeah, pretty rational... But I refuse.

If you've ever played enough RPG, you must have come across situations where someone close to the hero or heroine dies in the middle the story. You must have, right?

In terms of game progression, it was viewed as necessary for developers to bring the story to a climax, or stir your emotions. From a user's perspective, it was seen as the character dying due to unavoidable circumstances.

But I really hated that.

Although gamers played all kinds of genres—ranging from RPG to action and FPS—rather than simply enjoying them for the fun of it, some immersed themselves into their worlds and set out to overcome challenges and adversity to then come out on top. However, no matter how much effort was made, no matter how strong your character was, or how skilled you were, there would always be someone you couldn't save. Didn't that basically negate all the effort and emotional investment that a player poured into the game?

The heroine that couldn't be saved might have been a mere NPC, but have you ever thought about it from the heroine's perspective? How awful it must be to see your lover resign to your death tens of thousands of times, and abandon you just like that...

Thankfully, this game wasn't one where the future was decided just yet.

In this case, it wasn't bad that I wanted to take on the challenge to save my heroine. I was a gamer that laughed off difficulty levels no matter how high they were, was I not?

"If I liberate the village... there won't be any rebuilding costs. I'm not sure what the outcome will be, but would you allow me to try on my own?"

"You'd like to help even at your own risk...? This isn't a problem that only affects you, Kousaka-san. If those close to the labyrinth put themselves in harm's way, the labyrinth itself will be exposed to danger. As someone employed as a labyrinth manager, and a member of society, wouldn't you prioritize your work?"

Karumi-san shot me down with the truth, a look of indifference on her face. The tone of her voice was cold-hearted and down to business, but the curiosity-tinged gleam in her eyes was different, as if she was gauging my response carefully.

There was nothing wrong with what she'd said, rather, her sound argument couldn't have been more perfect.

There might be civil liberties and humanity problems on Earth, but it was completely different compared to the other side. Abandoning the easily replaceable villagers and securing the life of an important labyrinth manager seemed like the most natural choice.

And the only one that knew how to traverse between Earth and the other world was Karumi-san here. I couldn't force her to help me. This wasn't the time or place to get emotional and act irrationally. It would be a mistake to choose the "Raise my voice and say I want to save the villager's lives" option. At the very least... that wasn't my playstyle.

"It's because I look at it from a work perspective that I'm suggesting that we can get better results from acting now, instead of waiting to repopulate the village."

By this point, I'd grown out of spewing stuff like "I want to save someone important to me", or other impulsive and heroic one-liners. I was too old for that now.

I had to persuade Karumi-san that saving Ann and the villagers was in the company's best interests. Compared to my younger self that could do anything out of sheer strength or courage... That was too cringey. This was the way the game played out in the world of adults.

I took a flimsy-looking paper cup that looked like it would fall apart at the slightest bit of pressure, and put some instant coffee, sugar, and milk powder in it. Since the coffee enthusiasts out there would get angry if I called it coffee, we'll just say I wet my whistle with that coffee-based drink, and spoke once again.

"I went through the training, and just like you said, if I become a full-time employee, I'll officially become the manager of Labyrinth #228. In which case, there's barely anything as of now. I made a pathway, expanded the room, and created an exit connecting to the surface. But I'll need even more manpower to at least give it the appearance of a proper labyrinth. I think I'll go senile in that world before accomplishing any of that on my own with only a pickaxe."

Even though Ann and I tried our very best building the stairs to the surface every single day, it still took us a whole month. I didn't know how much time and labor would be required if the intention was to build a proper labyrinth on that plot of land.

To dig up a labyrinth with my own two hands sounded like a fun endeavor, though.

"You're right. The labyrinth was supposed to be completed by now after fifteen years of work, and a lot of funds were invested into it. The fact that not a single hole in the ground was dug despite it being reported as completed in the official documents is quite ironic, I must add."

"In these three months... It might be true that I've only come into proper contact in the last month, but I've assessed that the people I exchanged and dealt with have the mental and physical prowess to partner up with me to build the labyrinth. If there are new villagers that will come instead, they'll more than likely be preoccupied with trying to improve their situation in a new place. I'm not sure I can produce better results without knowing their qualities or disposition like I do with the current residents."

Mayor Hopper and the villagers might be a little scary at times, but they were ruggedly honest and hard workers to a fault. Never mind that I was together with Ann, they still accepted me with open arms. And the thought of learning to play and work with them seemed like fun.

"I see, what you say is reasonable indeed. However, don't you think you're getting your priorities backwards, so to speak? You would be wielding your qualities as a superior labyrinth manager and exposing yourself to a very real danger in order to achieve what you say."

Karumi-san stated the simple truth. I could see her reasoning as a gamer that pursued figures and efficiency. But people with their own wills and dreams lived in that world, like other players in a multiplayer game. And I didn't care about risking my life to save Ann, Sara, Deneb, or any of the other player's lives.

I may act and talk like an adult on the surface, but I was just a serious player in this game of life. Camping and playing like a coward wasn't cool, and it was literally better to die than live on with regrets your whole life.

"It's an honor to hear you say I'm a good labyrinth manager. As a superior labyrinth manager, if I'm to consider the future of the labyrinth's expansion, I need those people. I judge that the risk necessary to save them is one worth taking."

How about that? I gazed at Karumi-san to gauge her reaction when she grabbed a cup of the same sugary milk coffee and drank it up as if it were really delicious... She flashed me a delightful smile that I could only compare to blossoming flowers in spring.

"........."

Since she didn't show a hint of emotion ever since we'd met, the unexpected smile made me choke on my words for a moment.

"Looks like I'm defeated. That's a splendid facade. There's no room for complaints."

She said she lost, but I couldn't sense a hint of bitterness in her cheery tone.

"Our company—no, I have been looking for a labyrinth manager like you, Kousaka-san."

Was she testing me? Well, they were looking for people good at games, so I doubt they had been looking for the kind of adult bureaucratic person that could only deliver rigid judgment.

"Like me? What does that mean?"

"A person with the desire and will to make the desires of their heart a reality—without getting caught up in the concepts of good and evil," she said in a cutesy manner, tilting her head to one side. "See, since we're subordinates of the Great Dark Lord, we aren't exactly knights in shining armor material, right? And since we're more or less a company, we need people that can keep up appearances and act like adults."

I calmed down and tried to think back on everything. I was a human that was...

—Living in a country that's ruled by a Dark Lord... For the sake of the people of a country called Daemon... Trying to fight off humans.

There was the minor detail about Daemon also having humans among its population too, but we were certainly doing something akin to an evil organization's work.

"Although, I personally think you're more than what our company deserves as far as labyrinth managers go. But you're still the talented person I've been looking for so long. I won't hand you over to any other department."

There was an almost carnivorous grin on Karumi-san's face. I thought she was a more calm and collected person, but it seemed she was pretty expressive on the inside.

"I will accept the responsibility for your plan, but first I'd like to confirm one thing. It's kind of a regulation, you see... Well then, even if you were to retire here, your remuneration for the last three months of training comes to the amount of 500,000 yen, and the additional fee for your outstanding performance adds 180 million yen that will be paid to you."

That additional fee was wildly different, but it was a huge number, so... I couldn't complain.

Karumi-san raised her index finger and continued.

"However, this additional fee includes the current savings of the labyrinth itself, so it will decrease if the situation of the labyrinth worsens... In the worst case scenario, it could very well disappear entirely. Will you still take the risk regardless?"

It didn't seem like there was ill intent in her voice still. The obscene amount of money certainly was more than a mid-career person like me could ever dream of earning after just three months, but the silver ring I held right now was worth far more than that.

“This might be a little out of place, but... I choose ‘yes.’”

Karumi-san smiled as she heard my answer and nodded radiantly. You’d think she just fell in love.

“Kousaka-san, please don’t die. Our company... No, I expect great things of you,” Karumi-san said with a mischievous wink. “That’s why, I’ll give you a little advice for breaking the rules. Keep what I’m about to tell you a secret to everybody, okay?”

Karumi-san was... the very picture of a beautiful lady.

“I was allowed to look into you after sending you off to training, and there so happens to be a very unusual labyrinth manager in that world that manufactures golems and exhibits them in Tundra’s . Labyrinth #13, if I remember correctly. There’s a certain giant-sized manned golem currently listed which just happens to have a very high affinity with you, Kousaka-san. It’s designed to defend, but it also has offensive capabilities, so it may be useful for your current situation.”

Karumi-san snapped her fingers, and... I heard the creaky sound of a door opening right behind me and... Slam! At the same time I heard the door closing, I was left back in front of the little cabin sitting in the middle of the ravine I’d missed so much.

“Well, then... I guess I’ll go with that.”

I drank the remaining coffee out of the cup I was holding in my hand, and opened several UI windows around me, including Tundra’s catalog.

—Let’s try taking a look at the giant golem Karumi-san told me about first.

“Hmm... These two here look promising.”

After browsing the Tundra for about 30 minutes, I singled out the two most promising items.

Assault Golem Armor - Comet
(Height: 7 m / Weight: 6.5 t) == 13800000 DL
[Recharges automatically! Get up to six hours of battery life on a single charge!]
Seller: Manager, Labyrinth #13

Rating: ★☆☆☆☆
Reviewer: Manager, Labyrinth #201
- Amazing friccing speed! Pretty funky mecha bro! It goes to friccing fast I ended up pulling the emergency brake and coughing out blood! It'll pop like a popcorn if you so much as brush a wall you can't break, it's pretty fricced up!

Rating: ★★☆☆☆
Reviewer: Manager, Labyrinth #102
- I value it good as a pretty ornament. It's currently just sitting outside to scare a few loitering demons, but it's rather pretty to look at. I'll ignore reviewing it in regards to its functionality in this review.

Rating: ★☆☆☆☆
Reviewer: Manager, Labyrinth #601
- Bad stability. I heard it was 3 times faster than the other model this same person has up for sale, so I tried giving it a whirl, but 3 times faster also means 3 times harder to use, but that's not all, the armor is also 3 times more thin. It does have an option to fly using a flying unit, but controlling it is so hard I just gave up. I'm afraid of even trying to use the default jump unit.

I tried it out just because an acquaintance asked me to, turns out the attack power is quite high, but the equipment is specialized for close encounters. Why wouldn't it have shooting weapons? Besides, did the price lower compared to when I bought it? This is a selling off price, isn't it? This isn't even a golem, it's a goddamn robo... oh, looks like I got a visit!

Automatic Cursed Sword
(Height: 1.2 m / Total Length: 1.5 m) == 6800000 DL
Brand: Jr. Devil King Edge
Seller: Preceding Manager, Labyrinth #552

Rating: ★☆☆☆☆
Reviewer: Manager, Labyrinth #35
- Tough to use for older folks. A sword that bestows various faculties to the body of the wielder, it also bestows fencing abilities, tactic skills. This cursed sword gives you all those. You can use it without problem even if you don't know anything about wielding a sword, but there's a catch... if you're too rough using it you might die because of the muscular pain the next day...

Rating: ★★☆☆☆
Reviewer: Manager, Labyrinth #172
- It has a lot of value as work of art. The single edged sword image makes for a beautiful single piece, but the fencing abilities it gives are not very beautiful. It doesn't grant any kind of way to protect the body, so I wouldn't recommend it as a weapon for managers.

The giant golem from Labyrinth #13 that Karumi-san told me about was expensive enough to drain most of my savings, but I'd decided to go through with it still. It seemed it was hard to maneuver, but it had good performance, which was nice.

It seemed like the 'Comet' was more focused on looking intimidating than being aerodynamic. It pretty much looked like a futuristic set of armor. No one from Earth would see this and call it a golem.

The golem looked to be more difficult to steer than a robot, but when I thought back to robot games that were played in large cabinets, it was a riot for gamers even if they were a bit unwieldy. It was certainly a product that hit all my preferences, but I wondered what she meant by 'good affinity'.

Next thing was the supposedly cursed sword; it seemed like I could increase my physical faculties just by holding it. I'd fought using blades in games countless times, but this was a suitable item for someone that didn't have any kind of real swordsmanship or fencing experience.

The two things had a fair bit in common. They had high offensive power, high mobility, put burden on the user's body, had no defensive power, were hard to use—and both of them absolutely wrecked a labyrinth's budget.

I wanted as much mobility and offensive power as I could possibly get. It'd be indispensable if I were to face at least 30 or so armed soldiers alone, not to mention the metal giants... I needed offensive power to destroy those Extended Knight Armors.

I could do much about the budget problem. If a labyrinth manager was going to battle directly, you'd think that they'd place defense power and survivability at the highest of priorities, but neither of the two gave any of that, so I had nothing to worry about in that front.

If I wanted more defense while maintaining performance, the price spiked up more than five times. It wasn't like it wasn't worth it... I just didn't have the money.

—The problem is the budget. I'd like to buy both the sword and the Comet, but the total amount goes up to 25 million DL... I'd probably have to attach a firearm and flight unit as well... If I don't have the flying unit, I won't be able to take it out of this ravine.

The stairs were about two meters wide and were barely big enough for people to go up and down.

The sword may have been usable normally, but the fact its toll on the body was so high made me kinda unsure I wanted to rely on it completely. I had stamina potions, but I doubted I'd be able to recover if I ran out of steam, or one of my muscles snapped in the middle of a battle.

Since the money I had in the labyrinth right now was only about 15 million DL, I started looking for things I could cash out in the delivery box to get to the desired amount. But after living here for some months, I knew there was nothing valuable enough outside that'd give me the money right now... Or so I thought, until my eyes laid on a certain amber room decoration inside of the cabin.

The pretty waterdry amber I'd been picking up as of late. I didn't give them much mind because it was rare to even see money back in Milt Village, but amber was a precious stone. Could it be worth something?

"I can always collect more of them again... I need as much money as I can get, even if it's just a little more..."

The waterdry amber pieces within the glass container rattled around as I placed it inside the delivery box and closed the lid. It was a bit frustrating to do, but as long as I still breathed,

I could get more.

I heard the usual sound of coins falling, and when I opened the lid I saw something I'd never seen before—a rainbow-colored silver coin with an incredible luster. The engraving said "10000000 DarkLord Coin"...?

There were two rainbow-colored coins that were about the size of a 500 yen coin, and one golden 5 million DL coin, and a few coins of other denominations that seemed to be leftover change. In the end everything was worth about 28 million DL. I wasn't expecting to get such a huge amount of money.

—That was quite the decoration for a cheap cabin like this, huh? Was it that good of a decoration to stuff all of them in that glass container?

That was quite an unexpected surplus of money, but I could prepare both the Comet and the sword with it. I thought that the Comet alone might be good enough for the job, but when something this important was on the line, I didn't want to hold anything back.

I ordered the Comet, the flight and firearms units, which were sold separately, and the cursed sword from Tundra's . I put the coins I'd got before along with all the savings so far inside the piggy bank.

Since my savings were arranged in 10000 DL coins, it was a bit of a problem to move them all at once. Perhaps it was because the amount to pay was incredibly high this time around, but the back of the piggy's back spread out like a funnel to facilitate the insertion of money, making the payment far easier.

"Thank you very much, we appreciate your continued support! Bring it in, boys! Heave-ho! Heave-ho!"

This time it wasn't the usual carefree part-timer looking dude that usually appeared. Instead, it was a relatively older-looking, polite gentleman. Maybe the full-time employees came to say 'hi' when the purchases were big enough?

I heard a certain rumbling noise, and then... the door that appeared out of nowhere expanded greatly to give way to a giant cardboard box. The immense weight of the item made the soft earth sink slightly. I wondered if Tundra had a bit of an obsession about delivering things using cardboard boxes... The cardboard box the Comet seemed to be inside of didn't lose its size to the cabin we'd been living in this whole time.

"It'll be a hassle to unbox this one..."

Then out came a long and thin box with a sticker that said "Dangerous Goods". It was probably the cursed sword. The expanded door of sorts finally closed down afterwards.

"Good day! Thank you for choosing us!"

—Oh, the usual guy came too after all? That's kind of a relief.

I took apart the cardboard box and found the Comet already came assembled with the extra parts I'd ordered. I guess it was supposed to be operational as soon as you took it out of the packaging.

—I'm glad I don't have to assemble it... I wonder if it arrives finished because it's a golem.

I took the demon sword in one hand, an instruction sheet the size of an A3 paper in the other, and opened the Comet's chest cavity. I put the cursed sword inside the storage space and got inside. The chest armor opened and closed with a lever mechanism. Instead of going inside a robot, it was more like one giant set of armor you wore. The maker knew what he was doing with this, huh? Someone, somewhere probably got ripped off.

"The model is apparently a 'Fantasy Golem', how much did he remodel this?"

The wine red and black coated Comet was curvy and streamline in shape, but it also had a sci-fi feel to it as well. I'd like to stare at it a little more if I had the time.

I boarded the Comet and my body and limbs were fixed in place. At the end of my hand were a set of joysticks with buttons for each of my fingertips; there was also a foot pedal that got triggered by my ankle. It seemed the harnesses that held my body in place also had a motion sensor.

—This layout and piloting setup gives me so much nostalgia that it... Yeah, I see how this is a good match for me.

The switches on the tip of the joysticks had a certain hardness that made me think they were spring powered. I tried to confirm it with the tip of my fingertips, and... it was roughly the same as I remembered from normal joysticks.

You didn't see that many of them these days, but there used to be a really popular robot battle game that used a huge cabinet called "Master Arms" that had this kind of layout. It was quite the wallet slayer as it would cost 800 yen per play. It added up fast due to the fact that beginners needed to repeat the tutorial stage about 20 times before they could get a hang of the movement. The amount of freedom it gave, and the level of difficulty it had, made it quite popular.

—If this thing is anything like Master Arms, I think I'll get used to it pretty quick.

"Hah, I might even meet this golem's creator in a battlefield, somewhere."

I went through the startup procedure by repeatedly pressing the foot pedal and the finger buttons.

I was a sucker for sim games with cockpits. I was so obsessed that I got a part-time job solely to dump money into them. I played so much that I ended up being in the Top 20 ranking for the Kanto region.

Between the shape and weight of the joystick, the button layout felt a little out of place. It was basically the same kind of thing though, so I should be good to go. Master Arms used retinal projection to display stuff, but I didn't know how images were being projected in the Comet. A mix of English and Japanese letters flowed along on the internal gray armor plate, like it was beginning some sort of start up sequence... Then a screen popped up that said "Sugawara Heavy Industries".

—Is this really a golem? It even has a start-up logo! The guy that made this really is something else.

"Based on... 'Master Arms Ver.2.4'? That's not even the latest version. They updated it like half a year ago."

It appeared that a robot maniac had managed to become a labyrinth manager and was going pretty hard at it. But thanks to him, I could avoid charging in headfirst with only a sword, so I was grateful nonetheless.

Most of the launch settings of the Comet were automatically set. There was a pair of wings with jet engines attached to them that was probably the flight unit, which was sold separately. Also attached was the firearms unit, which consisted of a huge rifle with a revolver magazine, that clashed with this whole fantasy world we were in.

VER.2.4
Sugawara
Heavy Industries
©

Impatience started stirring within my heart as night began to creep in. If I got too hasty I probably would crash headfirst into the rocks and die. That wouldn't be all that great of a climax, would it? I fought off the urge to just get going as I waited for the progress bar to complete.

"No abnormalities in the various check sequences, and the optional parts are functioning properly. The assortment of gauges based on Master Arms is nice to see."

The monitor displayed the word "READY" and locked the joints, allowing for the Comet to slowly start moving.

When I first came to this world, it was a survival game where I searched for food and water. And ever since Ann came into my life, I enjoyed interacting with her, living together and making things, like in a crafting adventure game. When the horsemen chased after me, it was like an action game where one wrong move could end my life.

But now... it was a PvP game, where I bet my life against another player's.

Hostile players came and disrupted what was once a peaceful game. Everything changed into a completely different mode: one where you had to fight with the intent of killing another.

I still remembered the first time I played a game with other people. Yes, the first game in which I fought other players went offline a long time ago, but it was still a famous old MMORPG. Back then, I wasn't prepared at all. I got lured out of the safe zone and was ganked immediately; I just laid there, shocked at being attacked. I still remembered the tension and excitement of being assaulted by people with ill intent, and how wet my mouse got from my sweaty palms.

Compared to then, my palms weren't sweaty now; and I was holding onto the Comet's joystick instead of a mouse. And besides my worry for Ann, Sara, and the other villagers, I was quite calm.

"Heh... I can't help but smile, huh?"

My mouth warped into a smile, unable to hide the hunger to fight.

—Violent games are a terrible influence for children...

That overused phrase came to mind, but I laughed it off.

I couldn't tell you if all the games I'd played in my life were a good or bad influence. But what I could say is that thanks to them, I was now able to face danger in order to save someone precious to me.

"Well, then... Let's enjoy life."

I stepped on the feet pedals lightly and the flight unit started up. A blush-white light poured out of the wings as the Comet rose into the air with a metallic sound.

"This is more like riding a wild horse than I thought!"

I raced over a nearby wall at high speed with a gentle nudge of the joystick.

I tried to muster all the skills I had gained from playing Master Arms a long time ago. Lately there were less and less arcades that could take on the high maintenance cost, or the high cost of the cabinets themselves, so I was kind of rusty after not playing for a while. It didn't take long for my body adjust to it again, though.

No wonder the Tundra review page was filled with criticism. It was really hard to get a handle on how to maneuver it, as well as dealing with the response time. It was like raising your PC's mouse sensitivity two or three times. It wasn't outright unusable, but it definitely wasn't easy either.

I stopped the flight unit once I was out of the ravine. The power of gravity enacted and drove the decelerating Comet right into the ground with a heavy thud.

"(cough) Ugh! (cough)"

I may have been a gamer capable of piloting it, but my body wasn't used to the forces a real pilot went through. The impact I took from the landing sent me right into a coughing fit. Thank goodness I didn't have the chance to eat lunch at the village's market. I would've made a mess out of this thing if my stomach was full.

I really had the urge to just waste time to figure out how it moved and such. I took a deep breath to calm myself and maneuvered the left joystick... which caused the Comet to kick off the ground into the air. The parts attached to the back and leg portions of the machine made a high-pitched metallic sound as it created the propulsion to move, and I headed towards the village, halfway leaping through the air. A distance that would have taken me an hour by foot took less than ten minutes using the Comet.

“This robo— No, this golem armor really is strange in more ways than one, huh?”

When I got to the hill where I could see the whole village from, I stopped. In the middle of the village were those Extended Knight Armors from before.

Thankfully the raiders hadn’t left yet, if those Extended Knight Armors were any indication. I still couldn’t understand how those lumps of scrap metal managed to even move. I observed them for a bit, waiting for steam to spew out of them like they were some sort of steampunk machine. My eyes eventually wandered to a spot near the neck of one of them. A metal tube roughly two meters in length protruded out of it. Judging from the position and size, I reckoned that was the cockpit. It made sense if you considered the safety of the pilot, I guess.

As far as I could tell, there were three sets of armor in the village square, with soldiers and bowmen in the village’s entrance. Yeah. So flying all the way here was the Stage One, doing a surprise attack on the village’s entrance would be Stage Two, and eliminating the Extended Knight Armors in the village square would be the Final Stage.

There was no guarantee I had a happy ending waiting for me once I cleared all three stages, but I didn’t really have the time to dwell on it.

“Alright... Let’s get it on.”

I grabbed the Comet’s cylinder rifle firearm (sold separately) that cost 12 million DL from its holding spot at the waist. It looked like a futuristic, modern rifle but it seemed to shoot magic, as opposed to using some complicated firing mechanism. Not that it mattered how it worked. A gamer plays with whatever he’s given. The lore maniacs can deal with all the principles, diagrams, and mechanical parts in their own time.

“So to prime it I have to do... this? And if I switch to ‘Fire Mode’ a reticle appears and... Huh?”

When I positioned the Comet’s body sideways and held the rifle with one hand, a blue-colored magic square appeared at the tip of the rifle’s barrel and a new pop up appeared in one corner of my field of view.

[3 Rounds Remaining. Optional Firearm Unit: Activated. Aim Adjustment Engaged. Corrections Will Complete After Two Rounds Are Fired.]

—Well, I guess I can't do much about the adjustment when it's the first time its starts up.

I breathed a heavy sigh. In short: the shots would go where I wanted them to after I'd fired twice.

Or so it said...

But I only had three rounds. Should I expect to only hit once...? Even though I paid so much money? I wondered if it was because the creator decided to make a damn rifle instead of something more like a fantasy game like a bow, or something. While I had more objections, I figured that if I could take out at least one of those Knight Armors with a shot, it would be worth the trouble, at least.

The Daemon villagers were all gathered and handcuffed in the middle of the village's square. They were all tied together by the same rope in a straight line, waiting to get transported. The raiders were using a sturdy rope that had metallic threads braided into it, and they conducted themselves in a very organized manner, while the villagers looked miserable.

The humans that attacked the village were a raid party that came from one of the three human countries to the west of Daemon, but they weren't mere outlaws—they came looking for a commodity called... "Daemon Slaves".

And they'd gotten permission from the country to stock up on them. They were mercenaries employed by a major slave dealer. Even among human nations, the treatment of Daemon people varied between them, but in this case the only thing they saw were 'beasts able for labor and capable of speech.'

And that was the treatment all Daemon citizens received.

That being said, the raiders didn't run amok on the village, wrecking it like barbarians. They weren't so bored as to do frivolous things that could lower their commercial value, even if they did consider Daemons as beasts.

"Next one, step forward."

A bearded mercenary wearing a grim expression, with his head crammed into a metal helmet, called for the next villager to be added to the chain of others. A well-dressed female kobold stepped forward...

"Hmm...? Pretty good-looking and well-dressed... Are you a Daemon from another village?"

The middle-aged soldier looked puzzled when he laid eyes upon the kobold. She was in stark contrast compared to the villagers that wore nothing but ragged, patched up old garments. The girl didn't answer as she was startled and quivered in fear.

"We were celebrating her becoming an adult today. Why did this have to happen...?"

Another female kobold close by had spoken up. In truth, that celebration had ended about a year ago, but even then, what they wore in celebration paled in comparison to the well-dressed kobold.

"I see... You got unlucky," the middle-aged mercenary grumbled. "This is why I hate hunting Daemons. Talking them down like this sickens me."

The man moved to his work, but a rumble that shook everyone to the core interrupted him.

"What is it!? What happened!?"

Among angry screams and shrieks, what was reflected in the eyes of the middle-aged mercenary was a red light coming from the west. The light pierced through one of the Extended Armors sitting in the middle of the village square. The upper half of the reliable and intimidating giant hell apart and crashed into the ground with an earth-shattering roar.

A chill ran down my spine when the shot landed in the square... I completely understood the maker's intention now—he wanted to make a rifle that shot beams.

When I pulled the trigger a multi-layered magic square formed around the muzzle, and a blue light erupted out of it. The first shot landed on the roof of the house that was burning close to the village square, blowing it away completely. I changed my aim completely in a hurry and the second shot went into ground near the horsemen that were on standby near the southern exit of the village. I calmed down and took my time to aim the third shot after blowing up the horsemen, and landed it right in the center of the Extended Armor that was the farthest away from the villagers in the square.

I took a look at the display floating in a corner of my field of vision and sighed when I saw that hard mode was turned on.

[Aim Correction Complete. 0 Rounds Remaining. Recharge Time: 83 Hours, 59 Minutes 21 Seconds.]

“It would’ve been great to know beforehand that I could fire three shots every 84 hours!”

I let go of the now steaming rifle and let it fall onto the ground. I heard an astounding amount of screams and shouts while I cautiously headed towards the village. The iron-clad mercenaries seemed to be moving around the village in a panic. With the Comet I dashed past the mercenaries with a steady pace, desperately trying to hold back the desire to run in guns blazing. The thing that worried me the most right now was the potential of the mercenaries taking hostages. Even if we could overwhelm them with numbers, my chances of winning would be null if they decided to use them as shields. On the other hand, if I ignored all collateral damage and concentrated only on saving Ann, she would probably be sad about it. I didn’t really want to sacrifice the good people of the village either.

—How should I go about this? If I seem like I’m on the villager’s side, they’ll take them as hostages.

Luckily, the Comet was an enclosed golem armor that didn’t expose the pilot in any way, so they couldn’t see that there was a human inside. It looked kinda peculiar, but you could probably guess it was a golem by how hard the outer shell was.

—Yes... I should just swoop down like a monster, a random natural disaster. No idiot would try to take hostages in front of a blood-starved demon.

For someone from that human country, this must be a land where horrible demons lurk around. They probably wouldn’t be very surprised if a mad creature attacked them with a golem.

"Well then, time for Stage Two!"

As I approached the village entrance I was met by nine soldiers. Four were pointing spears in my direction, while the other five drew their bows. They looked scared still. Meanwhile the Comet's armor was basically like "Defensive power? Is it yummy?" I was curious as to whether or not the Comet could even deflect arrows, but then again it was still a golem that stood seven meters tall. It was natural to be scared when faced with an unknown quantity like it.

—I'll charge in once they fire off their bows...

I walked the Comet at a constant pace. Soon I felt the hand holding the joystick starting to sweat, waiting for the battle to begin. The archers released their arrows basically at the same time the Comet leapt forward.

The flying arrows arced right over my head. My body got pressed heavily by the force of the momentum as I leapt into the row of spearmen at full speed. I backed away a bit, kicked out the spearmen, and crushed two of the archers with both hands, then stopped.

"Now... Three more!"

I grabbed the remaining archers and flung them away towards the village square, effortlessly. I tried behaving like a monster to strike fear in them, but the burden on my human body inside the golem was taxing. The finely-detailed control of the golem was done through a motion sensor, so I had to...

"Bear it, come on!"

Since I was inside the Comet, I had to look the part. When I bent my body to match the golem's unreasonable posture, I could hear my joints creak.

Not only were they getting attacked out of the blue by a mysterious being, they were given a front row seat to see how a monster mowed down their forces like tons. About half the soldiers surrounding the villagers were thrown into a state of panic. And so, all the unlucky soldiers standing in my way were thrown about like playthings. I could see archers sneaking into houses facing the square in an attempt to hide, while others scrambled out the southern exit after dropping their weapons.

"Is that a Commander I see? There's one of them screaming at the ones running away."

I apologized to whoever owned the old-fashioned cart that was lying around as I grabbed it and threw it at the screaming soldier. The commander-like man finally shut up as the cart collided into him.

"Did the cart fall right where I wanted it to because I'm so good at handling the golem? I kinda doubt that's the case. (cough)"

—So now we're at the Final Stage. I'd sure like a save point right around now...!

While I was busy catching my breath from the coughing fit, one of the Extended Armors started moving.

"It's really freaky-looking seeing it up close, huh? It's roughly humanoid... but it's a robot. It'd be kinda dumb to call it 'humanoid machine', though."

At first glance, the Extended Knight Armor looked like a giant steel skeleton that used gears as its flesh and blood.

The gears interlocked and ground, causing the limbs to follow suit. There were parts protected by iron armor plates, but there were also some rusted spots and pieces of scrap mixed together in other places.

—Amazing...! I get to fight that freaky thing!?

I heard something resembling a voice echo through one of the metal pipes sticking out of it.

"I see. If you're gonna go against me, I have to get serious... Come on!"

I lowered my stance and waited for the next moment to strike. The Extended Knight Armor pulled out a lance as big as itself and lunged forward, trying to impale me. I leapt to the side with the Comet and dodged. I passed right besides the Knight Armor at high speed and deployed the Comet's fixed armament—a huge metallic blade built into the golem's wrist. I crammed the blade into the moving gears, which caused a sharp metallic grinding to ring out, and the Extended Armor imploded on itself.

"(cough) Tch...! (cough)"

The reverberations of the implosion impacted the Comet like a wave crashing into my body, causing me to cough. There was now a certain red liquid mixed up among my coughs, so I took my hand off the joystick, grabbed a vitality potion from my pouch, and downed it in one gulp.

"(cough) The... (cough) float like a butterfly, sting like a bee (cough) phrase is cool, but if your opponent is sturdy and heavy, then the constant impacts are enough to make you want to die! (cough) I wouldn't mind fighting at half speed if it meant I had some armor to take a punch of me, at least then it wouldn't wreak my body!"

I left the dilapidated Knight Armor as it collapsed onto the ground, scattering gears all over, and headed towards the village square once again. As far as human soldiers were concerned, the Comet was simply a monster that appeared out of nowhere. I couldn't afford to show them the toll my body was taking. I'd been battling nothing but... humans this whole time, taking them down with my own hands, but I was still surprisingly calm about it.

I used to read novels and comics back on Earth. One such story you'd often see was of a boy who was good at games, then killing people in cold blood like it was nothing. They were made to emphasize the difference between fictional games and reality, and I'd always wondered why they did that. While you typically were crushed by the feeling of guilt in killing someone in real life, the same didn't apply when you did so in a game.

Be it games or whatever, was I not prepared to murder people with my own two hands? When I realized that I had become the monster those stories spoke of, it hit me so hard that I didn't want to continue on anymore. To say I was doing it to save someone—to save Ann—would be selfish and just shift the blame. I couldn't justify my actions with that. In order to satiate my selfishness I was willing to cover my hands in blood, no matter if it was in games or reality.

The mere thought of continuing my life forward with regret of not saving what was precious to me, because I'd gotten distracted, sent a chill down my spine.

◇

"Maybe now..."

Ann stealthily untied the rope holding her hands down. The main reason the village adults didn't resist in any way was because of the human soldiers pointing spears at the village's children in order to subjugate them. But most of them had escaped, and the last two soldiers left were just staring in disbelief at the Extended Knight Armor's demise in front of them—their heads anywhere but there.

"I'm stronger in my human form... I'm sorry for breaking our promise, Auntie," Ann murmured as she reverted from her kobold form.

She grabbed the two soldier by their ankles, raised them into the air, and tossed them aside with all her might. Originally, Ann's status as half-human and half-kobold made her naturally weak, but in the two months she'd spent with Aoi, her body became sturdier, and her strength increased dramatically for some unknown reason.

"If Aoi was here he'd probably say something like... 'Since you've been working at the labyrinth this while time, maybe you leveled up or your status increased.'"

The soldiers Ann had thrown slammed right onto some mud walls. When the cloud of dust cleared, it was obvious they wouldn't be going anywhere anytime soon.

"Mister Gald! Everything's fine over here!"

"Got it!"

As soon as the tied up ogre saw the children were held hostage, his rock hard muscles tensed up as he swung his tied up arms, knocking out a nearby soldier.

"Hey, you guys! Ann's doing all the work! We have to step it up too!"

All the villagers started rebelling at once, and held down all the remaining soldiers. The villagers would normally be helpless against trained soldiers, but Ann was at the vanguard for them. Being protected by the children they were supposed to be protecting seemed to encourage the adults greatly. There were also soldiers that tried to stop Ann since she looked like nothing more than a little girl; unnatural power or not, Ann would have been easy prey for a rear attack due to her lack of battle experience.

"Gwah!"

A soldier that tried to attack Ann ended up with an extremely deep dent in his helmet, and crumpled down to the ground.

"Ann~ Your back's exposed, be careful~"

"Miss Deneb! Thank you!"

Deneb struck the soldier's head with a giant stone pot she was wielding in one hand. It was normally just a cooking utensil, but she seemed strangely used to this kind of thing... Or maybe her usual calm demeanor was all a ruse.

"Protect the families and the fields!"

The most important thing for the farmers living in the frontier were their families and fields, and Gald's roar rallied them to that end. The usually peaceful giants that always opted to shy away from conflict broke away their restraints and joined the fray.

The supposedly powerless Daemons fought back. Once the Extended Knight Armor that was supposed to suppress got taken down, it didn't take too long for the remaining soldiers to get routed. A moment of happiness reflected on the villagers' faces, but was dashed away almost as fast as it came.

"Filthy Daemons! Don't resist if you care about this piece of filth's life!"

A soldier wearing gaudy armor restrained Sara and stuck the edge of his sword to her neck.

"Sara...!"

Ann's scream sent a chill down the spines of the surrounding villagers.

"You ogres there, stop! All you Daemons need to shut up, or do you wanna see this little girl die!?"

As soon as I entered the village square, I saw a soldier clad in a pompously decorated set of armor holding Sara with one arm, with a sword pointed at her throat in the other.

"He took a hostage, huh? So he thinks it might be useful despite there being a raging monster running amok? Or was he just regurgitating the only thing he knew how to do?"

My intuition told me it was the latter. He may have been born that way, but the soldier seemed to exude an aura of cruelty—he reeked of it, even.

I continued to edge closer, bit by bit, to the soldier that took Sara hostage.

"Stop! Do you not understand me!? Enough!"

His fear couldn't have been made more evident. I crept ever closer to him without a hint of desisting.

—I know this must be scary, Sara, but hang in there. Things might get worse if I stopped now.

"Cease! No! Stop! Damn it all!"

As soon as I was close enough to reach him, he tossed Sara out of the way and tried to make an escape. I was astonished he had kept up the rotten act thus far. I almost wanted to praise him. But really, it all the more reason to squash him like the rodent he was.

"S-Stop! Don't come closer! STOOOOOOOP!"

I took one step forward with the wrist blade extended and held it above the soldier... And swung downward until the blade was stopped by the ground.

Sara, who had fallen on the ground, looked up at me in horror... I would have called out to her, but... Yeah.

—I have to change to the motion tracking mode to control my right hand better... I think I just have to do this here and... I think I got it.

I made the Comet kneel down and extended its hand towards Sara. When she saw me swiftly stick out the golem's ring finger her dumbfounded expression shifted to one of understanding, and eventually one of joy. Thank goodness she understood me. She opened her mouth and muttered something, but I was unable to hear due to the armor. I thought must have been something along the lines of "It took you long enough!"

I circled around the square one last time in search of any stray soldiers. There didn't seem to be any. Off in the distance was a trail of lances and shields heading south. The raiders must have ran away towards the sea that I'd heard so much about.

"Wasn't there one of those Knight Armors still around? Where'd it go? I can't see it an—GAH!"

As soon as I let my guard down, the remaining Knight Armor broke through the nearby buildings facing the square and threw itself at me. I was blown away to the other side of the square, into the wood storage house. The building had stopped my fall.

"Ugh! (cough) So... (cough) He stayed in hiding waiting for his own chance to strike, huh? I thought I cleared the Final Stage, but looks like there's a hidden bonus round."

The surprise impact sent me into another coughing fit. A display flickered open informing me that various parts of the Comet's internals were heavily damaged.

—I didn't think it had much defense considering that one Tundra review, but I expected it to at least be able to take more than one hit before becoming useless!

I closed the various warning windows and gripped the joystick once more. I had no intention of going out with a fight.

"AHHHH!"

The villagers screamed in anguish as the Knight Armor blew away the red and black Comet. They felt fear. Fear of the unknown. Two giant bodies fought before them, one of ill intent and one against it. Their sense of comradery was put into question. As the Knight Armor moved to wrap its hand around the neck of the now immobile golem, the villagers covered their faces in dismay.

Ann ran down to where Sara had fallen. From there she called out to the golem at the top of her lungs...

"AOI! DON'T GIVE UP!"

Ann's voice had been carried by the wind and miraculously reached my ears inside the golem. I could feel my mouth jerk into a smile.

My body screamed in pain despite downing a vitality potion just now. Ever since Fez and I had separated and I was chased by the horsemen, I hadn't stopped putting my life in danger. Every fiber in my body ached and pleaded for me to stop, to slow down, but

I couldn't. The difficulty was set to its absolute maximum and it'd been nothing but a barrage of challenges. There were no choices or hints, no strategy guide or wiki either. It was a brutal game that had no save slots or continues—a game where my very life was at stake...

"Even so... Life's still pretty fun."

I wasn't done yet. I still had to teach that evil, oblivious little girl how to be a proper lady, for my sake, and for the world's.

I took the cursed sword and slipped out of the Comet's cockpit and ran up the nearby wall using the physical abilities the sword had granted me. I jumped up above the hand of the Knight Armor which was around the Comet's neck. I could hear Ann's voice as I was being dragged down by gravity. I took a deep break and shouted back to her...

"LEAVE IT TO ME...!"

Using the momentum of gravity, I aimed myself towards the metal cylinder on the Knight Armor's back. I slashed away at the metal tube, in an attempt to sever the connection between it and the armor. Perhaps it had noticed my resistance, as the Knight Armor moved its other hand towards me. At the verge of being squared by the hand, I managed to cut the connection of the cockpit with my sword.

"Knock it off already, you piece of crap!"

I relaxed my body slightly and gathered my remaining strength into one final stab. The Knight Armor slowly came to a halt as I hit, and soon collapsed into the ground with an earth-shattering impact. A cloud of dust was kicked up by the impact, and I took cover under the now powerless arm of the machine. As the dust cleared, I stood there, sword in hand, one eye closed off from blood. The villagers began to cheer, having realized the identity of their would-be savior.

I didn't really want to say what actually happened as I fell off the back of the Knight Armor, since I'd landed right on my head and ended up a bloody mess. I hoped that the giant dust cloud managed to mask my embarrassing blunder. It was impossible to show off perfection like a real hero since, after all, I was just a simple gamer.

Amidst the aftermath I managed to move closer to Ann.

"......!"

She said something and then embraced me. I hugged her back and finally lost consciousness.

◇

"Aoi!"

I woke up the next morning on a bed inside Jenny's house. Apparently I had been sleeping for more than half a day's time. What was waiting for me as I finally opened my eyes was an embrace from Ann in human form. It seemed like she had been waiting in the bed with me this whole time. Sitting in the nearby chair wasn't quite enough for her.

"How long has it been?"

"It's the morning after. We've been all taking turns watching over the village, but the mayor told me we could switch turns."

I was kinda worried about whether they would come back or not after escaping, but everything seemed to be okay.

"I see... One more thing, why are we naked?"

"Hm...?"

I wanted to think it was safe because we were both covered in sheets, but neither of us were wearing any clothes. I was a little concerned for my chastity, but I trusted in Ann.

—That's okay, right?

"Auntie told me that if you want to nurse someone really special to you, you need to be on the same bed naked."

—Another one of Jenny's traps!?

"Yeah, I think Jenny got that wrong. Let's put some clothes on."

"Okay~"

She obediently got off the bed and started putting on the clothes she'd folded nearby.

Ann was pretty intelligent. I couldn't help but wonder why she was only clueless when it came to relationships between males and females.

My clothes were also neatly folded as well. I put on my now blood-stained white shirt and ragged formal suit. I checked my potion pouch and noticed that one of the vitality potions was empty. I realized then that I felt no pain and that there wasn't a single wound on my body from yesterday.

—I'll just overlook this for now. Yeah, it's better that way...

I quietly put the empty bottle back in the pouch. I was kind of afraid to ask who got me to drink it, and how, while I was out of commission.

As we went out afterwards, Ann was back in her kobold form, and we met the mayor along the way, who proceeded to thank me endlessly.

"You're truly our village's patron. I don't know how we could ever hope to repay you!"

I understood he was grateful, but I'd like to keep a little distance between me and his minotaur face since it honestly still scared me.

I tried to boot up the Comet, but all I was met with were a bunch of warnings and no movement. Fortunately, there was a sort of self-healing function, so it would eventually repair itself. The only downside with that was the minimum wait to base functionality was two weeks, and a full recovery was two months...

I locked it up near the village to prevent any children from getting inside, and left the rifle alongside it. Thankfully, the mayor and the villagers gracefully agreed to help me in safekeeping the Comet while it was there.

I also helped with guarding the village, cursed sword in hand, but Fez eventually came along with city sentinels and mercenaries in tow. With security taken care of as well, Ann and I headed back for the labyrinth.

"Welcome back, Kousaka-san."

As we reached the bottom of the stairs to the ravine we were met by the sight of Karumi-san standing in front of the cabin. Oh, how I missed that shabby thing.

"I made a bit of a mess back there... Is my training score intact?"

"Naturally. You proposed a plan that would generate further profit, and you produced outstanding results. You're a desired person by our company, by all means."

Results were required in the adult world. Even if you said you'd do you best, you wouldn't be appraised by your heartfelt intentions, more so the actual results you produced. That's just how the world worked.

"Allow me to repeat myself from a few days ago: will you retire and go back to the 'safe world' and accept the salary and remuneration you've earned so far? Or will you become a full-time employee and continue living on in this danger-ridden world?"

"Aoi..."

Ann clasped the hem of my shirt with a lonely expression on her face. I stroked her head in response just like always.

"My answer is..."

I recited my answer as Karumi-san stared daggers at the little thing around my waist.

Strongest Gamer
Let's Play in Another World

Chapter 5

A week had passed, and I walked to the front of the train station, dressed in my brand new business suit.

It wasn't a custom-tailored luxury suit, it was just one I'd gotten from a store for a reasonable price. It was so new that I still had the tight feeling around me that you felt when you wore new clothes for the first time. I rolled my bag over and arrived at my office near the bus stop. I had a monthly salary of 180,000 yen, with overtime and holiday pay calculated separately. My transportation expenses were even covered, and there was a semi-annual inspection for salary increases, with bonuses awarded for getting certain milestones. There were even 4 days off a month, and 20 additional vacation days per year. No extended leaves, though, but there was annual paid leave.

It was pretty typical to stay late at work during the busy season. My hours would be high, but they would be added up as overtime in the end. Lodging was paid for by the company as well, along with various utilities like water. I had landed some pretty amazing working conditions; fewer and fewer people got deals like this in recent years. There was also a clause in the contract that stated it had to be firmly protected and maintained, though there shouldn't be a problem with upholding that.

On the neck of my suit was a rainbow-lustered silver metal pin with a blue dragon carved into it. It was the company badge that had been provided to me. My family said it looked almost like a toy.

"Good morning."

I knocked on the door of the office building and went inside.

“Good morning. This'll be your first day as a full-time employee, right? Here, this is your exclusive key, Kousaka-san.”

I greeted my seniors at the workplace and received a key that shined with the same luster as the company badge.

While I walked towards the back of the office, I couldn't help but mutter out loud.

“By the way... What's the deal with Karumi-san?”

“So you finally ask, huh? Well, since you're a full-timer now, let's just say she's a relative of the Great Dark Lord. She joined the company thanks to her connections, but managed to mess up badly one too many times, so she couldn't actually get a managerial position. Thanks to that, she ended up becoming a regular office lady.”

“Ah, so she's his daughter, huh?”

—Maybe she failed at the survival training?

My mind wandered among various possibilities as I inserted my key into the door at the back of the office. The door looked like it was made of plastic or some other kind of synthetic material. Its hinged creaked as I opened the door.

I stepped forward. My feet land on soft ground and I heard the sound of the door as it closed behind me. A pleasant and nostalgic wind, which carried the scent of fresh soil, nature, and pure water reached my nose as I now stood at the bottom of the ravine.

“Aoi!”

I turned back when I heard her voice. The sight of a lovely girl standing in front of the old cabin made me wonder if this was how happiness felt.

“I'm back, Ann. I can answer you now... Would you mind staying with me forever? I don't know much about this world... And it seems like I'm no good without you.”

“You're so hopeless! You really don't know anything at all! That's why I worry so much... But yes, I'll stay with you forever.”

The sweet girl embraced me as tears rolled down her face. I wanted to believe they were tears of happiness rather than sadness.

"Now we can be together forever, right? I don't mind if I'm not your number one, just let me stay close to you, okay?"

—Excuse me? That was a weird turn.

"Now that you gave me your answer, I'll be your mistress starting today, right? So we can always be together even if you fool around or get a wife, right?"

"Wait a minute, Ann... Where did you come up with that idea!?"

"Auntie taught me a lot about it, why?"

"JENNYYYYYYYYYY!"

"Hm?"

My roar echoed out once again across the bottom of a ravine in another world.

This was my life. I had no complaints.

The difficulty setting was set to the extreme. There were no choices or hints, and no saving or loading. But... it was so unbelievably fun that I just wanted to keep playing.

I think I'll keep living and playing seriously, having as much fun as I can, until the very end...

Epilogue

Have you ever heard of role playing? Its origins may be lesser known, but it has served as the basis for the RPG genre we know today. To 'play a role' may conjure up an image of actors performing on a stage or on a movie screen, but this isn't a story acted out on a grandiose platform. No, it's much simpler, more basic, yet still expansive and filled with endless possibilities.

Role playing happens a lot in everyday life, whether you notice it or not. From innocent games of make-believe and house as children, to interacting with strangers and eventually your seniors and teachers as we age, a mask is put on—a role is played. We incorporate those masks into ourselves, and sometimes they can even warp our personalities. But we don't have to let the roles we play define us...

"You're heading towards the city in a horse-drawn carriage... It's been two days since you left the village. As you near the dark path that leads into the forest, dirty men jump out of the bushes on the side of the road! They block your path, stopping your cart, and aggressively shout out to you, 'This is Mountain Dogs turf! Hand over all your gold and valuables, or else face the consequences!'"

"When then... I jump out of the carriage wielding my lance, and strike a battle pose and respond with, 'There are no rich passengers on this carriage. This is the only means of transport they have! If you mean to do us harm, then it is you who will face the consequences!'"

"The bandits stare at you with your lance and beautiful armor, then move in to attack. The fight is on! Alright... since it's a fight, let's prepare the paper to write on, and the figures."

"Okay!"

This was one such game that involved role playing on a smaller scale—a make-believe tabletop adventure that I played together with Ann.

The experience was greatly enhanced with the use of a pen, some paper, and dice. All you needed to know how to do was speak and perform basic arithmetic. A game so timeless that all ages could enjoy. It transcended the ages, existing long before the age of electronic smartphones, and will continue forth long past their expiration.

Labyrinth #228 was in a sort of fantasy world, where the literacy rate wasn't that high, and finding people that knew arithmetic beyond counting their fingers was rare. Simply being able to do basic math functions set you above the rest of the populous.

We let Fez handle the task of obtaining pen and paper for us to use. Despite how expensive they were, the quality was still rather poor. We could use charcoal to write and have slabs of wood or stone as the writing surface, but that was incredibly unwieldy. Plus, there was a certain level of romanticism when it came to using pen and paper for this sort of thing... The cultural differences between modern Earth and this fantasy world were pretty huge, so I figured this sort of game would be hard to popularize in Milt Village. Nonetheless, I had no problem playing with Ann, a girl so brilliant she would put adults of this world to shame.

Ann and I were using the free time we had between dinner and bedtime to play. Ever since I came to this world and met Ann, we played card games made with thin pieces of wood, and board games with handmade pieces. Our favorite game of them all though was one called "Labyrinths and Dragon's Feast". She asked me before why I liked this one so much, to which I told her that while card and board games were fun, being able to make your own adventures and characters in "Labyrinths and Dragon's Feast" was way more enjoyable for me.

"With two bandits taken down, they are at a disadvantage and feeling desperate, so one tries to take a hostage. What will you do?"

"I won't let him do that and use 'Galewind' to stop him!"

"You might not make it in time so you'll have to roll for that."

"Okay, so I throw two die and have to get more than a five and... An eight! I got it!"

"You manage to move so fast that no one can see you cutting between the bandit and the woman he was trying to take hostage."

"I look at them with a fearless smile and say... 'It's useless to try and take hostages, you guys never learn. Do you even care for your own lives!?'"

Tabletop Role Playing Games (TRPGs) had the unique feature of being able to play with premade characters, or creating your own. There were a lot of games on PC and such that let you choose basic things like your occupation or gender, but not many that let you customize everything down to personality quirks and individual stats. I wish there were more games that did this. It was really interesting to play with your own custom character and go off on adventures. There were some games that had Yes or No choices for story progression, but they typically were still confining when it came to player flexibility.

In our game here, Ann had created a character named... "Anne". It was pretty easy to determine a person's preference and tastes by the characters they created. And in some cases, the player bases their character off the idealized version of themselves.

"So you defeat the bandits, all the passengers of the carriage lavish you with gratitude."

"Well, I smile at them and say, 'I just happened to be on the same carriage as you all, but maybe this chance meeting was one of fate. One destined to happen.'"

Ann's character was a 19-year old female warrior who was tall and had an extremely nice figure. Anne had a very caring personality and a strong sense of duty—she also had hopes and dreams of her own.

My heart was warmed by Ann's cuteness as she tried to play out her gallant imaginary character. She even came up with cool one-liners, but then would get shy whenever she recited them so— No, that's not important right now.

"You march straight into the bandit's hideout. There, a man that seems to be the boss is lying in wait and greets you. He mockingly says, 'Yer jus a trav'ler, ain't cha? Watchu doin' protectin' dis sorry lot? Dey can even save der sorry asses.'"

"I say, 'That's right, I'm just a traveler that has nothing to do with them, but the tears of the children you caused with your misdeeds is more than enough reason to fight!' while striking a pose and lunging at the boss bandit with my sword."

I become worried as I look at Ann's sparkling eyes filled with passion and joy.

There were various players that projected their idealized selves as TRPG characters. Anne was a gallant female warrior that wore plate armor and wielded swords and lances. Did she represent Ann's ideals? There were no characters that could do absolutely everything in the world of TRPGs or MMORPGS. Typically there were a variety of roles ranging from tanks and healers to damage dealers, and they all came together in a party to fulfill their various roles and advance towards a similar goal. I had made this "Labyrinth and Dragon's Feast" game so that even a beginner like Ann could enjoy it while keeping those basic rules in mind.

But Ann hadn't chosen a healing profession, or even concentrated on healing skills, despite having such a sweet and gentle personality as Anne. It wasn't like I was one of those people that equated female players as always being healers. But Ann didn't so much as look at the healing system before she dashed straight for shields and swords. I was surprised she chose the role of an attacker without hesitation.

Ever since then, I began observing Ann and her preferences and playstyle of her character from the role of the facilitator of the adventure—the Game Master, if you will.

"The mayor of the village you saved bows his head deeply and thanks you. He says, 'Thank you so much, traveler. These are all the silver coins we collected among all the villagers. Please take them as a token of gratitude,' and he hands you a bag with 48 silver coins inside."

"Umm... let's see... 'That's really nice of you, but won't the village be in trouble if I take this? I'll accept half of it as thanks, but please take the other half and repair the village.' I take 24 coins and give back the rest to the mayor... Aoi, I can make it to next town with three silver coins, right?"

Ann's sense of economics was quite nice. She was neither too modest or greedy. So even in her ideals she was pragmatic as well?

"I give Wata five silver coins and say, 'Here, have this. You're always helping me with the recovery potions.'"

Anne might excel in attack and defense as a warrior, but she had no way to recover herself. So I made an NPC companion for her named Wata, a doctor character that specialized in healing, and urged her not to forget about him. His occupation may involve healing people, but there was an expense that you had to keep in mind, as medical ingredients depleted as they were used.

It was surprising to see her interact with Wata, but she wasn't handing all the money for him to manage, she managed her own money and gave some to him from time to time.

Right now I was giving Ann an allowance we called a 'salary,' but I took care of her food, clothes and living expenses as well. Basically, I was raising her myself. Would Ann have the independence and capacity to take care of herself even if I wasn't looking after her?

I had come to realize Ann's capacity to live was quite high in the time we had spent together, but... Actually, that wasn't all that strange in hindsight. Considering how Jenny was, it wasn't all that difficult to figure out how Ann had become so independent to the point where she learned how to read, write, and do math.

This wasn't like Earth where there were various welfare services for people. We were in another world that didn't seem to have advanced much past the middle pages. I became all too aware of that fact when Sara got sick and her mortality was very much up in the air. With this in mind, it made sense to me that Jenny tried to raise Ann in such a way that she could fend for herself in the event that Jenny died or became unable to work. The last time I asked, Ann told me that Jenny was her only family left, which was all the more reason to be motivated to learn.

Even if crisis was to befall Anne, Ann was a really good player, and her responses always surprised me.

"A knight in imposing black armor clashes swords with you and says, 'You know the difference in our power, don't you? It'd be a shame for you to die here, so why not become my minion? I will help you if you submit to me...'"

My game didn't have any rebirth mechanics or anything like other games had. Once your character died, that was it. So even if it was just the life of the character that was on the line, the fear of death was always around the corner.

"I'll let my sword answer! 'I won't give up. I won't be able to keep on living if I lost who I am. I will defend my humanity at all costs!' Yes, if I use all the magic tools I have, there's about a 50% chance of winning!"

She had the strength to confront death head-on, and the pride to treasure her dignity.

"Zzz..."

I remembered something I had noticed from observations of Ann, as I looked at her happy, sleeping face. She glued herself to me and dressed lightly when we went to sleep, so it was kind of difficult to keep my head cool. While the female warrior Anne played out in the game, the thought of Ann projecting herself through Anne made me feel somewhat lonely, but also happy.

Right now, Ann was the one being protected by me, but if Anne represented her true ideals, then she wasn't very satisfied with how things were right now. Even if she wasn't unhappy with them, it wasn't something she'd want to live with forever. Which reminded me... She'd been devoting herself to helping me with potion making and doing housework. Judging from her attitude towards Wata the NPC, she seemed more eager to protect than be protected. She would probably want a partner that could stand on equal ground with.

If Ann told me someday that she wanted to me to be her 'equal partner'... What would I say? What kind of face would I make? Would

I feel happy or sad? Which one of us would overcome the other? She may even find someone that wasn't me to be her partner... I wanted to believe in the relationship we developed between each other over the last few months. I could rest easy if she chose me as her partner, right? The feelings swirling within me were a mix of 90% expectation and 10% anxiety—just like when you came across a cool-looking game with a large update coming.

I slowly closed my eyes and fell asleep before the warm feeling inside my chest dissipated.

Life may have tons of difficult events in store, but there will always room to have fun and play around.

Afterword

"Do you like games?" That was the first phrase that came to mind when it was time to write the afterword. Hello, nice to meet you. I'm the game-loving author, Shinobu Yuki.

This novel tells the story of our protagonist, Aoi, a gamer that dedicated his whole life to enjoying the games he loves so much, and the people he meets along the way. I hope you enjoyed it!

What happens when you devote your heart and soul to living games? I think there are various ways to answer that, and my conclusion was that I wouldn't neglect playing real life while still actively enjoying games. I'd be very happy if you could enjoy the story of our protagonist, who doesn't discriminate between real life and games, and takes both as seriously as he can.

Some time ago I found myself asking, "Once I become an adult, why would I play games?" To which I would've liked to respond with, "If my play time goes down, so will my youth!" It's a good time to be alive, though. There are plenty of adults that endeavor to play multiplayer games and such late into the night, even after a long day filled with work and commuting.

It's the middle of summer as I write this, but... "I'm slaving away at work now so I can play this open world game that lets you wander a devastated world at the end of the year. I'll take my full vacation then!" I'm sure there are lots of people that have this kind of Aoi-esque thought inside their heads.

Although one part of that crowd might be going, "If I study for the entrance exams, I won't be able to play 'til next year! I'll have to shoot for getting recommendations now!" It's not all too uncommon among students, at least. Surprisingly enough though, Japan seems to be gradually moving into the future in areas unknown. Ah, I'm starting to ramble on now, so I'll move on to thanking everyone that made this possible.

First and foremost, I'd like to thank my editor, Mr. K. You helped me more times than I can count. I still remember the countless times you told me "Let's make this novel even more perfect!" I'd like to also thank Katou Itsuwa for delivering such beautiful illustrations, and Hiiragi Ryou for drawing such an amazing cover, together with Itsuwa. And a thank you to all the judges that valued this world and awarded it in the second Overlap Novel Awards.

To every single person that bought and read this book, I thank you from the bottom of my heart for helping me get to where I am today. All of you have my most heartfelt gratitude!